WELCOME TO

ABYSS

The Abyss line of cutting-edge psychological horror is committed to publishing the best, most innovative works of dark fiction available. ABYSS is horror unlike anything you've ever read before. It's not about haunted houses or evil children or ancient Indian burial grounds. We've all read those books, and we all know their plots by heart.

ABYSS is for the seeker of truth, no matter how disturbing or twisted it may be. It's about people, and the darkness we all carry within us. ABYSS is the new horror from the dark frontier. And in that place, where we come face-to-face with terror, what we find is ourselves.

"Thank you for introducing me to the remarkable line of novels currently being issued under Dell's Abyss imprint. I have given a great many blurbs over the last twelve years or so, but this one marks two firsts: first *unsolicited* blurb (I called *you*) and the first time I have blurbed a whole *line* of books. In terms of quality, production, and plain old storytelling reliability (that's the bottom line, isn't it?), Dell's new line is amazingly satisfying . . . a rare and wonderful bargain for readers. I hope to be looking into the Abyss for a long time to come."

—Stephen King

Please turn the page for more extraordinary acclaim. . . .

P9-EJU-227

MICHAEL BLUMLEIN

A Dell Book

Published by
Dell Publishing
a division of
Bantam Doubleday Dell Publishing Group, Inc.
1540 Broadway
New York, New York 10036

ISBN: 0-440-21374-6

Printed in the United States of America

Published simultaneously in Canada

November 1993

10 9 8 7 6 5 4 3 2 1
OPM

My gratitude to Michael McDowell, Jeanne Cavelos, and David Wallin for, variously, their insight, enthusiasm, and encouragement.

This book is dedicated to Hilary

Liebe Ist Rache

All Mine

When Tiresias was a young man, he came upon two snakes coupling in the dirt. He struck them apart with a stick, whereupon he was changed into a woman. Seven years later he came again upon two snakes coupling, and again struck them apart, whereupon he was changed back into a man. Hera, Queen of the Gods, then descended from her throne to pose him this question: which sex has the greater pleasure in love?

"Woman," Tiresias answered, at which point Hera raised her arm and struck him blind.

1

Late at night the girl is dancing. She is on a platform of polished oak ten feet long and five feet wide. At each end is a full-length mirror. The platform is six feet off the ground, and she is dancing to a song about love and female attraction. The drumbeat is mechanical, comforting in its relentlessness. It has been months since she has heard the words.

Beneath her, running the length of the platform and then some, is the bar. Fronting it is a long row of stools, most of them filled, and behind them some booths. The bartender is a ruddy and earnest-looking man in his sixties. It is past midnight, and he is working hard. The customers are drinking tonight. The people need their liquor.

The girl dances in high, spiked heels. It is a requirement that she wear them. She has long legs, strong from dancing. It is a requirement that she shave them. Where her legs meet in front and back is covered by the slimmest of g-strings. It is purple, sequined in silver. Above it she is naked. She has firm breasts that move very little when she dances. They tend to disappear when she raises her arms. On her face is an expression of disinterest and faint amusement. She is quite drunk, and the panic is far away.

When she dances, as much as possible she is supposed to face the customers. For those who like tits this means she has to face forward. For the ones who like ass, backward. Rarely, when she has the energy, she spreads her legs, aims her ass at the customers and bends over. Then the ones who like tits can see tits and the ones who like ass can see ass. Her legs are always on view, as is her hair. Her face comes and goes.

When the bar originally went topless, the owners, knowing something of women, realized that the dancers would not have an easy time of it. A girl could go crazy watching drunken men leer at her hour after hour. So they put a mirror at each end of the strip. Then, when the men got old, when they turned into creatures better off not seen, the girls could watch themselves. In the mirror, at least, would be a partner they knew.

The song ends, but the drum machine beat does not. Seamlessly, it moves into the next song. The girl dances on, tired but dragged along by the music. It is still thirty minutes to her break.

The bartender reaches up and slides a folded bill into her g-string. He taps her two times on the calf to signify it's a ten and points to a man sitting down the bar. The girl slides a leg out in rhythm to the music and follows it with her body. Her eyes glide over the man who gave her the money. He nods and smiles at her.

She turns back to the mirror and dances with herself, waiting for the shift to be over. All the dancing and sweating have sobered her up. She needs another drink.

When the next dancer comes up, the girl climbs down as fast as she can and hurries to the dressing room. The place smells of smoke and sweat, and the first thing she does is take a hit from a bottle of Jack Daniel's she carries in her purse. The warmth drives out the cold in her belly, and she takes another, then screws back the cap. She pulls the bill out of her g-string, unrolls it and zips it into a pocket of her purse. She starts to feel a little better.

Next to the door is a rack of gowns provided by the management. All are of the same fabric and style, sleek, sleeveless, with a generous cleavage in front. She chooses a red one her size and slips it on. It clings very close to her skin. She stoops to the mirror and makes sure nothing is terribly wrong with her face. The eyeliner and lipstick are holding up pretty well. She squeezes some drops into her eyes to take away the redness, fixes her hair, takes a deep breath and leaves the dressing room.

She finds the man who gave her the ten and sidles in next to him at the bar. She slips a cigarette out of his pack of Viceroys lying on the counter and holds it upright between her first two fingers. Glancing at him and smiling, she cocks her head and waits.

The man is in his fifties; he wears a bow tie and a narrow-brimmed hat with a feather in its band. Putting down his drink, he fumbles in his pocket for a lighter. The girl gets the light and drags on her cigarette, blowing smoke toward the ceiling. The man lights one of his own and offers her a drink. She accepts.

"Make it a double," she tells the bartender.

"I'll take a refill," says the man.

They get their drinks and talk. The girl puts it in gear. She listens, asks questions, laughs when the time seems right. The man loosens up. Despite himself, he thinks that maybe, just maybe, this might be someone. He screws up his courage and touches the girl's hand. She does not move it away. Instead, she orders another drink.

The bar has a strict policy concerning performers and clientele. The girls are expected to mingle between sets. They are expected to be friendly, gay and accessible. In this way they encourage the patrons to buy more drinks. They are allowed to drink themselves, and if their affability is further rewarded in the form of tips, the money is theirs to keep.

Most of the men who come to the bar assume that the girls are cheap and easy. They assume that the bar is a bordello. Nothing is further from the truth. The girls are neither required nor encouraged to turn tricks. Being one of the commodities that give the establishment its value, it is in the owners' interests that they be protected and relatively happy. So when the man in the bow tie and rising fantasy puts his hand on the girl's, she is not frightened. She knows she is protected. There is always a bouncer nearby.

The man, of course, is not privy to these rules. The liquor, the music, the naked girls encourage him to fantasize. After holding the girl's hand for a few minutes, feeling the moistness of her palm, the warmth of her skin, he is ready to try more. He downs the last of his drink and wipes his wet hand on his pants. Staring into the deep cleavage of the dress, he inches his hand up the girl's arm. He touches a breast. It seems to draw away from him and he presses harder.

The girl looks up. She has been playing with a cigarette butt, trying to remember how much longer she has to dance. The liquor has removed much of the feeling in her body, and it takes her a moment to realize that the man is fondling her. She takes his hand and pulls it away. She tries to do it nicely, thinking if she plays it right, she may get a little more money. The man, however, has crossed his border. All his trains have left; he is in the city for the night. In the city and on the loose. As soon as she takes his hand away, he puts it back.

This does not make the girl happy. It is a hassle. She tries to get some understanding going with her eyes, but the man is seeing landscapes of his own. She says something nice, which at first he doesn't appear to hear. She repeats it, and he growls.

"You got my money. Now you put out."

The girl sighs and motions to her bouncer. He is six foot three, weighs two-fifty. In seconds he is at her side.

"Some kind of problem here?"

"Lover here's getting a little too familiar."

He steps between them. "That right, friend? You getting too familiar with the lady?"

"She took my money. I'm only asking what's right."

The bouncer glances to the girl, who shakes her head. He turns back to the man. "We need to have a little talk. There're some things I got to explain."

He grips the man by the elbow and lifts him off the bar stool. The man makes a halfhearted attempt to resist and quickly realizes he's in way over his head. Besides, he's not the belligerent type. The girl watches them go, then turns back to the bar. She feels shitty. The guy was lonely. He thought he knew the rules, and he was reaching out. She knows the feeling. It's a sad situation all around. She finishes her drink, then goes in back to get ready for her last shift.

When it comes down to it, up on the platform is the best place to be. It's safe, and she doesn't have to hassle with other people's feelings. She has a kind of power, and can be as unconscious of the world as she wants. She dances now, slowly, sensuously, pretending that she's making love to someone who loves her more than anyone's ever loved her in her life.

A short time later her man comes into the bar. He blows her a kiss, and she responds with a little move of her hips. It's near closing time, and the bar is no more than half-filled. Most of the remaining patrons are regulars. The ones who come to get drunk are now drunk, and the ones who come to see flesh have seen it. The girl feels more comfortable, almost as though she's among friends. Work is nearly over; in half an hour she'll have money in her hand and her man beside her.

Fifteen minutes before closing time two strangers enter the bar. They are dressed expensively, and once they've settled down and ordered, the girl dances over to have a look. One of them is wearing a fat ring that glints when it catches the light, and in her mind the girl starts thinking money. Despite her weariness she figures it's worth a shot, and standing in front of them, she starts dancing the best she knows. She shimmies her top and rolls her hips to make the tassels on the g-string twirl. Not knowing what they like, she gives them ass and tits and legs. Everything she can think of. It's kind of fun.

One of them notices her first, and he taps his friend, the older of the two, on the shoulder. Just as the man looks up, a siren wails by outside. An ambulance maybe, or a fire truck. The man frowns, as if taken by surprise. He stares at the girl. The girl stares back. There is a moment between them. A puzzled, then terrified look in their eyes. All at once the man slumps to the bar. The girl grabs air. Tottering on the spikes of her heels, she collapses to the floor.

2

Suter's, the bookstore where Terry Connor worked, took its name from Adolf Suter, one of three brothers who emigrated from Germany in the mid-nineteenth century. Josef, the eldest of the three, was lost on the journey in a brutal North Atlantic storm, and Emil contracted tuberculosis a year or two later. Adolf, the youngest, was forced to take on a second job, and the first thing he could find was at the New York Medical Society, cleaning and restocking the library shelves at night. Many of the books were in German, and Adolf often found himself staying late, poring over a medical text. When Emil died several years later, Adolf quit his daytime job. By then he was fluent in English and had an encyclopedic knowledge of the texts housed in the library. He soon received a promotion and got involved in purchasing. One thing led to another, and on the eve of his thirtieth birthday he left his sinecure with the Medical Society to strike out on his own. He opened a medical specialty house in a tiny storefront on Antiquarian Row that soon grew to include texts of all the sciences. But medicine remained his primary interest, and his knowledge of the field was such that physicians anxious to know the latest treatment for neurasthenia, gleet or the gout freely consulted him.

Adolf died in 1925, and his son took over the business. He had less love for it than his father, but it afforded him a good income and he had a family to support. He managed it competently if unimaginatively, passing it on to his own son at the earliest opportunity. This Suter, though he had never met his grandfather, shared Adolf's love of books and took to being a bookseller like a surgeon to a knife. Unlike his grandfather, his interest lay less in science than it did in fiction, and he began to bring these titles into the store. Poetry followed, and then the swelling genre lines. The store expanded to the rear in the seventies, but ten years later it faced another crisis of space. Books on sex, money and diet were crowding out the texts on science and medicine. It seemed only a matter of time before the latter would be gone.

But grandson Suter was a traditionalist at heart: he would not cut the roots on which the store had been built. Against the advice of his accountant, who quite reasonably pointed out that rents in the area were rising precipitously, that other bookstores were folding left and right and that a major investment of capital at that time would be more than just a little risky, young Suter expanded once again. This time it was downward, into the cavernous basement of the ancient stone building. Here there was ample space for the scientific texts, for all the fat and over-sized volumes of observation, research and speculation, while upstairs would now have room for the best-sellers on whose legs the store's viability depended. Suter did not seem to care that a certain portion of his customers were intimidated by the basement room, as though its vast store of information posed a threat to their well-being. Nor did it bother him that others found it irrelevant. Intuition told him he was doing the right thing, and for the sake of tradition he was more than willing to take the risk.

Had Terry Connor known of the man's idealism, he wouldn't have cared a bit. The time when he would have was past, or so he thought. He took the job because he needed work. He knew something about science, and he had read his share of books. At the beginning he was stationed upstairs so that Pinkett, the evening manager, could keep an eye on him. After a month he was transferred to the basement and a couple of months later put in charge of purchasing for that area. For reasons both priggish and self-serving, Pinkett liked to keep the sexes separate. Women worked upstairs with him, men down below. Terry didn't object. Though he hated windowless rooms and fluorescent lighting, a voice told him that the basement was exactly where he deserved to be. Tucked away. Closeted. Over time he got used to it, especially when he was stoned, although working with the medical texts was never easy. Leafing through any one of them filled him with wildly contradictory emotions, all knotting into a rope of ill luck from which his life seemed to hang.

It was better now that he had Frankie. She gave him purpose the way medical school had. It was coming on three years since he'd been thrown out. Three years and counting.

Terry checked the clock on the wall. It was a slow, mid-week evening, the last day of March. Except for a bearded man in an overcoat Terry was alone on the floor. He watched the man for a while, trying to imagine who he might be. He was in his fifties and seemed well fed, carried a fancy-looking cane and leather gloves. A businessman? Perhaps a widowed professor from NYU. He was reading a book on cannibalism, primitive and modern-day. Anthropologist? Cook?

The man closed the book and opened another, in a single fluid motion slipping the first between the buttons of his overcoat. He went on reading as if nothing had happened. It was smooth, and Terry almost missed it. His heart sped up a little at the drama. He took a step from behind the counter, then changed his mind and stopped. It was almost closing time, and he didn't want to get involved in a scene. He was already starting to think of other things besides work. If he called the man on it, it could get ugly. Accusation, denial, enforcement. He might have to listen to the man's real story, or a heartbreaking one of his invention. Either way it was bound to be unpleasant. He decided to let the man leave his department. When he got caught at the electronic sensor inside the door on the main floor, someone else could deal with it. If the man found a way to demagnetize the book before then, he was welcome to it. As far as Terry was concerned, ingenuity was to be re-warded.

The man eventually left, after a glance and curt nod in Terry's direction. It was about a quarter to eleven. Terry marked the book he had been reading and began turning off the lights. On his way out he asked Brenda, the cashier, if she wanted to get something to eat. He had some time to kill before Frankie finished at the club, but Brenda was already booked. With her head she gestured toward the front door.

Standing just beyond the sensor was the man from downstairs. Flanking him on one side was Pinkett and on the other, a uniformed security guard. The man's arms were folded tight across his chest, and his face was flushed. He was protesting in a strained voice. As Terry passed him, the man glanced his way, as though begging help to halt this humiliation. Something in his eyes made Terry want to stop, but he kept going. Nothing he could have done would ultimately have mattered.

He walked up to Fourteenth Street, on the way passing a trio of mannequins in a tacky store display window. For a moment he thought one was alive. It was a mistake he'd made more than once, long before the fashion had become to use live models to simulate mannequins. Each time that it did, he ended up feeling degraded. Tonight they were modeling cotton dresses and bathing suits. It was forty degrees outside.

He crossed over to Union Square, whose darkness and lack of commerce were a relief, and went around to the back of the pedestal that supported

George Washington and his horse. From a pocket he pulled a skinny joint and fired it up. After a few drags he palmed it and came out from his hiding place. Across the street beneath the Village Voice building was a billboard filled up with a curvy blonde. Lying on her side with her head propped on an elbow, she was dressed in the sheerest of lingerie. Her smile was beguiling, and Terry got an inkling why Washington sat so tall and stiff in the saddle. He was familiar with the unattainable object, with the frustration, whether by character or circumstance, of being denied. Certain things were inevitable. The guy who got nailed in the store would live through it. Disappointment and humiliation were part of life.

Terry turned and headed through the park, sneaking a few more tokes on the smoldering spliff before stubbing it out on a tree and eating the roach. The night was cold but nice, and his mood started to improve. He thought of seeing Frankie and later, getting her in bed. He unzipped his jacket and let the air run over his chest. The world had a message. He felt potent and strong.

On a whim he decided to visit Marcus, a friend who worked swing at Park Memorial. He jogged along East Seventeenth, virtually empty at that hour, until he got near Beth Israel. Turning uptown, he passed a man hobbling on a foot whose filthy bandage was unraveling. Farther up the block he ducked around a couple speaking rapidly in Spanish. Ten minutes later he arrived at Park Memorial.

The hospital's main entrance was closed at that time of night, and he circled past the emergency room to the rear. Next to the loading docks was an open door, which Terry entered without being seen. He got to the locker room just as Marcus was closing his locker. Terry leaned against the door jamb and caught his breath.

"Hey."

Marcus looked up. He was a tall, dark man with a handsome face that could be menacing one moment and boyish the next. When he saw Terry, he broke into a smile.

"Hey, man." He finished buttoning his shirt and stood up. Terry went over and the two of them embraced. His head barely reached Marcus's shoulders.

"Thought I'd drop by," he said.

Marcus nodded.

"You off?"

"Off and running."

Terry grinned. "Want to get high?"

"Well," Marcus said clownishly, letting his head drift toward his chest then jerking it up. "The fact of the matter, the absolute truth is I am. And I do."

Terry pulled out another slim number and struck a match, but Marcus blew it out before the joint got lit.

"No no no," he said, taking Terry by the arm and leading him from the room. "You gotta be cool. The man's everywhere." His eyes shifted. "Behind doors, under benches, in the trenches. He's got eyes and a nose. When he wants, he bites you with his big teeth."

"There was no one in the room," Terry said. They were walking down one of the underground tunnels of the hospital. Several large pipes, covered with dust, ran close above their heads. The hum of a generator echoed off the concrete walls.

"You didn't **see** no one," Marcus corrected him. "What you see is different from what is. You just follow me, we find a place what's safe."

Terry didn't argue. He was used to Marcus's cautiousness. Early in their friendship he had thought it crazy and paranoid that he owned guns and padlocked his doors. But over the years he had changed his mind. Marcus had grown up in violence. He had been to Vietnam. His caution was not paranoia, not pure paranoia anyway. It had taken Terry, in whom impulse and impetuosity were instinctive, a long time to understand.

Marcus took him to a door at the end of the tunnel that led to a tiny dead-end courtyard, created several years before by the expansion of one of the hospital wings. Save for the door there was no other access, and a concrete overhang kept it out of sight from above.

"You always get high at work?" Terry asked.

"Only way I can work. The man doesn't want me to think. Which is like telling a bird not to sing. The sentence is twenty plus five. I got to leave him behind."

There were other methods Marcus used to protect himself. At work there was a certain evil, half-demented look he could bring into his eyes on command. A supervisor, on his way to give the janitor some bit of nonsense, would find himself facing a very large black man, hands gripping his broom like it was a weapon, face hooded and clenched, as though at any moment he might snap. Nine times out of ten the supervisor would pass this menacing character by, deciding there were others to whom he would rather give his orders.

"I once got high when I worked at the hospital," Terry said. He sucked on the joint and handed it to Marcus. "It was too weird. Everyone was so exposed. So blatant. The patients, me, the nurses. It was too strong. Too heavy a dose of something."

"Now that's different. I just mop the floors. They don't want me thinking about nothing but the trash and the little bits of dirt in the corners. It's a different thing."

"Yeah," said Terry. "People are different than floors."

"There you go." Marcus finished the cigarette and opened the door. The atmosphere in the tunnel was dense and subterranean. Terry hung back. Sneaking around the bowels of the hospital made him edgy. The last time he'd snuck, years before, he'd been caught.

They made it to the street without incident, and Terry invited Marcus out for a drink. His friend declined.

"Aunt Orphah's visiting from down South. I told her I'd be home 'bout midnight. Where's Frankie at?"

"Working. She doesn't get off for another couple of hours."

"She still at that place?"

"Virgo's? Still is."

"I like that girl," said Marcus. "You see she keeps out of trouble."

Terry laughed. "Sure thing, Marcus. You kiss the next old man you see."

Marcus bent his big frame, pushed out his head and puckered his lips. He made a flourish of kissing the air. He turned in a circle, kissing in all directions. Then he lifted his hand and elegantly pressed it to his lips.

"You come back again," he told Terry, backing down the street. "And bring that good stuff."

Terry watched him go while he decided what to do next. He was a little hungry, a little lonely. The pot accentuated both. In lieu of other, ameliorative drugs that weren't in his possession, he zipped his jacket and hurried over to Third. Near Thirtieth was a Chinese restaurant that stayed open late. Food would have to do. On the way he passed a ragged black man with a swollen face and a coat ripped down one side. He was holding a Styrofoam cup, which he shook as Terry walked by. It occurred to Terry that he had passed a half-dozen such men since leaving the hospital, men he routinely ignored, men, in some cases, he had stopped seeing altogether. It was a way of survival, like learning to blank one's mind to a persistent pain, and it had a price. At that moment, maybe because of his own fleeting sense of fragility, it was not a price he was willing to pay. He returned to the man and dropped a couple of quarters in his cup. The man muttered something unintelligible and asked for a dollar. Terry looked him in the eye, hesitated, then said no. The man did not protest, and Terry walked away.

The restaurant was a hole in the wall, narrow as a boxcar, stuffy, dim. Bare bulbs encased in accordion paper lanterns hung from the ceiling. Painted on the lanterns were pastoral scenes of ancient China, a mountaintop rimmed with snow, a boatman poling across a stream, a field of rice. Hunched over a table in the rear of the restaurant were two black-haired children, pencils in hand, deep in concentration. As late as it was, they were still doing schoolwork. Terry was dismayed. Adult life was serious enough, and these were only kids. It seemed a kind of reverse negligence that they weren't in bed, dreaming.

His food came, and he ate greedily. He felt better after he finished and better still when the slip of paper in his fortune cookie promised an unforeseen advantage. He glanced again at the kids in back, poring over their books, preparing for a life strung between paper lanterns and video games. It was a big distance to cover. With proper feeding the human spirit was a pliant and marvelous thing.

He paid his check and left. It was five minutes to one, still a little early for Virgo's. Frankie wouldn't be finished her final set for close to an hour.

To kill time he decided to check out the hookers. They used to hang out around Virgo's, but since the Master Plan to rid midtown of its more pungent elements had been in effect, things had changed drastically. Now to find them Terry had to go all the way over to Eleventh, in the dead zone just above the Lincoln Tunnel. They were as easy to spot as birds on a wire because no one else was on the street. Terry guessed that it was probably good for business that way, but it made him feel more an interloper than he had when he was one of a crowd. He walked from just above the Javits Center to Forty-fifth, staying on the east side of the street. The ladies were on the other side, better to snare a late night commuter before he hit the tunnel and home in Jersey. Tonight it was relatively quiet. A limousine pulled over, then a red sports car and a pickup truck. Terry played a game with himself, trying to figure out which of the ladies were men and which women. Most of the time it was easy, though with some he could never be sure. The women were taller these days, and the men much better with clothes and makeup. A lot of them took hormones, and some had had surgery. Close-up, even touching, it was not always a sure thing.

When he started to get cold, Terry called it a night, walking up to Fiftieth, then over until he got to Broadway. Virgo's, which he could see from where he stood, had once been surrounded by flashy top-less clubs—the Den of Love, the Marquis, the Pink Chalet—but now it stood alone. Across from it a huge new multipurpose high rise was going up, commercial units on the bottom, condos up top. It was the kind of place where a person could live and die without ever having to leave. The block above the bar was rubble, awaiting some young architect's dream, and the one below was boarded up. Terry marveled at how Virgo's itself had survived.

It had started out at least fifty years before as a neighborhood bar called Ted's Can Do, turning top-less only after the sexual revolution of the early sev-enties had forced its hand. In seventy-four the own-ers had changed its name to Virgo's and commissioned a fancy marquee that featured a painting of a Godiva-like creature with blond tresses covering her bosom and privates. Now the painting was faded and cracked, though the red neon that spelled Virgo's was still relatively bright. Much brighter, thought Terry, than the bar's future.

When he got there, a drunken flock of businessmen and wives, wearing plastic, pig-shaped badges exhorting the world to "Buy Pork," kept him from entering. They were massed outside, peering through a slit in the heavy curtain inside the door. Some of the women stood on tiptoe to see over their husbands' shoulders. A man in front grunted several times in quick succession. A pig in heat? The others laughed.

Terry got pissed and pushed his way to the front. Several people got shoved to the side. They swore at him.

"Get the fuck out of here," he said heatedly, determined to defend his lover's honor. Some of the men grumbled and made signs of attack. Terry sneered. "I said go, you assholes. You swine!"

He bared his teeth and began to hyperventilate. His eyes got wild, and then he started to grunt.

The Buy Porkers were at a loss. The ones in front backed away. "Let's get out of here," someone said. "Can't you see the guy's crazy?" They moved off, keeping their eyes on him. "He's probably on that drug, the one they talked about in *Time*. What's it called?"

When they were out of sight, Terry stopped his act. It took a while to wind down. He was enormously pleased with himself, and snorted one last time. Laughing, he entered the bar.

Jerry Cox, the bouncer, wasn't far from the door.

He was dressed in typically impeccable fashion, camel hair jacket, fitted navy pants, tasseled leather shoes. Tonight he wore a beige turtleneck, which hid his gigantic neck.

"Been chained to the Nautilus again, Jerry?" By way of greeting Terry patted him on the shoulder rather than risk being crushed by a handshake.

Cox chuckled and sucked in his breath. The lapels of his coat slid apart, revealing a chest like a chunk of marble. "You should join me, little man. So they don't kick sand in your face."

Terry tapped his chest with a thumb. "No one's kicking this man. Not tonight." He told him about the scene outside. Cox wasn't impressed.

"You get in trouble you start unloading your mouth like that. It's bad for business."

"Trouble is my business," he postured.

Cox eyed him. "You go easy tonight, Terry. You hear me? Just lay back and stay cool."

Terry was too full of himself to listen. He shuffled his feet and playfully sparred with the big man. Cox wasn't in the mood. He reached out and grabbed Terry's arm below the shoulder, squeezing it as easily as a loaf of bread. The pain was instant.

"Hey, man, let go." Terry tried to twist away but the grip was steel. Cox pulled him close, then leaned into his face.

"What you do outside is your business." His mouth reeked of breath freshener. "What you do inside is mine. I'm thin tonight, Terry. Be cool and don't give me trouble." He released the arm and patted Terry on the shoulder. Smiling, he turned away.

Terry stood there, dazed, rubbing his arm. His fingertips tingled. His sense of well-being was gone. He made his way to the bar, where he ordered a beer. Half a bottle later he felt a little better. Cox was an asshole. Frankie was the reason he was here. She looked good tonight, fresh, loose and sexy. He blew her a kiss, to which she replied with a slow grind of her hips. He smiled, smug that this fly lady was going home with him.

Near closing time a couple of well-dressed guys came in. Terry heard them before he saw them, their laughter piercing the pounding dance music that never stopped. He turned on his stool and watched as they passed. One was blond with a reddish mustache that curled over his lip. His hair was cut conservatively, with sideburns sliced even with his ears. The other was older, in his early to mid-fifties. His hair was flecked with gray, and he wore a fancy suit that bore the look of a custom job. There was a gold pin in his lapel, a handkerchief in his breast pocket and a fat diamond ring on his finger. The two of them took stools at the bar and ordered drinks. The older man looked around, as though noticing where he was for the first time.

Terry glanced at Frankie to see if she'd seen the men. Often she was too drunk to notice anyone but herself. This time, however, she was already at work, grinding, shaking, giving it what she had. The blond was the first to notice. He nudged his friend, causing Terry to smile. He was already counting the money Frankie would entice from these rich daddies.

After finishing his beer, he slid off the bar stool,

deciding it was time to make up with Cox. It didn't pay to be at odds with the guy. On the way past the door he heard a siren. In his current state of mind it sounded more piercing than usual. Probably some new cop device to paralyze the criminal mind. It reminded him of the bone-chilling screeches of crack-addicted babies. He shivered and looked for Cox.

Out of the corner of an eye he saw the rich man at the bar freeze. From behind he couldn't tell why. His gaze shifted to the platform, where Frankie had stopped dancing. Something was wrong. She too had frozen, her face pinched in disbelief as though the mind behind it had been gripped by a frightening and irresistible command. Suddenly, life seemed to drain from her. She flailed at the air, and her legs buckled. Slowly, like a cut flower wilting in the sun, she sank to the ground.

Terry was on the platform in seconds. He held her head and called her name. He slapped her cheeks. Nothing. He yelled for someone to stop the music and stuck his ear to her mouth. He heard air move, saw her chest rise ever so slightly. Her breath had the edgy smell of whiskey.

With Cox's help he got her down. The big man carried her to the dressing room. By then her eyes were open, but the eyeballs were roving independently of one another. The muscles of her face twitched randomly, like blinking lights on a circuit board. Other parts of her body moved in a similar fashion, in disconnected tics and jerks. It occurred to Terry that she was having a seizure, but it didn't look like any he had ever seen.

"Lay her down," he told Cox, making a space in the middle of the room. He pulled a bunch of dresses from the rack and spread them on the floor. Cox lowered her gently then stood back up.

"You think we should call an ambulance?" he asked tentatively.

Terry didn't answer. He was crouched at her side, watching the ripples of the muscles as they contracted, then relaxed. It was as if she were some shell, or an empty piece of hardware being programmed.

"She drank a lot tonight, Terry." Cox rummaged in her purse and pulled out a bottle of Jack Daniels. It was three-quarters empty.

Terry nodded and brushed the hair out of her eyes. The flicker of muscle movement over her body was gradually subsiding. Her breathing was more steady. The eyes had clicked back into synchrony. Now she looked more like a run-of-the-mill drunk.

"Maybe I should just take her home," he said.

"Yeah," Cox agreed quickly. "That way everyone stays clean. Here . . ." He unpeeled some bills from a wad he kept in his pocket. "I'll flag a taxi."

After he left the room, Terry tried to rouse Frankie again. This time her eyes tracked to the sound of his voice, but the look in them was still glassy. She did, however, move to his command, and he managed to sit her up and get her into her clothes. When Cox came back, they got her on her feet. After several stiff-legged tries she was back walking again. She moved like a drunk.

The bar was empty when they went through it, the

music off and the lights on. Ted looked up from behind the counter as they passed.

"We finally got the stiff in a cab," he told Cox.
"She okay?"

"Yeah. She just got excited seeing her old man."
He winked and with his free hand punched Terry on
the arm. "The guy's a stud."

"It's a shitty job," Ted muttered, going back to
cleaning glasses. "She should be home raising
kids."

"Home is just where she's going," said Cox. He
helped Terry escort Frankie to the cab and get her in.
By now she was moving better but still had not spoken. She sat where she was put, and Terry got in
beside her. He told the driver where to go.

"When she comes out of it, tell her to take a couple days off," said Cox. "Get her legs back."

Terry nodded and shut the door. The taxi took off
down Broadway, which was pretty fast that time of
night. The driver didn't talk. He kept a pencil behind
his ear and at stoplights worked on a crossword puzzle he kept on the dash. Terry spent the trip trying to
get Frankie to talk. She'd turn to his voice, but to his
questions and pleas she was mute. When he stopped
speaking, or sometimes in the middle of a sentence,
she'd look elsewhere. Her movements seemed disconnected, her affect devoid of recognition. Like a
baby, thought Terry, seeing the world for the first
time.

He kept his arm around her the whole trip, drawing her against him with a steady pressure. She neither resisted nor nestled up to him naturally. When
she was drunk, she was usually more compliant.

"Frankie," Terry finally said, "you rest now." He moved his hand to the back of her head, forcibly pushing it to his chest. "You've had enough for one night. Rest. We're almost home."

She resisted the pressure of his hand, but only for a moment. When she gave in, something seemed to go out of the drama. Terry felt better. He was reassured by her closeness and the mingled smell of alcohol and sweat. He ran his fingers through her hair and heaved a sigh.

The driver turned at Houston and again just past Lafayette. He slowed, and Terry pointed out his building. It was an old brick walkup, sandwiched between a warehouse and another walkup. A few doors down was the Wing Luen Trading Company and next to it the Yin Lung Fruit Exchange. Both were dark. Terry paid the driver with one of the bills Cox had given him then bundled Frankie out, not waiting for the change. He shouldered her into the building and up the four steep flights to their apartment. He got her inside, closed and locked the door and turned on the light.

They were standing at the head of a narrow hall, made narrower by cinder block and bare wood bookshelves along one side. The ceiling was high, curved and riddled with cracks. A plated brass fixture held three naked bulbs, one of which was dead. Opposite the bookshelves were two doorways. The first led to the bedroom; the second, the bathroom. The far end of the hall opened into the living room, beyond which lay a compact kitchen.

Terry went into the bedroom by habit, dropping his coat on the floor and turning on the television.

Their bed was a mattress on the floor, and he flopped down, waiting for Frankie to join him. After a minute or two he called to her. She didn't answer. He called again, then got up and went back into the hall. She hadn't moved.

"C'mon," he said, taking her by the wrists and pulling her into the bedroom. "You must be exhausted."

He steered her to the bed and sat her down. The television seemed to attract her attention. She watched with a fixed stare, face motionless save for the eyes, which darted with each flicker of image. Terry brought her some food, which she accepted wordlessly, chewing and swallowing without taking her eyes from the tube. Her expression never changed, and his worry returned. Maybe she'd really flipped this time. He tried to remember neurology lessons but couldn't think of a thing. He was angry at her for drinking so much.

He turned off the TV. Frankie kept staring at the screen. Her face, even in its emptiness was lovely. Dark, wavy hair, crescent eyes, full, red lips. Terry started to get aroused.

A moment before he had thought there was something wrong, but now he saw her posturing for what it was. A game. She was tempting him, luring him on with her beauty and restraint. He liked that, and touching her chin, turned her head until it was facing his own. He kissed her on the cheek, then the lips.

"You're beautiful," he murmured. He found her dead tongue with his own. "I love you."

He had to carry it all. Laying her on the bed, he

removed her clothes, and as before, she neither helped nor resisted. Sometimes she was like this when drunk, but Terry usually didn't make love those times. Tonight was different. He felt uncommonly aroused.

He handled her gently, beating down another wave of anger at her helplessness and the thought that she might be doing this intentionally, enfeebling herself as a way of avoiding him. The power of love soon took control, banishing all doubts. Terry pumped away, past the late night fatigue, through the alcohol and pot until he made his climax. It wasn't great, but it was enough to calm his nerves. He turned off the light and rested a hand on her thigh. In moments he was out.

Frankie did not sleep. The parts of her brain that allowed such activity had been knocked out, at least for the night. She was too busy processing information. Sound, smell, sight. This strange place, the touch of the body next to her. Something had happened to the world, some crack had opened. She had moved down a fault line, moved, maybe disappeared. Everything was the same and different. She was a baby, and growing up fast. Soon, maybe as early as morning, she would be a man.

Siren

There is an inclination when faced with the inexplicable and preposterous to call on some dogma or system of values for aid. Religion has, for the greater part of human life on this planet, served in this capacity.

In the past eighty years it has been supplanted by science. Logic stands in place of spirit; methodology above faith. We are content with knowledge and control, pleased when the voice of instinct grows dim, when the taste for raw meat and blood fades. We are relieved to secure our thirsts in boxes, behind walls, in locked drawers beside pills. We say, I believe in science. Science, from sciens, *having knowledge. The past participle of* scire, *to know. We want this word in our vocabulary. It gives us strength. Few of us recall the kinship of* scire *to* scindere. *Scindere, to cut. Latin brother to* schizein, *to split. Schizophrenia. The head that is split. The one that equals two.*

The siren is a device for the production of audible frequency sound waves by the regular interruption of a jet of compressed gas or vapor. It was invented in 1819 by Cagniard de la Tour, a tone-deaf Frenchman who nonetheless was an avid music lover. In his later years he became acquainted with Hector Berlioz, who used the siren's concept in a number of his orchestral works. The device was originally designed to measure the vibrations of sound, and De la Tour was the first to accurately quantify a wide variety of tones. He ascertained that the buzzing wings of a mosquito move at a rate of fifteen thousand beats per second and went on to measure the range of dozens of musical instruments, bird songs, dog howls and the like. Single-handedly, he developed the theory of acoustico-coital synergy, in which he attempted to link the pitch of peri-coital vocalization (i.e., the sounds produced during arousal and intromission) with coital outcome. His research, unfortunately, was cut short, and interest in the siren waned for many years.

In the latter part of the nineteenth century the instrument underwent a fundamental change in form. This resulted in a device capable of producing high levels of fluctuating or warbling sound, and it changed the siren's function from measuring tool to signal producer. Warning sirens were developed and used successfully in air raid defense, ambulance calls and policework. The power of these newer devices is such that they are capable of projecting intense and often disturbing sound for miles.

Recently, there has been new interest in the effect of such sound. A study from Great Britain in 1989 found a three-fold increase in neurologic disease in those who lived in London during the years 1941 to 1945 as compared to a matched cohort living in Cheltenham. This finding was attributed to the frequent use of sirens in London as warning signals during the war. Those who lived a half a mile or less from such sound sources were particularly prone to neurologic disease, manifesting itself commonly by lapses of short-term memory, behavioral changes and affective disorders. A study from Finland the same year corroborated the British findings. Additionally, in the autopsies of seven of the subjects, investigators found evidence of neuronal reorganization and piecemeal degeneration throughout the frontal lobes. The changes were similar to those observed in mice subjected to varying degrees of high-pitched (80,000 Hz) siren stimulation over a period of several weeks.[1]

In the United States there have been similar reports. Most are anecdotal, but recently, the National Center for the Study of Disease has released epidemiologic data of significance. Three population clusters (com-

prising a total of one hundred and thirteen cases)
have been identified, each of which has been exposed
to high levels of siren sound over a period of ten or
more years. The inhabitants of two of the clusters (one
in Chicago, another in Houston) live within a three-
block radius of a busy firehouse. Those in the third
(East Los Angeles) reside within a block of a police
station. In all groups there is nearly a 30 percent inci-
dence of Alzheimer's disease. Borderline states,
hebrephrenia and infantile autism exist in much
higher proportions than normal. Arrests for sexual of-
fenses—prostitution, sodomy, indecent exposure,
transsexuality—are ten to fifteen times the national
average.[2]

In contrast to their European colleagues, the inves-
tigators locate the pathology in the limbic system.
They reason that the auditory apparatus is in inti-
mate contact with this area of the brain, which is
precisely the region that governs emotion. More im-
portant from an epidemiologic standpoint is their
suggestion that we are seeing only the tip of the ice-
berg:

"Siren-associated sound," they conclude, "pene-
trates the human neurologic apparatus deeply and ef-
ficiently. The changes it produces, whether by synap-
tic re-organization or destruction, are just beginning
to be appreciated. Given that thousands, perhaps mil-
lions of people are exposed to such sound on a regular
basis, we should expect to observe a striking increase
in neurologic disorders. Primarily these will be of the
temporal and/or frontal type (i.e., disturbances of
emotion and mentation), but practitioners must be
alert to a full range of presentation."[3]

In both African and South American tribes much attention in the warrior classes is given to voice. Whoops, shrieks, wails and howls are practiced assiduously. Certain pitches and patterns of sound are known to cause fear, even paralysis in enemies. During battle, prior to engagement, one tribe will siren its foe. Voices are raised, joined, sent forth. When successful, the enemy tribe will swoon, become disorganized, flee. This is the siren as a social tool. A tool of war.

Other Sirens inhabit the sea. They live on a remote island and sing a bewitching and heavenly song that promises comfort and unimaginable delight. Sailors have driven themselves mad in pursuit of it, crashing their vessels on the rocky shore, forfeiting their lives.

These Sirens are women, their song a poem of female power and attraction that no man can resist. To give in is to be consumed. To give in is to die. The only possible salvation for a man, the only hope, is to deafen himself to the most beautiful song on the face of the earth.

3

Frankie de Leon dropped out of college her third year and moved to New York City. Neither her father, who was dead, nor her mother, who insinuated a dark and uncertain future, could stop her. She moved in with her boyfriend to a roach-ridden, leaky dive on the Lower East Side. Heaven and hell, they lasted two months. "The East Coast is a wound," he told her the day he moved out, meaning that he couldn't stand her face anymore. "I need to check out the West." Frankie got images of Colorado and California, and maybe the boy did too. Six months later she heard he got a job in his father's company in Hackensack, about as far west as she could spit. The news made her laugh, and then she went out and got drunk. She passed out and the next night got drunk again. It was nice knowing the liquor was always there. She had been doing it since high school.

Frankie met Terry at Suter's. She had gone to the basement in search of a book on cosmology, and having found it, had slid it down the front of her jeans. Terry saw the whole thing and called her over. He found her appealing, especially the way her eyes met his openly. He was rather stoned.

"You should put the book back," he said.

Frankie gave him a blank look. "Huh?"

"The book," he repeated. "In your pants."

She stared at him, trying to gauge how far he would go. She looked away for a moment, then fixed him again with her eyes.

"What book?"

Terry took a breath and blew it out. "C'mon, lady. I saw you lift it. Put it back and walk away."

"Prove it," said Frankie. She crossed her arms and puffed out her chest.

Terry sighed and got off his stool. He went around the counter, until he was face to face with her.

"What do you want me to do," he said, "feel you up?"

"Do your job," she replied carelessly.

Neither of them moved. Then Frankie smiled.

"You're stoned, aren't you?"

Imperceptibly, the lines of force shifted. Frankie took his hand and placed it under her shirt, about two inches above the top of the book. She held it there.

"Find it," she challenged.

The hand trembled, and Frankie let go and waited. A moment later it began to inch down between the book and her crotch. When it reached her pubic hair, it hesitated, then pulled out.

"Find anything?" she asked innocently.

Terry shook his head. He wanted to fuck the woman right there on the spot.

"Then I guess I'm free to go."

Unconsciously, Terry lifted his hand to his face, smelling the tips of his fingers. He felt as if he were acting a part someone very clever and unforgiving had written for him.

"You leave now, they'll get you in front. There's an alarm."

Frankie weighed the information. "You got a suggestion?"

"Fuck me now."

Despite her pose, the words startled her. She took half a step back and forced a smile. "I'm on my way to work."

"Later then."

She regarded him. "You got a pencil?"

He handed her a pen.

"Turn around."

When he was looking the other way, she slid the book out. On the title page she wrote her name, toyed with giving a fake phone, then wrote the real number and handed him the book. Terry dogged her on the way out, but she didn't look back. She had made her decision, now she wanted to forget it for a while. Terry was left holding the book, which was still warm. On his fingers he had her smell; in his pants, a huge erection. He went into the stockroom and beat off against a stack of Encyclopedia Brittanica. Afraid of ruining the books, he kept his cock inside his pants. As a consequence, things got a little sticky and wet. His squirmy walk on the way out was a dead giveaway, and he hurried behind the counter.

He found her name on the title page of the book. *The Big Bang*, and right below it, Frankie de Leon. He ran the spine of the book through the machine to demagnetize the alarm code. There were still a few hours of work left. By the time he was ready to leave, his pants would be dry. Then he'd be able to lift the book himself.

Their courtship lasted six weeks. By then they had it figured they were well enough suited to live together. Frankie moved in with Terry, whose place was bigger and had less roaches, and a few months later she got a job at Virgo's. Terry stayed at Suter's. They did all right together, holding each other up by turns. Sex was good, and the rest was what it was. Over time, as happens, they got closer. There were fun and games and periods of real happiness. On occasion they even talked of love.

Morning came. Frankie stirred. He had been neither asleep nor awake, but rather in some hazy region of processing and information exchange. He sat up and looked around. Things by day were clearer: colors were colors, objects had names. Sounds outside the window made a certain amount of sense. He understood that he was a person, separate from a world around him. He knew he was in a room, on a bed. There were clothes on the floor, books, a clock radio. He could name these things, although nothing was familiar. He did not recognize the place by sight or smell, nor by any other sense. He did not recall how he had arrived. Worst of all, he could not remember his name.

He stumbled out of bed, bracing himself against a

wall until the dizziness passed. His head felt like the aftermath of an explosion, his tongue like sand. He groped his way out of the room, instinctively moving toward the smell of coffee. It was at the end of a hall, in a small kitchen. There was a man there.

"Morning." The man glanced up from his paper. "Aren't you cold?"

Frankie stared at him.

"How do you feel?" The man poured him a cup of coffee and held it out. "You sure were fucked up last night."

"Who are you?"

The man chuckled, then got up and rummaged in the refrigerator. "You know, I was asking myself that very question not five minutes ago. Who the fuck am I and where is my life going? You read the paper, you get all sorts of crazy ideas. Like this man, he's crawling from California to New York on his hands and knees. Blessing the earth and its creatures. Ants, dogs, birds, lizards, the guy's got it figured out. He's doing something with his life. It makes one helluva lot of sense."

He pulled out a couple of eggs and some margarine. "Fried or scrambled?"

"Who are you?" Frankie asked again. "What is this?"

"What it is," Terry replied, cracking the eggs in a pan. "This is it, Frankie. The big I—T."

Frankie put the cup of coffee on the table and grabbed Terry's arm. "This isn't a game. Who are you? Where is this?"

There was panic in the voice, and Terry turned from the stove, simultaneously unpeeling Frankie's hand from his arm. It still hurt where Cox had grabbed him the night before.

"You still tripping?" he asked.

"Tripping?" Frankie's eyes darted around the room. "What the hell's going on?"

"You got a hangover is what. A million cells are dying every day, Frankie. You got to cut down."

"You keep calling me Frankie."

"You got it bad this time, babe." He shook his head. "Blackout, a little amnesia." He made a motion with his hand, like turning a key in a lock. "Switching off the lights. You got to stop."

"Who's Frankie?"

"Good question. Who is Frankie? You tell me."

Frankie grabbed the man again in the same place, digging his nails in. Terry winced and twisted out.

"Don't do that," he warned.

"Tell me who Frankie is."

Terry eyed her. "Frankie de Leon. The Lioness. Queen without a throne, seductress, breaker of hearts, lover. Frankie is you, babe."

Frankie shook his head. "That's not me."

"You don't know who you are."

"I don't know my name. But I'm not a woman."

Terry snorted. "No? Then what are those things hanging on your chest? And what was it that wrapped so nice around my cock last night?"

Frankie followed Terry's eyes to his body. He saw feet, smooth-shaven legs, a patch of hair where his thighs met. Rounded hips, a flat belly. From his chest hung two fleshy globes. They had weight, a sensation he was not used to in that part of his body. Breasts?

"I'm not a woman," he repeated.

Terry shook his head and turned to the eggs, which were burning. "Woman enough for me."

"No," Frankie said, his voice tremulous but firm. "I'm not a woman. I'm a man."

A Newborn Creature

Memory, like many functions of the brain, is most precisely studied in conditions in which it is most conspicuously absent. Its loss can take many forms. Sacks describes the case of a man who, as the result of a stroke, developed a profound visual amnesia:

"Forthwith this patient became completely blind— but did not know it. He looked blind—but he made no complaints. Questioning and testing showed, beyond doubt, that not only was he centrally or 'cortically' blind, but he had lost all visual images and memories, lost them totally—yet had no sense of any loss. Indeed, he had lost the very idea of seeing—and was not only unable to describe anything visually, but bewildered when I used words such as 'seeing' and 'light.' He had become, in essense, a non-visual being. His entire lifetime of seeing, of visuality, had, in effect, been stolen."[4]

A. Luria, the famous Russian neuropsychiatrist, presents a far more devastating case of amnesia. The Man with a Shattered World *is the autobiography of a man injured in the war. His memory dysfunction is extreme, at times agonizingly so:*

". . . I couldn't visualize a cat, dog, or any other creature after I'd been wounded. I've seen dogs, I

know what they look like, but ever since my injury I haven't been able to visualize one when I'm asked to. I can't imagine or draw a fly or a cat, can't visualize the cat's paws and ears—I simply can't picture them.

"If I try to get an image of a thing (with my eyes opened or closed), I can't do it, I can't visualize a person, animal, or plant. Except that sometimes I have a sense of something that resembles them, though it fades very quickly. What I really see are some specks or tiny bodies.

"I tried to remember my mother's and sisters' faces but couldn't form any image of them. But when I was finally sent home and saw my family, I immediately recognized my mother and sisters. They were overjoyed that I was home, threw their arms around me, and kissed me. But I wasn't able to kiss them—I had forgotten how . . .

"I can't understand how wood is manufactured, what it is made of. Everything—no matter what I touch—has become mysterious and unknown. I can't put anything together myself, figure anything out, or make anything new. I've become a completely different person, precisely the reverse of what I was before this terrible injury . . .

"I've become a very peculiar sort of person since I was wounded—sickly, but on the other hand a kind of newborn creature. Everything I learned or experienced in life has just dropped out of my mind and memory, vanished for good since that awful head wound. I have to try to identify everything I see all over again, even things in my daily life. When I leave the hospital for a while to get some air, to get a little closer to nature—flowers, trees, lakes—I'm not only aware of

*something new and unclear that's hard to under-
stand, but also something that makes me feel terribly
helpless, that doesn't really let me grasp and understand what I see.''*[5]

This man suffered an incapacitating form of amnesia. He was unable to properly receive and process
sensory information, and was impaired in his ability
to express himself. His intellect was severely crippled.
Not only was he unable to remember, but he had forgotten how.

Other forms of amnesia, equally as profound, produce far less effect on cognition. Intelligence is pre-
served, and behavior to the undiscerning eye may appear virtually normal. Korsakoff's syndrome, a
unique and rare disorder of memory, is one of these. It
is characterized by two salient features: retrograde
amnesia, in which there is an impaired ability to recall events prior to the onset of the illness, and
antegrade amnesia, in which there is an impaired
ability to acquire new information, that is, to learn or
to form new memories. It is, in essence, a "pure"
memory disorder. Unlike the cases described by Sakhs
and Luria, other parts of the brain continue to function competently.

In the vast majority of cases Korsakoff's syndrome
is caused by chronic alcoholism. Few recover completely.

Patients who suffer the severe form of this illness
are unable either to recall a past or to create one
anew. They become literally stranded in the present. A
face, a word, a gesture known one minute is forgotten
the next. With each blink of the eye the world seems to
pop into existence for the first time.

If left alone, these people may wander helplessly in a house or city they have known from childhood. Destination melds with origin; each is whatever the next step brings. They may not know their own names, much less the names of others. Often they forget even the names of common objects.

To fill these perplexing and embarrassing voids, they confabulate, drawing with keen eye and ear on other people's cues to fashion for themselves a place in the world. Lacking a history, they devise marvelous stories, as convincing as they are preposterous. Through surface wit and imagination they charm their acquaintances and keep the world at bay. If ever they are sad, they forget it a moment later. Self-awareness is fleeting. So too are despair, hope, love, fear . . . the words are impossibly long. Their world is an ever-changing, anesthetic present. Their lives are the stories they tell.

It is not known whether any Korsakoff patient has ever claimed to be of the opposite sex.

Terry dished out the eggs, then sat down and began to eat. Frankie did not move. Every so often Terry glanced up and shook his head. At length he motioned to the other chair with his fork.

"Have a seat."

Frankie frowned, then did as he suggested. The act of sitting at a table with a plate of food recalled the act of eating. He noticed the clumps of yellow-brown egg and realized suddenly that he was famished. He began to shovel it in.

"I want some more," he said when he'd finished.

"There's another in the fridge."

"Scrambled. Like this."

"Do it yourself."

He didn't move. Terry looked up from his plate.

"Did you forget how to cook too?"

Frankie stared at him, barely registering the mockery. At length he got up and opened the refrigerator door. There were some old greens inside, an opened carton of milk, some margarine crumpled in its foil and various plastic bags. Nothing looked the least bit familiar. Searching for the egg, he began to get cold. The air from the refrigerator streamed against his skin, hardening his nipples and causing goose bumps to appear on his arms and chest. It came to him that he was naked, and he turned to Terry.

"Where are my clothes?"

Terry shrugged. "Where they always are."

Always meant nothing. Frankie glared at him.

"In the room," he said, gesturing down the hall. "Why don't you get dressed, and we'll start over. Page one, new beginning. Whad'ya say?"

Frankie turned and went back the way he had come. At the first door he stopped and looked in. There was a sink, toilet and bathtub. Seeing the toilet recalled a need other than food. He went inside and shut the door. Lifting the toilet seat, he stood in front with his legs veed open. In a few seconds the urine flowed.

It wasn't a bad shot: nearly half made it into the bowl. The rest hit the rim and the floor, with a sizable portion running down his leg. Frankie frowned. This was not right, nor were the wet beads that re-

mained on his pubic hair. The nightmare was per-
petuating itself. He began to panic.

He gulped air, each gulp making him want another. Soon his fingertips were tingling, and then his
muscles started to twitch. He felt like he was suffocating and breathed faster. His head became light.
The room spun. Moments later, he collapsed to the
floor.

A minute or two later he came to. He was on the
floor of a bathroom, naked, wet and foul with urine.
He managed to stand up and get in the bathtub.
There was an old yellow shower curtain, streaked
with mold, which he pulled around the tub. He
turned the water on hot and waited. The shower
head sputtered a few times, and then the water hit
his back, cutting a line of pleasure down his spine. It
was the best he had felt since he could remember.
He wanted to cry.

He showered until there was no more hot water,
then dried himself and got out. Above the sink was a
mirror, misted with water vapor. It occurred to him
that he might need a shave, but he wanted some
clothes first. Wrapping the towel around his waist
locker-room style, he left the bathroom for the room
in which he'd begun the dream, tendering the vague
notion that if he backtracked, he could start everything over the way it was supposed to be. He still
had a headache, and every so often ripples of nausea
rose halfway up his throat before being swallowed
back down. Maybe the sickness, too, would vanish.

In the bedroom he sat on the mattress. Next to it
on the floor was a crumpled pile of women's clothes
and a purse, from which the neck of a bottle was

sticking out. Frankie grabbed the bottle, and without thinking or knowing why, unscrewed the top and took a slug. It burned going down. He took another.

Five minutes later the headache was gone. He felt steadier, not about to retch every time he moved. He undid the towel and got up, looking for some clothes to put on. There was a bureau against a wall and next to it a closet that smelled of sweat and cigarette smoke. He went through one hanger after another, looking for something to wear. He found dresses, vests, blouses and skirts, mules and slingbacks on the floor, hats on hooks, but nothing whatsoever to suit a man. Finally, jammed at the end of the clothes rod, he located a herringbone sports coat and slacks. He pulled them out, got some underpants and a wrinkled button-down shirt from a drawer in the bureau, then sat on the bed and put them on.

The underwear fit okay, but the rest of the clothes were ridiculous. The jacket and shirt hung on him like seaweed, and when he stood up, the slacks slipped down to his thighs. Angrily, he pulled everything off, wishing he could continue past the clothes to the skin itself. He glared at the bureau and the closet as if they were enemies. Then he started over.

In the back of the bottom drawer was a worn-out pair of jeans. The cuffs were frayed, and there was a rip across each of the knees, but they fit well enough; even the wrinkles seemed to conform to his body. Hitching them on his waist and locking the zipper, Frankie felt for the first time that something was right. In another drawer he found a faded tee shirt with writing and a picture on the front that he ignored. It was loose and baggy, all the better to hide the curves of the body, deny the contours of this alien land.

He took another nip from the bottle, which was nearly empty. Briefly, he wondered where he had developed such a taste for alcohol. It seemed to calm the little tremors, and it straight out flattened the headache. He threw down the last half-inch and dropped the bottle on the bed. Bracing himself, he prepared to face the man again.

He was still in the kitchen, feet propped on the table, browsing through the newspaper. He looked up as Frankie entered.

"Feeling better?"

Frankie sat in the other chair, businesslike but wary. "We need to talk."

"I thought you hated that shirt."

Frankie looked down. Painted on the shirt was a picture of a man fishing from a boat, with a mermaid circling his underwater hook. Above the man's head, in capitals, were the words, "GONE FISHIN,'" with the "F" crossed out and a "W" scratched above it. Beneath the mermaid's tail, in parentheses, was written "any fish'll bite if you got the right bait." What that bait was was not clear: the hook had nothing on it.

"The empty hook," said Terry, grinning. "The allure of endless possibility. Of course, that was before I met you."

"I'm not who you think I am."

His grin widened. "Your checkered past, you mean."

"I'm not this woman Frankie you keep calling me. I'm not a woman at all."

Terry wagged his finger. "Bad start, Frankie."

"I'm not Frankie." Despite the alcohol, or because of it, he was starting to get worked up. He leaned on his elbows and raised his voice. "I'm a man."

Terry heard the pitch of Frankie's voice and sensed danger. He had the urge to dig his face into the paper but feared that that would only incense her more. "Why do you keep insisting on something that's obviously false?"

"I insist because it's true. Something's happened to me. I don't know what, or how. I don't remember anything before this morning."

"Before this morning you were tanked up to the lid. Dead drunk. The stuff obviously reamed out your brain."

Drunk? The accusation gave him pause. "I don't remember liking to drink," he said, straining without success to recover something of the past. "But just now, back there, it seemed so natural. Automatic."

"You're a boozer, babe. An alcoholic. Your body craves it."

"But this isn't my body. It's someone else's. Hers."

Terry slapped the paper down. "What the fuck, Frankie. What are we saying here?"

"I don't know. You, me, this place. I don't know any of it."

"And what else?"

"This isn't my body . . ."

"Of course not. Anyone can see. You're a man."

Frankie glanced at him. "You're laughing at me."

"Fuck I'm laughing. I'm crying. I'm bawling." He feigned pulling out his hair. "This is pathetic."

"It's a nightmare."

"What are we saying here, Frankie? It's over, is that it? You've had enough? You want out?"

"I want this to end."

"Then end it right. Don't jerk me around with some bullshit about not knowing who I am. You want to erase something, erase this bullshit. Don't erase me."

"It's not bullshit."

"I'm a man," said Terry. "I can take what you've got to dish."

Frankie shook his head. "I don't understand this at all."

Abruptly Terry stood up, kicking his chair over backward. He hammered the table with a fist. "You listen to me. I'm talking about respect. Don't fuck me around on this, Frankie."

He felt like lifting the table and throwing it. The way Frankie cringed made him even madder. He swept the newspaper to the floor, then grabbed his plate and tossed it at the wall. It shattered, and he stormed out of the kitchen. Moments later he was at the front door.

Frankie remained in his chair. He was frightened and bewildered. When the door slammed, his whole body jumped. He waited for something more to happen, but the minutes passed without incident. Still, he was afraid to move.

Gradually, he understood that he was alone in the apartment. It was a relief. The man neither understood what had happened nor seemed to care. He made jokes and got mad. He insisted on things that weren't true. His presence was a complication.

Frankie made himself another cup of coffee, got the egg from the refrigerator and fried it up. He found a loaf of bread in a drawer and had two slices with the egg. He tried to concentrate on the act of eating, whose sensations were basic and unthreatening. It afforded a certain measure of comfort, but then it was done. The thoughts came back. And the questions. So many questions.

If he could just find out what had happened, then maybe he would understand. Calamity begs for a reason, and he assumed there was an explanation. If he could discover what it was, then maybe he could alter the outcome. His mind cleaved to that idea. There was order, and in the discovery of that order there was power. So rational a thought, so fatuous and reassuring. C followed B, which followed A. Reason would be his guide, and knowledge the first step.

He returned to the bathroom to look himself in the eye. The steam from his shower had long since dissipated, and the mirror above the sink was clear. Was a mouth. A gate. He quailed. The thought of seeing his face terrified him.

He leaned against the door to gather courage. He tried to blank his mind. Drawing his breath, he stepped forward.

It was actually quite lovely. Neck-length wavy dark hair swept past the edges of the forehead, framing blue eyes that were flecked with gray. The nose was strong, the lips wide, the top one slightly overhanging the bottom. There were smile lines at the corners of the mouth.

The face was young and pretty. Frankie could see that. But it was not his. Someone's skin had been sewn atop his own. Beneath it other tissues had been grafted. Cheeks, jawbone, teeth. A stranger looked at him, blinked when he blinked, frowned when he did. It watched his every move, knew his every thought. It was ruthless.

Frankie covered the face and turned away. Where had he gone? What had invaded him? How was he to get himself back?

When he looked again, the girl was still there. He grabbed at her with his fingernails, red fingernails, not his. He scratched the cheeks, which hurt. Tears collected in the eyes. The face registered pain.

Again he hid behind his hands, not willing to weep. When he looked back, the face was tense and hopelessly bewildered. Before his eyes its ignorance grew. The pupils ballooned. Slowly, like a sea, panic broke across its surface.

Frankie stumbled away. He was as far from understanding as before. Farther, because the shred of hope he had constructed was gone. To keep calling his condition a nightmare would be semantics. What was happening had all the texture, all the feel of reality.

The tears came. He huddled in a corner like a wounded animal, rocking back and forth, sobbing miserably. He had been violated. He was a prisoner. There was no exit.

He cried until he could cry no more. Then, like a

running gag, a persistent itch, the allure of reason returned.

This time he ordered his thoughts, forming them in his mind as simply as he could, giving each a number.

1. I am a man. This I know.
2. I have the face and body of a woman.
3. I do not know my name. I do not know where I live or what I look like. (At this point he began to breathe more rapidly; it took some moments before he had calmed himself sufficiently to continue.)
4. I do not remember anything before this morning. The man said I blacked-out. Was he telling the truth? Who is he anyway?
5. This body's name is Frankie. What is she to me? Is she occupying my body as I am hers?
6. Why has this happened? Whose victim am I? How?

These final questions put a rapid end to his program of enlightenment. Logic could not sustain itself in the face of such bewildering ignorance. Reason was a clown's fixed grin. He pushed himself out of the corner and headed down the hall. Maybe he could find out something of substance before the man returned.

On the floor of the bedroom he noticed the bottle of Jack Daniels and picked it up. It was empty. Alcohol, he thought. Okay. He held out his hands: they were pretty steady. Maybe all he had needed was a good cry. The idea seemed funny. He looked around.

Most of the bedroom was taken up by the mattress, on one side of which was a small television, on the other, a clock radio. Above it was a window covered by a faded cloth. The only piece of furniture in the room was the bureau, which was black except on the side next to the radiator, where the heat had peeled the paint to reveal an undercoat of lime green. There was the closet, whose rack of female clothes disturbed him almost as much as seeing his face in the mirror. He closed the door and went to the window. He had to step on the mattress to push the cloth aside.

Outside was a metal landing with stairs going up and down from it. Several stories below was the street and on the other side a tall brick building blackened with age. Frankie made out people through its grimy windows, all of whom seemed to be women. They were sitting at machines, sewing.

For no apparent reason one looked his way. She wore a scarf on her head and her face was deeply wrinkled. For a moment they locked eyes, then Frankie panicked, snapping the curtain shut. Backing away, he fled the room.

The hall was lined with books. Medical texts, science, romances, politics. Only the medical books had names in them: Terry Connor was printed on the inside cover of each one. Was he the man in the kitchen? A doctor? It didn't seem likely. Some of the science books had parts that were marked with yellow ink. There was one on quantum mechanics, another on solid state physics, a third on botany. A fat compendium purported to list all the plants of southern New England.

Frankie wondered which, if any, were his. He looked at the covers of some of the romances, dark and unruly haired men clutching the slender waists of full-bodied, tormented women. Nothing was familiar. He skimmed a page that seemed to have been marked with a slip of paper, searching for clues. A woman was coyly flirting with a man who was undressing her with his eyes. He shut the book in frustration. It was an impossible task, trying to find out about someone this way. Out of the whole book only a few sentences might ring true. And true for whom?

He left the hall, wishing his mind would go blank again. He didn't want to know this woman. He despised her. She had stolen his mind and sealed it off. When he found her, he would make her pay.

He went into the living room. What wealth existed in the apartment seemed concentrated there. An overstuffed green armchair and a frayed brown sofa with wide arms dominated the room. Above the sofa hung a poster of the President with his head replaced by a rocket launcher. On the opposite wall was a built-in wooden cabinet with glass doors, beneath which was a counter with a stereo. Two big speakers sat on the floor, and between them ran a long line of records. Frankie looked through them, but like the books they gave him little clue to his identity. There was such a range of style. Jazz, rock, industrial, R & B. In a box were some tapes, most of which were labeled. On an impulse he took one that wasn't and stuck it in the cassette player next to the stereo. He turned the machine on and waited. There was the hiss of tape noise, then some giggling in the background. A man's voice came on.

"I, Terry Connor, have been asked to speak of love. The lioness, naked before me, creamy and magnificent, has so bidden. Presumably, she wants comments directed to herself." There was the sound of a rapid intake of air, followed in ten seconds by a loud exhalation. A leonine roar.

> On my back, my feet,
> in a crouch I love you.
> On a hill, floating,
> rolling, your eyes tumbling
> I love you.
> Ass backward I love you,
> That smile;
> Buttocks like currant jelly
> Hips the dream of cavemen.
> Irresistible this is
> Urgent. Obscene.
> The c word, the f
> 'Taint love;
> 'Tis, so what the hell.
> FUCK FUCK FUCK
> I love your mind, lioness
> I want to fuck, lioness.
> The calabazoo
> That sweet calabazoo;
> Your smell, your heart,
> Your organ meats.
> How have I lasted without?
> How made the day?
> Slept nights, took breath,
> Tumbled in dreamy sleep?
> Cooked, washed, bathed,
> Stripped, uttered word,
> Groomed my looks . . ."

Laughter in the background halted the recitation. There was the uncertain sound of movement.

"Give me that," a woman's voice said. There were crackling noises.

"I'm not done."

"You're done all right." Giggling, more crackling noises, the sound of air through fine metal mesh.

"The lioness speaks now," the woman's voice said. "She speaks of the jungle. Her pride, the men who follow. Her prowess."

"What men? You're mine, De Leon."

"C'mere."

Moments of silence, followed again by crackles, like static. Then breathing, and the faint sound of a drum, deep in some chamber.

"Do you think it picks up our heartbeats?"

"Let's see what it gets down here."

Rubbing, the sound of water over pebbles.

"Stop." A pause, and then a loud crack. Giggles. From a distance, voices, trailing off.

". . . in here. Yes. God, Terry. Yes . . ."

The tape hissed on emptily. Frankie finally punched it off. He had heard the woman speak; it was as if she were alive in that very room. For the first time he felt ashamed. He had snatched her body; she was as gone as he. It was murder, both ways.

The thing to do, he thought, was to get the two of them together. Him and the girl. Ask some questions and work out the connection. He frowned. Which girl? And what connection? The whole thing was absurd . . .

He had to stop himself from going further.

He wanted a drink. He searched the apartment, including the bedroom, and found nothing. There were moments when he felt like screaming, but fear and a sense of doom kept him quiet. He kept eyeing the telephone, which sat like a stone on the living room floor, proof of his dementia and isolation. He remembered nothing, no names to call, no numbers. That gate, like all the others, was locked. He returned to his corner, which, because it had walls, boundary, definition, was something. He hunkered down and rocked, feeling hopeless, alone and forgotten.

The phone rang.

He jumped. It rang again. He quivered. Three, four, five, and still he could not move. On the eighth ring, forcing life to limb, he grabbed for it.

"Hello?" a voice said. "Frankie? Is that you?"

He did not recognize the speaker, a woman, but the voice did subtle things to his body.

"Hello? Is this 555-5217?"

He glanced at the dial, nodded.

"I'm sorry. I must have the wrong number."

"Wait."

"Frankie?"

"Who is it?"

"It's your mother. What's wrong?"

"My mother?"

"Yes. Is that so hard to believe?"

"Mother?"

"You sound far away. Put the phone closer to your mouth."

He held it against his lips.

"What's the matter?" The voice was more urgent. "Something's wrong."

He had nothing to say.

"Are you on drugs, Francesca? Please say you aren't."

"I'm not."

"Where's that boy? Terry. Is he there? Did you have a fight?"

"He's gone."

There was a pause, an emotional one, and Frankie hung on to learn what would come next.

"You don't give me much," the woman said.

"I don't know much," replied Frankie.

"It used to be different."

Frankie nodded, silently amazed at the woman's insight.

"I'm talking about family, Francesca. You make jokes. To me it's not a joke."

"It's not one to me either."

"I'm glad to hear that. I'm coming down the week after next. Thursday the nineteenth. I thought we could see each other."

"What do you look like?"

There was an icy silence on the other end. "God strike me down, but I can't wait until you get old. It's not all peaches and cream. A person wants to do something to look nice, that's her right."

Frankie wanted to ask another question but was afraid he'd make the woman mad.

"I've got some shopping to do," she said. "I'm not going back until mid-afternoon."

"Back where?"

"Home. Where else?"

Frankie thought about it. The woman seemed so sure. "Maybe I should meet you."

"I'll be close to the Regency. How about lunch? Twelvish?"

"You have things to tell me, don't you? Maybe you can help."

"Let me make sure." There was the sound of paper being turned, the pages of a book being flipped. "The nineteenth. Thursday. Is that what I said?"

"Thursday?"

"Try to look nice, dear."

"You know how I look?"

"I know how you can. You were always a beautiful girl, Francesca. As pretty as they come."

Suddenly, Frankie had misgivings. He felt trapped in a web of other people's knowledge and expectation of him, while he at the center knew absolutely nothing. More than before he felt invaded, naked to all eyes but his own. Without thinking, he muttered the thought aloud.

"Well put some clothes on," the woman chided. "Honestly. The way you people live . . ."

Frankie tried to back out of the date, but the woman interrupted before he could get the words out.

"I've got to run, dear." She smacked her lips near the receiver. "I love you." The line went dead.

Frankie stared at the phone, not moving until the operator came on ordering him to hang up. Again he felt like an insect caught in a web. Or pinned to a collector's board, while strangers gathered round, murmuring words, reaching out, touching him with unbidden fingers. He wanted to scream.

He needed a drink.
Some help.
A friend.
More than anything, he wanted to fall asleep and wake up the man he was.

4

Terry didn't come home until afternoon. Cradled in an arm he carried a long-stemmed flower, wrapped and stapled in green tissue paper. He called out when he got inside, then dropped his coat in the empty bedroom and went down the hall.

Frankie was asleep on the couch, still wearing the torn jeans and mermaid shirt. The sun slanted down on her face. As always, Terry was amazed how peaceful she looked in sleep. He loved her that way, as a child, a fairy tale. As a woman too, though in that form love was more problematic. He went to the kitchen, where he unwrapped the flower and put it in a jar. The momentary groan of the pipes as he filled the jar with water woke Frankie.

"Who's there?"

Terry came out of the kitchen bearing the flower. "For you."

Frankie sat up and rubbed his eyes. "I fell asleep, thank God."

"It's a gladiolus," Terry said meaningfully. He handed her the flower. "I want to make up."

Frankie turned the thick stem in his fingers, working up the nerve to speak. "Terry," he began, but the word caught in his throat. Using the man's name was an admission that they had some link. It gave him pause. He tried again. "I need your help."

Terry went immediately to the couch. Kneeling down, he took Frankie's hands in his own. "We're a unit, babe. What you need, I need."

Frankie, who had instantly stiffened upon being touched, could barely respond. Carefully, lest he irritate the man, he extricated himself from the grasp. "I want to speak freely," he said. "I don't know where else to turn."

"You don't need to turn, Frankie. We fight, we make up. It's dialectical. What I don't have, you don't need."

This disturbed Frankie. Again he felt circumscribed, as though he were someone else's plan. He wondered briefly if this was the man's way of encouraging him.

"You're not going to like it. It's going to make you mad."

"So make me mad. What's mad anyway but love. I get angry because I care." He put a hand on Frankie's thigh, and this time Frankie couldn't take it. He jumped up and went to the other side of the room. He tried to stay calm.

"I'm lost, Terry. Really, truly lost. This is not my home, you aren't my lover, these pants, I know they fit, but they're not mine. This body is someone else's. Frankie de Leon's, whoever that is. I don't know why, or how, but something's happened. Something terrible." He gestured frantically. "None of this makes sense. Nothing. I need help. Please. Help me. Tell me what's happened."

"You've flipped, that's what. How can you not be Frankie? Look in the mirror."

"I have. It's someone else's face. This body . . ." He grabbed his breasts as if to tear them off. "It's not mine. I've never been a woman. I know it. In the deepest part of me I know I'm a man."

"That's crazy. You're so sure, tell me your name. Your age. Tell me where you live."

"I don't know. I can't remember."

"You've got amnesia, Frankie. You got loaded last night, and now you can't remember. It happens. It doesn't mean you're not you."

"I am me. But me's not this." He slapped his chest. "Not this." He squeezed the skin of his cheeks between his palms as if to push it off his face. "I'm not a woman. Not this one, not anyone."

"How are you so sure?"

"I just am, I can't explain how. How is anyone?"

"That's easy." Terry grabbed his crotch. "I got the equipment, that's how. Never been a doubt."

A gauntlet, it seemed, had been tossed, and ineffably, Frankie felt obliged to take it up. But when he grabbed his own crotch and felt the smooth, knobless seam between one leg and the other, all manner of retort caught in his throat.

Terry, watching from the couch, sensed an advantage. He stood up and began to unbuckle his belt. "Mister's right here, Frankie. Humble, but not shy."

He dropped his pants and gestured for Frankie to do the same. Frankie shook his head.

Enjoying himself, Terry pulled down his under-pants. He stood with his legs spread, briefs around his hairy thighs, pants down by the ankles. He folded his arms across his chest.

"Proof of the pudding's in the eating," he said provocatively.

Frankie flicked an eye across Terry's mid-section. "This is ridiculous. Put your clothes back on."

"You wanted proof."

"I wanted help."

"Sure. Help yourself."

"Get dressed."

Terry reclothed himself with a triumph muted by his inability to loosen Frankie up. This thing about being a man was so weird. He wondered what it meant.

"If you're so sure you're a man, prove it."

"What proof would you accept?"

"What do you have to give?"

Frankie considered the question. He tried to recall what men did together that made them know they were among their own. Was there a joke? Some bit of secret lore? A rite? He could not remember.

"I have no proof. Only my word."

Terry regarded him. "It's hard to swallow, Frankie. I mean, shit, what would you do in my shoes?"

"I wish I were. I'd be a lot better off."

Terry kicked one across the room. Frankie was not amused.

"C'mon," wheedled Terry. "Where's your sense of

humor? You've got to admit there's something funny about all this.''

"Not to me. I need help, not jokes. You don't believe me, fine. You don't want to help, I'll find someone else.''

"And who would that be?''

"I don't know. I'll have to look. It's not as if I'd be giving up years of work.''

Terry reflected on that. He sat back on the couch and ran his fingers through his hair. Several lines of thought occurred to him.

1. Frankie had flipped. She needed hospitalization and probably medication too.
2. She was faking the whole thing. She had another lover, wanted to split and was too chicken-shit to say so.
3. She had become a dyke.
4. This whole thing was some kind of test of his love. Like Job. She wanted to see how far she could push, how far he'd go for her.

The second, in a sense, would have been the simplest. He could have accused her, gotten angry, felt hurt and betrayed. But Frankie wasn't the type to hide something like that, nor, until today, had there been any slackening whatsoever in her affections and desire. Of the four, he suspected the last, although a small voice urged him to go look in one of his medical texts to see if something like this had ever been described before. But did it really matter? The question at the moment was not whether her preposterous claim was possible, or even true, but what he had to do to keep her from leaving.

"Fuck it," he said. "This is how you want the show to run, this is how we'll play it."

"You'll help?"

"I'll help."

The words cut a path to Frankie's heart.

"When do we start?"

"I think we have."

"Yeah?"

Frankie nodded. "When you're happy, Terry, or maybe just a little less unhappy, what do you do to celebrate?"

Frankie wouldn't allow what Terry had in mind. He was immensely relieved to have found a friend, but light-years from allowing the friend to touch him in a manner any more familiar than a handshake. In lieu of flesh, Terry suggested champagne. Frankie readily agreed.

Terry went out for a bottle of Cold Duck, came back with two and a bag of chips. He popped the plastic cork in the living room and took a hit straight from the bottle. Frankie, as was her custom, used a cup, running her tongue along the rim as if not to miss a drop. Terry had always teased her for this, what he called her false economy, never quite understanding. But today there was no teasing. Terry simply registered the gesture for later, when he would systematically tear her ridiculous charade apart. For now he drank along with her, and two thirds of the way through the first bottle he asked her what, if anything, she had in mind to do.

"I don't know. I guess we could start by your telling me about Frankie de Leon. Maybe something will click."

"What is there to tell? She's my lover."

"What does she do?"

"You mean her work? She's a dancer." It was more than a little strange being face to face with her, yet talking as though she were absent. He had to keep reminding himself that this was a game.

"She works . . . worked . . . whatever . . . in a bar called Virgo's. She dances there."

"In a bar?"

"It's a topless joint. She does topless." He downed another glass of champagne, then leaned forward. "You don't remember this, Frankie? Really?"

He shook his head.

Terry burped. "Then let's get drunk." He filled their glasses. "Maybe when we wake up, everything'll be like it was."

"My constant hope."

Terry raised his glass. "To hope."

"Tell me what happened last night. You said she blacked out or something."

"She was drunk. Collapsed up on the stage. I had to carry her off."

"Has that happened before?"

"The woman likes her alcohol. Says she needs it to do a job like that. It was weird. She grabbed her ears, like she was being hurt or something . . ." The memory gave him the shivers. "There was a man at the bar who did the same. Then she fell."

"What happened to the man?"

"I don't know." He gave Frankie a look. "I was paying attention to the girl."

"Who was he?"

"Some bozo who beats off to girlie magazines. How the hell do I know?"

"What I was thinking," Frankie replied evenly, "is that if I'm in Frankie's body, then Frankie's probably in mine. It stands to reason."

"Reason?" Terry burst into harsh laughter. "What the fuck's reason got to do with any of this?"

"Nothing," Frankie agreed.

"Damn right nothing." He belched. "At least I'm getting drunk."

"I say we look for the man."

"What man? We don't even know who the asshole is."

"You have a better idea?"

"Sure I do. We send you to a doctor. Get you straightened out on the difference between a prick and a pussy." He chortled to himself, spraying droplets of saliva on his chin. Frankie's icy response made him clamp a hand over his mouth, but the laughter continued.

"C'mon, Frankie. Lighten up. This shit's too heavy to keep boxed."

"Too bad we can't change places, Terry. Give you a taste of the box."

"Damned if I don't love you, babe."

"You think I'm crazy, don't you?" He slid along the couch until he was face to face with Terry. Cupping his hand on Terry's chin, he squeezed until the man's cheeks were flat up against his gums. "I'm not. I want you to understand that. No matter what." He tightened his grip until Terry gave a yelp. "No bullshit, Terry. I'm not crazy. You remember that. Keep it tight against your heart."

He let go and returned to his corner of the couch. Terry stared at him, too stunned to retaliate.

"Don't do that," he muttered.

"Don't make me."

"Because I'll tell you something. I can play that game too."

The menace in his voice sent a chill through Frankie. Reflexively, he drew his legs to his chest.

"I say we try to find the man."

"I say you watch your manners."

Frankie eyed him. Suddenly, Terry laughed.

"Hell, I'm crazy too. And you know about what. You don't need that guy. Your man Terry's right here."

"I get the point. You think we can move on now?"

"Look, babe. The man's long gone. He was just a guy in a bar. A nothing."

"Sure. And Frankie was just a girl."

The seeming simplicity of the statement choked Terry up. "Damn champagne," he said, wiping away tears. "Fine. You want the guy? You tell me how we're going to find him. We don't know his name, don't know where he lives, don't even know what he looks like. New York's a big place."

"We could start at the bar. Find out if anyone remembers anything."

"Cox was too fucked up. Maybe Ted."

"Who's Ted?"

"The bartender."

"All right. So we start with Ted."

Terry wasn't thrilled.

"You got some problem with that?"

"Nope. No problem."

"Stop bullshitting me. You don't like it, say so."

The Frankie Terry knew rarely swore. Then again, that Frankie had never laid a hand on her man in any way other than affection. "What exactly are you going to say to him?"

"I'll tell him the truth."

"Right. You do what you want, Frankie, but I'll tell you something. Not everyone's as understanding as I am."

"You're being modest."

"Actually, I'm trying to help."

Frankie thought it over. "Okay. Maybe you're right. I sure as hell don't want to have to go through this shit again. Maybe you should go."

"And say what?"

"I'm sure you'll think of something."

This drew a smile. "You're giving me license to make up stories about you?"

Frankie failed to see the humor. "Look. I didn't ask to be here. For all I know, you've been making up stories already."

"Just telling what I know," said Terry.

"So will you go?"

"Did I say I'd help?"

"When?"

"Tonight, I guess. After work." He looked at his watch. "Uh-oh."

He rushed out of the room, returning moments later with a clean shirt. Quickly, he rolled himself a joint from the stash in the cigar box in the cabinet.

He slipped it in his breast pocket, buttoned his shirt and, without thinking, leaned down to give Frankie a kiss. Frankie ducked away, and Terry ended up with air. It was a humiliating moment.

"Nice," he muttered, recovering his balance and edging out of the room. From the doorway he gave her a last, bitter look, then turned and left.

Once again, Frankie was alone. The first bottle of champagne had barely given him a buzz, and he took the second between his legs and worked the cork up with his thumbs. It blew out and hit the ceiling, and immediately, he covered the mouth with his lips to keep the bubbly from spilling. This time he drank straight from the bottle. It was hard to do fast because the champagne bloated his stomach, but finally, he began to feel the glow. It was faint but unmistakable, like the embers of an old fire. Little by little the heat reached out, spreading through his body. By the time it reached his brain, the madness had dulled. Dimly, he realized that getting drunk might not be in his best interest. He needed to stay sharp and alert. A different voice told him he had to travel with what companions he could find. Right before he passed out, he had a vision. There was a vessel. It held a secret. He nearly had it, and then it was gone.

The Twenty-third Pair

The twenty-third pair of human chromosomes determines sex. In females it is comprised of two X chromosomes; in males, an X and a Y. The X is large: it contains nearly three times the genetic information of any of the other chromosomes. The Y is less than half its size.

For the first month and a half of life an embryo is sexually unspecified. It has the capacity to become either male or female. In the sixth week a gene on the Y chromosome begins to express itself, causing the fetal gonads to differentiate into testes. Shortly thereafter, a second gene stimulates the testes to begin male hormone production. Nearly all cells in the male bear the mark of this second gene, and nearly all are affected by their exposure to male hormones.

In the absence of the Y chromosome and its testis-determining gene, the fetus develops into a female. The gonads differentiate into ovaries, which subsequently produce female hormones. These bathe all the cells of the fetus, causing their own profound effects.

Certain regions of the brain in normal rats show marked sexual specificity. Cell density, dendritic formation, synaptic configuration of the male are different from the female. When presented with two solutions of water, one pure, the other heavily sweetened with saccharin, the female rat consistently chooses the latter. The male does just the opposite. Female chimpanzee infants exposed to high levels of male hormones in utero exhibit patterns of play different from their sisters. They initiate more, are rougher and more threatening. They tend to snarl a lot.

Sexual differences of the human brain exist, but they have been obscured by the profound evolution of this organ in the past half-million years. Humans have speech and foresight, consciousness and self-consciousness. We have art, science, and religion. In *a language whose meaning men and women seem to share, we say we are different, but equal.*

Different, yes. Structure proceeds function. Equal?

Recently, normal-appearing males have been described whose sex chromosomes through some genetic trickery are XX, and normal-appearing females have been found who are XY. The cells of these XX males lack the typical male marker, while those of the XY females possess it. In other words, an internal environment exists completely at odds with external appearance. One might reasonably expect unusual twists of personality and behavior.

Unfortunately, data to this point are lacking.

5

Terry caught the Lexington line at Spring, dozing off almost immediately. The champagne weighed him down and he almost missed his stop, struggling awake just in time and groggily mounting the stairs. He stopped at a little Korean deli on Fourteenth for a cup of coffee, gulping it down and scalding his tongue. He was already fifteen minutes late, and by the time he got to Suter's it was twenty. Brenda was at her usual place in front. Today she was wearing bangle earrings, a paisley head scarf and pink lipstick. Yesterday it had been a cotton blouse with a Peter Pan collar and fake pearls. Her fem look, she called it.

"Pinkett know I'm late?"

She motioned toward an enclosed office at the rear of the store. "He's been locked up with a new sales rep. Fresh out of school. She's got him salivating."

"Which says nothing about the woman."

"Not a thing. Our Mr. P.'s a purebreed." She rang

up a customer and sent him on his way. "So how's by you?"

"I've seen better days."

"Tell me about it. I've decided to go live on a mountain. Become a nun."

"Can you still do that?"

"Why not? Celibacy's always in style."

"I mean you."

"The Church has always had a special place in its heart for its black sheep."

"I know what you mean about the mountain. Somewhere high and very far away."

"And cheap," said Brenda. "No frills."

"Sure. Where the women are women and the men are men. You think there's a place like that?"

"I doubt it."

"Maybe I'll check out the travel section."

"Hey, Terry, you think you can lend me five bucks?"

"No problem." He handed her ten.

"Five's plenty."

He waved her off. "Keep it. Get something nice for Rhonda."

She started to reply, then stopped. "Forget it. You don't want to know."

He took her word for it and headed downstairs. On the way he found himself wondering what it would be like with Brenda. Awkward as hell and probably a ton of fun. Not that she'd do it, but then again you never knew. Something was definitely in the air. People were going off right before his eyes.

He found Sal where he always found him, behind the counter playing with a pocket video game. The one today was called Thudder, but they were all the same. Hand-eye coordination, sensory stimulation direct to subcortical pleasure centers. Sal was a junkie, and a Master. Terry had seen him get to two thousand with his eyes closed, just listening to the programmed beeps of the stick characters moving across the screen. He could play while watching the floor, even talking to a customer. The guy was a jock. A split-brain preparation. Terry loved him.

"Sorry I'm late." He stuffed his coat on a shelf under the counter, careful not to jostle Sal's arms. "How're you doing?"

"Three thousand two hundred sixty. Sixty-one, two . . ."

"Anything happen today?"

"People came in, looked at books, bought books, left."

"No shit."

"I ate lunch, had a Coke, you were late."

"You're turning into a machine, Sal."

He smiled without looking up. "It happened long ago. I'm a highly evolved creature."

"You've got a brain the size of a slug's."

"Three thousand three hundred twenty-eight, twenty-nine . . ."

"Sal, go home. There isn't room for the two of us back here."

Sal nodded, grabbed his coat without losing his rhythm. "You want me to leave this with you?"

"How would you ever make it home?"

"I got another in my pocket."

Terry shook his head. "You're too much, Salvatore. Sure, leave it."

He handed the game to Terry. "Here. Keep it going."

"Don't do that," cried Terry, but it was too late. He fumbled with the buttons, and in a matter of seconds the game was over. He cut Sal a look.

"You shouldn't have done that."

"Don't take it so seriously." Sal was smiling. "It's just a game."

"You know what I think," said Terry. "I think you got it up high just so you could give it to me and watch me fuck up."

"Why would I want to do that?"

"To prove that you're better."

"I *am* better."

"Yeah." Terry pushed the game away. "So take it home."

"You mad?"

"I'll live."

"Want to try again?"

"Beat it, Sal. Go home."

He left, and Terry went into the storeroom for a few tokes. He felt better when he came out, and to pass the time he got a copy of *Grant's Atlas* off the shelf. Leafing through the pages, the painstakingly beautiful renderings of bone, vessel and organ, awakened familiar yearnings. From childhood he had been fascinated by the human body, its mystery, wonder, precision. At eight his treasure had been the see-through man, each organ of which he had meticulously painted a different color. Every day he removed the organs, scrambled them, then fit them back like a puzzle into their translucent shell. Later, he got himself a beat-up microscope that he used to study insects, leaves, drops of blood and pieces of skin. His boyhood hero was his doctor, who seemed far more understanding than either of his parents. At times he feigned illness just to engineer a visit. At sixteen he got a job washing test tubes and at seventeen went to college, and after that, medical school. There the learning was cut short. The prank with the tank, as he thought of it now. It was not a pleasant memory.

"Excuse me," a voice said.

Startled, Terry looked up. In front of the counter stood a woman in a somber suit, black gloves and a veil pinned to a narrow-brimmed dark hat. She had young-looking eyes, but the spots on her skin told an older story.

"I'm looking for a book," she said, then stopped. She squinted at him. "Aren't you the young man who helped me before?"

"Before what?"

"That book with the line drawings," she said. "The old etchings and intaglios of the human figure. Wasn't that you?"

Terry struggled with the memory, and then suddenly it was there. The woman had come in a week or two before. She had been on the verge of tears, and he had been drawn by her helplessness. Now she seemed another person entirely.

"The Dürer," he said defensively. "It's a beautiful book."

"I need something else today." She took a folded piece of paper from her purse and opened it. "A neurology text," she read. "Do you have one?"

"We have many."

"Which would you recommend?"

"It depends on what you want. Are you interested in neurobiology, neurosurgery, neuroendocrinology, clinical neurology . . ." He stopped. "It goes on."

"Something basic," she said, unintimidated by his big words. "With an intelligent audience in mind."

"An intelligent audience," he repeated, wondering briefly what she meant by that. "Of course."

He led her to the neurology section, a shelf just above eye level containing a number of imposing texts.

"It would help," he said, "if I knew a little more of what you had in mind."

"It's a private matter," she replied bluntly.

Terry shrugged and concentrated on the books. It was hard not knowing what she wanted, but at length he decided on one of the general texts and pulled down his favorite, opening it at random. It didn't take but a second for him to get absorbed by the language. The woman cleared her throat.

"Perhaps I should look myself."

Terry pulled himself away and handed her the book. She perused it, then turned her attention to the shelf. It was above her head, and she had to reach for the volumes, some of which were quite heavy. Terry wanted to help but got the sense she wanted to do things on her own. Watching her, another memory fell into place.

"You had a brother who was sick," he said.

The woman did not reply.

"A coma. Something like that."

There was an audible sigh. "The doctors are in

disagreement. Some say coma, but others seem to think it's something else. The fact is," she said, sounding angry, "no one's willing to say anything for sure."

"It's already been a while, hasn't it?"

Her face clouded, then dropped. She looked weary. "They say it's an unusual case. He lapses in and out of what seems like sleep. Except that he doesn't wake up. Sometimes at night, when his eyes start moving under his eyelids, it looks like he's dreaming. Like when he was a boy . . ." She stopped, unable to complete the sentence. It took a moment to get herself under control. "It's not a coma if you still have dreams, is it? Doesn't that mean that your brain is still working?"

"Sure it is," said Terry.

"Even when his eyes are open, he doesn't talk. I'm not even sure he knows we're there." She shook her head. "The sleeping periods are getting longer and longer. Now he hardly ever opens his eyes."

Terry was at a loss for words. He touched her on the shoulder, a gesture she acknowledged with the feeblest of smiles.

"I'm sorry. I didn't come here to make a scene."

"It's no scene," he said.

"I keep thinking that there's something I'm forgetting. Some key, or clue . . . if I could just think of it, they'd be able to solve his case."

"You feel responsible."

"I'm his sister. He's not married. When the doctors talk, I want to understand what they're talking about. At least more than I do now."

"It doesn't seem like a lot to ask."

"No, it doesn't."

Terry caught sight of a thin black volume on the shelf, the words *Stupor and Coma* written on its spine. He pulled it out.

"Here. Maybe this will help. It's a classic work."

He found a small medical dictionary. "There're words you'll have to look up, but you should be able to manage. It'll give you something to do to pass the time."

"There's plenty of that," she said in a hollow voice, leafing through the text. Up at the counter she gave Terry a credit card and after the transaction offered him her gloved hand. In the palm was a five-dollar bill.

"You've been very helpful," she said.

Terry unfolded the bill, stared at it an instant, then handed it back. "I can't take this."

"Please. As a measure of gratitude."

He shook his head adamantly, until she was forced to take it back.

"I feel somehow cheapened," she said, snapping her purse shut.

"Don't." He had an impulse to offer her his phone number in case she had questions about the book. It was a silly thought. The lady had her own doctors to ask. Real ones.

After she left, he put the books away and worked on inventory. It was a slow evening, but he didn't go back to the atlas. Enough was enough. At quitting time he had a few more tokes, splashed cold water on his face in the bathroom, then headed uptown to Virgo's. In his head he rehearsed what he would say to Ted and Cox. Telling them the truth, whatever that

was, was out of the question. He wanted to leave
Frankie out of it but didn't see how he could. Maybe
he could make a joke of the whole thing. From a
distance it did seem laughable, as from a distance
certain debacles did. Laughable, and pathetic.

It was near midnight when he got to the bar,
which was two-thirds full. The music, as always, was
loud and insistent. On stage was a slender,
bleached-blond girl he hadn't seen before. She
moved awkwardly, like a colt, and had a timid smile.
Terry doubted it was an act. He found her innocence
sad and therefore unappealing. The boys at the bar
didn't seem to share his opinion: the girl had a
whole row of bills stuffed in her g-string.

Terry took a stool and got Ted's eye. A minute later
the bartender brought him a beer.

"Evening," he said, wiping off a glass and setting
it next to the bottle. "How's Frankie?"

"Still a little shaky."

"It's no life for a lady. This one," he nodded
toward the stage, "Janet, Janice—I don't even know
her name—she's barely nineteen. What kind of life is
that? I tell you I'm happy when I see them leave. Get
a regular job, stay home at nights."

Terry poured his beer and took a sip. "You got a
wife, Ted?"

"If I had a wife, would I be here? I'd be home,
watching TV. God knows, maybe I'd even be
asleep."

"You'd still have to work."

"You know where I live? In a flea-bag hotel, single
room, bed, sink, hot plate. I got an old black and
white TV. You know why I work nights? Because

nights are when everyone else at the place works. The pimps and the pushers and the hookers. The drunks who wake up in time to get drunk again. You want to sleep, you do it when the sun's up. Now what woman's going to marry a man like that?"

"You got values, Ted. There're always women looking for a man with values."

"I got opinions. If by the time a man reaches sixty-three he doesn't know what's right and what's wrong, he's a sorry case. What I don't got, and what I could use, is money."

Terry smiled. "Who couldn't?"

"Not a lot. Twenty, maybe thirty grand. Something to set me up for when I get old."

"In place of a wife."

"That's why I play the lottery. It's guys like me that win. Poor slobs who don't know what to do with all the money. First thing I'd do is hire a lawyer. Then I'd get a new TV."

"Ted, I got something to ask you."

"Trouble is, I ain't never been the lucky type." He shook his head. "Just a minute."

He shuffled off to fill some orders, and Terry took the time to look around. He didn't see Cox, which was a relief. It was going to be hard enough as it was.

"So," said Ted when he returned, leaning on the bar and scanning the room, "what can I tell you?"

"Last night. When Frankie fell out, there was a guy at the bar. He was near where she was dancing."

Ted nodded, waiting for more. A guy called for a

drink, and Ted pointed at him with a finger to let him know he'd heard.

"I'm trying to find him."

"One of the regulars?"

"I hadn't seen him before."

"What's he look like?"

"I don't remember."

"Beard? Moustache? Old guy? What?"

Terry was at a loss. "He grabbed his head at the same time Frankie grabbed hers. Right before she passed out."

"I didn't see nothing like that. But there was a guy . . . right after Frankie fell. He was flat on the bar like he'd been shot. His friend kept calling out his name. 'Jonesy, Jonesy,' he kept saying, but he couldn't get him to move. We ended up dragging him outside and stuffing him in a cab." He shook his head. "The guy was dead weight. I'm too old to be hauling a load like that. If he hadn't been breathing, I would've swore he was a stiff."

"What did he look like?"

"I don't know. Forty-five, fifty. Dark hair. Not a bad-looking face."

"What about his friend?"

Ted gave it a moment's thought. "About the same age. Going bald. He combed his hair down on top like guys who are losing it sometimes do. He had a big nose too. A drinker's nose."

"That's it?"

Ted gave him a look. "What's the big deal? Two drunk guys. It happens all the time."

"Frankie's paranoid," Terry said glibly. "She

thinks one of the guys was following her. Wants to find out who he is."

Ted frowned, and Terry realized he had just opened something that could turn sour fast. In the years since going topless, Virgo's had taken on some silent partners who might not take kindly to the thought that one of their girls was being tailed. He was about to rephrase what he'd said when someone clapped him on the back. The force of it nearly pitched him off the stool.

"Cox," he said without turning.

Cox squeezed beside him until he was flush with the bar. "A night's not a night without your pretty face, Terry. How's Frankie?"

"Frankie's fine," he said, shooting a glance at Ted. The bartender left to tend to business.

"Glad to hear it. How do you like the new talent?"

"Robbing the cradle, Jerry."

Cox picked at a tooth. "She'll grow up. It's better than turning tricks on the street."

"Is that where you picked her up? Or maybe she's a friend . . ."

Cox turned to him, and Terry felt a quickening of danger. But the big man only smiled.

"You got a lousy attitude, Terry. I don't know why, but still I like you." He leaned forward, until his face was only a few inches from Terry's own. His breath smelled of Sen-Sen, an odor that was almost defeated by the strong cologne he used.

"Maybe some day we can get to be friends." His crotch was now touching Terry's thigh. "You know, really get to know each other."

Terry had seen the man high, plenty of times, but

never like this. Was this a new drug he hadn't heard of? Or maybe Cox was turning over a new leaf, trying to be nice. Only the scene didn't feel nice. It felt sinister. Terry realized that this was the first time Cox had seen him without Frankie. He wished she were with him.

"I gotta take a leak," he said, easing off the stool. He hurried to the bathroom, where he took his time, but when he came back Cox was still there. Terry remained standing, making a point of keeping the stool between Cox and himself. He wasn't sure if Cox got the message. The smile never left his face, and one hand was playing in his pants pocket. Terry managed to smile back, while he reached in his own pocket and threw a bill on the bar.

"Get yourself a drink, Jerry. I gotta go."

He quickly edged to the other end of the bar before Cox had a chance to respond. He got Ted's attention.

"I gotta split, Ted. Cox is after me."

"You shouldn't play games with him. Get yourself hurt."

Terry shuddered at the thought. What games?

"The guy's got a mind like a TV tube," said Ted. "Leave him alone."

"That's all I plan to do. Look, about that guy . . ."

"Which guy is that?"

"The one you helped into the cab last night. You didn't happen to catch where he was going."

Ted stopped what he was doing. "Frankie's in trouble? This guy, he's got something on her?"

"No." Terry shook his head. "It's nothing like that."

Ted looked at him suspiciously, with eyes that had seen a thousand different lies. Terry held up his hands as if in surrender.

"Honest," he said. "It's weird shit, Ted. You gotta trust me on this."

Ted essayed him, deciding at length that whatever was going down was neither his business nor his problem. "We put the guy in a cab," he said. "That's all I know."

"Where to?"

"I got no idea."

"What kind of cab?"

"A cab. Wha'dya want?" He started away, then stopped. "Wait a minute."

"What?"

He pinched his forehead in concentration. "Metro. It said Metro on the door. Big letters, like a newspaper headline."

"Metro."

"Yeah." He nodded slowly to himself. "I've seen it before."

"You're sure?"

He was put off by Terry's asking him a second time. "What's sure? I said I saw it."

"Right," said Terry. "It's a start anyway." He thanked Ted. "You're the sanest guy I know. You want my advice, stay single. Then you won't have to go running around trying to flag down your girl's wacked-out brain."

Ted shook his head sadly. Life hadn't done great by him, but he was glad he wasn't young again. The kids seemed really to have lost track of something. Their minds seemed unconnected to so much of the world as it was. He had his dreams, sure, but he knew them for dreams. He was grateful for what he had in hand: his room, his TV, the clothes he wore on his back. The kids acted sometimes like they wanted to be out in the cold. To be lost. He didn't understand. Why would anyone born of the earth give up the chance to be part of it?

He poured himself a shot and knocked it off. Terry was on his way out. A man handed Ted a five spot for the dancer. He stared at it uncertainly for a moment, then with a hand that seemed to reach across time rather than space pushed the bill toward the dancing girl. She bent to receive it, and he slipped it through the spangled string. In doing so he touched her skin. It was warm, and youthful. But her face, it was something else.

He turned away and poured himself another drink. Tonight he would buy ten lottery tickets. Twenty. Strike it rich for sure. Retire. The young these days were too young, and he was far too old.

6

When Terry got home, he found Frankie
asleep again on the sofa. Her hands were
folded under her cheek, her legs tucked against her
chest. Both bottles of champagne lay on their sides
on the floor.

He brought a blanket from the bedroom to cover
her feet and bare arms. He was hungry but didn't
eat, afraid that the noise would wake her. There
would be questions to which he had not yet decided
the answers. Better to let her sleep and wait until he
was sure.

He went to the bedroom, undressed, turned on the
TV and got in bed. He was too preoccupied to sleep.
A rerun of "Dragnet" was on. Jack Webb was strad-
dling the edge of a desk, his back as though it had
been nailed to a two-by-four. He was asking questions tough and getting the answers. His crisp, stac-
cato voice was informative and oddly soothing.
Terry was soon asleep.

He woke in the morning to a talk show whose

guest was extolling the virtues of reconstructive surgery. The man held up a disfigured hand, missing
two or three digits, and showed how, with a big toe
for a thumb and a pinkie for an index finger he could
write, shuffle cards, even thread a needle. He was
diffident but proud of his accomplishment, and the
audience, in what to Terry seemed remarkably bad
taste, applauded. He punched off the tube, pulled on
his pants and went to the bathroom. When he was
done, he looked in on Frankie. She was sitting up,
her hair matted down on one side, her face still puffy
with sleep.

"Morning," said Terry.

"What time is it?"

"Nine. Ten."

Frankie shook her head to clear it. "I've really
been out."

"Feel any better?"

"I'm thirsty."

Terry headed for the kitchen. "I'm making coffee."

"Did you find out anything?"

"Not much." The sight of Frankie freshly wakened
stirred desires that were difficult to stifle. He turned
his back.

"What?"

"Nothing."

"Tell me."

"There was a guy who fell out about the same time
you did," he said.

"What guy?"

"I don't know."

"What did he look like?"

"Ted didn't remember. His friend was bald."

"That's a big help."

"Yeah, I thought so too. The guy couldn't walk. Ted and his friend helped him into a cab."

"What kind of cab?"

Terry hesitated. He didn't like the way Frankie was on his case, and he figured the more he kept from her, the more he would get back in control. It was meager compensation for the lack of sex and sanity, but at least it was something. So he told her Ted didn't know.

"What do you mean, he didn't know?" She licked her dry lips, then rubbed them with the back of a hand. "He put the guy in it, didn't he?"

"The guy was dead weight. Ted was doing all he could to move him." He handed Frankie a cup of coffee and sat at the table. "It's a bitch, isn't it?"

"What about the other guy?"

"What other guy?"

"The bouncer."

"Cox? I told you he was too fucked up. He wouldn't remember anything."

"It's worth asking. What else do we have?"

"I thought I'd talk to a friend," Terry lied, thinking of Marcus, making it up as he went along. "He used to be a private detective." In fact, he'd been a security guard. "He's bound to have some ideas."

Frankie glanced at him. "You backing out?"

"No way," he said quickly. "I want to handle it myself is all. Gives me a chance to do something useful."

"I think **you** should talk to Cox."

Terry shook his head once, firmly. "That's out of the question."

"Then I will."

He looked up. Frankie was slouching against the stove the way she did when she had her morning coffee. But her eyes, normally still glazed from the night before, were watchful. Terry shrugged, unaccustomed to such scrutiny. "Suit yourself."

"I'll go tonight."

"He doesn't work tonight. Tuesdays he bites the heads off chickens in private."

"Then tomorrow," said Frankie, putting down the cup and absently picking at one of her knuckles. "How come you don't like the guy?"

"He's got a Tarzan complex. And he likes to hurt things."

"Should I be afraid?"

Terry found himself nodding, then realized he was thinking of himself. "Women he treats okay. It's men he likes to frighten."

"I am a man, Terry."

"Then, my dear, you best act like a woman." He smiled at the irony. "Not that Cox has the imagination to think you're anything else."

He gazed at the person standing before him, the youthful body so full in the hips and chest, the dark hair and dreamy eyes, and realized that he, too, lacked the imagination. This was Frankie, his lover. He knew her soft tongue, her lips, her smell better than his own. His desire resurfaced, stronger than before. He started to get hard.

"Don't you want it, Frankie? Not even a little?"

"Want what?"

"This," he said, rubbing his pants. "And these." He wet his lips. "You used to love my lips."

"No." Frankie shrank back. "I don't. Keep them to yourself."

Terry muttered something unintelligible, then kicked the chair back. "I'm gone."

"Wait," said Frankie, following him to the bedroom, where he put on shoes and a shirt. "Where are you going?"

"Out. Before I do something you wouldn't like."

"And what am I supposed to do?"

"Do whatever you want. You're a big girl, or whatever the fuck you are. I'm sure you'll think of something."

He slammed the door behind him and hurried down the stairs, ignoring Frankie's calls from above. At the bottom of the stairwell he stopped, listening for the sound of pursuit. His erection was gone, but his frustration, if anything, was worse. He cursed Frankie savagely and hit the wall. He did it again, hurting his hand, which he blamed on her. Then, feeling a little better, he left the building.

It was a warm day, and he crossed the street to be out of the sun, passing the garment factory, where a long rack of newly sewn shirts was being wheeled from a freight elevator into the back of a truck. At Broadway he bought a pretzel from Fat Tony, who was just setting up for the day. They had their obligatory chat about the Knicks, of whom Tony was a diehard fan.

"You see the game last night?" he asked, fastening his mustard-stained apron around his belly. "Ewing was a monster. An absolute monster."

"They win?"

"At the buzzer. Baseline jumper. Three guys in his face."

"Hey, Tony, you're a man of the world. You know anything about crazy women?"

"What's to know?"

"That's what I'm asking."

"All my girls, they turned out good. And Isabelle . . ." He shrugged. "The wife has her days. But all in all, I got no complaints."

"So maybe it's me."

"You want a soda to go with?"

"But I can't figure out what I did."

"Too much thinking gets a person in trouble. You want my advice, don't think so much. You got a good heart, things'll take care of themselves."

Terry figured his heart was as good as anyone's. It was his head and temper sometimes he couldn't control. He felt like talking more, but another customer took Tony's attention, so he headed off. A couple of blocks away he found a phone booth where he got directory assistance to give him the address of the Metro Cab Company. It turned out to be in Manhattan, on West Twenty-fourth near the river, and Terry decided the walk would do him good. SoHo at that hour, with all the trendy shops and galleries closed, was tolerable, and he took Spring over to Thompson, where he turned uptown. Some boys were playing handball in a concrete playground surrounded by a fence, thwacking the ball against the side of a building that was painted with an enormous Puerto Rican flag. In the court next to them a group of younger kids were running a game of free-for-all, and at the end of the yard three guys were passing a joint. Terry took Bleecker to Sixth Avenue, skirting the Village over to Ninth, which he took uptown. In fifteen minutes he was at Twenty-fourth, a cobblestone street in a neighborhood of warehouses and auto repair shops. Between Tenth and Eleventh ran the abandoned New York Central tracks, gathering rust, growing weeds, hanging against the sky like a forgotten promise. Looking west Terry caught glimpses of the Hudson, and beyond it Jersey. The water and the tracks made him feel for a moment like he was out of the city. It reminded him that there were kinds of life different from the one he lived. Change was not impossible. It only seemed that way.

He found the cab company near Eleventh in an old brick building, one side of which was covered with the faded painting of a giant cockroach, beneath which were the words "We Get What You Got." Terry thought of AIDS, TB, gonorrhea and other epidemic diseases. The ad, for a company whose name was no longer visible, had been prescient. He entered the building.

The cab company was on the second floor, at the top of a steep and worn flight of wooden stairs. It consisted of one large room partitioned into two by a waist-high railing about ten feet from the door. Part of the railing had been built up into a counter. Two dirty windows overlooked a fenced-in parking lot at the side of the building. Inside the lot were a row of gas tanks and some cars, most of which were cabs.

Toward the back of the room was a man at a desk.

He glanced up when Terry entered, then went back
to the phone. As soon as he hung up, it rang again.
In a corner of the desk was a dispatch radio whose
ambient static was interrupted at intervals by the
crackle of voices. When he had to, he answered
these too. At his elbow stood a tall bottle of Maalox.

Terry waited for further acknowledgment. It was
some time coming. At length the man ignored the
calls long enough to address him.

"What can I do you for?" he said in a harried
voice. On his upper lip was a chalky, white film.

"I need some help."

"Job applications are over there." He pointed
toward the counter before lifting the receiver on another call. "Don't bother if you ain't got a license."

"I didn't come for that," said Terry, moving up to
the rail. The man finished the call, then twisted the
radio knob until the static was barely audible. With a
loud exhalation he leaned back in his chair and ran
his fingers through his hair. What was left of it was
tawny brown. His sideburns were flecked with gray.

"My girlfriend lost a ring," said Terry. "A couple
of nights ago. She thinks it fell off in the cab."

"No rings've been turned in."

"It was small." Terry hesitated. "Gold. It was our
engagement ring."

The man studied him and wiped his lips with his
hand. "And let me guess. You don't know the cab
number or the driver's name."

Terry shook his head, looking contrite.

"Was it a dispatch?"

"We got it on the street. Outside a bar. About two
in the morning."

The man reached for his bottle of Maalox. He took a slug and turned the radio back up. A call came through on a wrong address. He told the driver to forget it and after consulting a sheet of paper barked out a new one. He looked at Terry.

"We got a hundred and four cabs on the street. Twenty-four hours a day. You take each one apart looking for your ring means money. A man working by the hour ain't gonna be happy. Not to mention his boss."

"Maybe I should be talking to him."

The man was not intimidated. "You are."

"Oh." Terry swallowed.

"Look, buddy. I'm real busy today. My dispatcher's been out for a week with hemorrhoids. I'm working on an ulcer. I'm sorry about the ring." He answered the phone, took the address and sent it out on the radio. The interview seemed at an end.

Terry looked out one of the windows. He could see the river; it was picking up pieces of sun. Lots of water, without regard for mankind's blunders, was rolling to the sea. What the hell. The worst that could happen was he'd get thrown out.

"Don't the drivers keep a record of their pick-ups?" he asked. "I could look them over, find which one has the right address."

"Half of them are made up," the man said without looking up. "They do it at the end of their shift just to have something on paper."

"Would it hurt to look?"

"C'mon, buddy. Gimme a break."

"My girl. It'd make her so happy."

The man made a noise, exasperated but not unfriendly. "Over there." He pointed. "The way-bills are in a pile. Don't mess 'em up."

"I won't. Thanks."

Terry went through a gate in the railing and sat at the desk the man had indicated. He took the thick pile of way-bills in his lap, then thought better of it and returned it to the bin. One by one he started through the sheets.

At the top of each was the driver's name, the number of the cab and the date. On ruled-off lines beneath were the pickup spots and destinations. At the end of each line was the size of the gate. Terry quickly realized that he could easily be there for hours. Each way-bill had between twenty and twenty-five entries; with a hundred cabs a shift, it came close to five thousand entries to check. Most of the writing was in pencil, some of it smeared, much of it illegible anyway. Pickups and drop-offs were often nonspecific, like "Broadway and 22nd" or "75th near Lex." The more Terry looked, the more his hopes faded. The drivers' names—Hamadeh, Wong, O'Reilly, Castillo—floated in his mind like a storybook, a consanguineous ark of a taxi embracing the world. His task became ludicrous, but he dogged on. Past Kalinovsky, Patel, Drinkwater, Daggoo. He stopped. John Daggoo. April 1, 2 A.M. Scribbled on the nineteenth line: "Broadway near 50th."

Terry looked over to the drop-off address. Smudged across it was a dried coffee stain. Numbers were visible, but no street. He held the sheet up to the light, but it was no better. He swore.

He wrote down the man's name and the number of the cab, and was about to leave when a disconcerting thought occurred to him. There were other places near Fiftieth besides Virgo's. The pickup could have been from somewhere else.

He sighed and returned to the way-bills. It was laborious. An hour and a half later he had gone through them all. No other entry came close to the one he had. He got out of the chair and stretched.

"Find what you want?" the man asked. He had a cup of coffee alongside his Maalox.

"I don't know. Maybe." He read off the driver's name and cab number.

"John D. He's been driving fifteen, twenty years."

"I'd like to talk to him."

"Why? You got the number of the cab."

Terry scrambled. "Maybe he already found the ring. Hasn't gotten around to bringing it in."

The remark did not induce an outpouring of good-will. The man looked hard at Terry.

"Buddy, you show up at five, I'll give you ten minutes with the car. You can't find your ring you go home." He swallowed some coffee, grimaced, chased it with a slug of Maalox. "I'm growing an ulcer sitting here. Five o'clock. If it's there, you find it."

Terry was relieved to get out. He resented having to lie on Frankie's account. Twice now, and the way things were going, there would be more. The payoff had better be good.

It was near noon when he left the building, and he had nowhere to be for five hours. Longer than that if he decided not to come back to talk to the cabdriver. It was his day off, and the truth was he'd had enough of Frankie's errands. Another day or two wouldn't hurt. Let the woman stew a little.

He walked over to Twelfth, which he took until it dead-ended at a chain-link fence on Fifty-ninth. Beyond the fence was a parking lot and beyond the lot a good half-mile of open space. He found a gate in the next lot over, at the rear of which was another fence, part of which was down. Once Terry got past it he was walking on dirt. Overhead ran the West Side Highway. To his right was a weed-infested field that ended at a concrete wall bordering Eleventh. Sixty feet to his left, its edge hidden by gray reeds, was the Hudson. Sparrows tittered in and out of the brush. Out over the water a crow circled, then landed on the charred skeleton of an old dock. Terry kept in the shadow of the highway, picking his way past twisted pieces of chrome, faded beer bottles, broken glass. His thoughts kept coming back to Frankie and her bizarre story. It was a sick way to dump him, if that's what it was. He couldn't understand. He felt blindsided, and inevitably, his mind returned to the other relationship in his life that had ended in such abrupt and unexpected fashion.

In medical school he'd had a friend named Zack. They'd met unforgettably, during one of the first-year sex education seminars. Everyone had been watching a film on paraplegic sex when Terry had had to leave to take a leak. In the bathroom he'd met one of the seminar's guests, a wheelchair-bound man who needed help fixing his catheter. Open-minded in those days and eager to learn, Terry asked what he could do.

"It's slipping off," said the man. "I'd fix it myself, but I'm getting spasms in my hands."

Even to his untrained eye, Terry saw that he was speaking the truth. His fingers were stiffened into claws, and every few seconds his arms jerked spasmodically.

"What can I do?"

"It's a condom catheter." With his head the man gestured toward his lap. "There's some kind of adhesive at the end that makes it stick to skin. If you could straighten it out and make it stick, I think it'll work okay. Until I can get a new one at home."

Terry glanced around the bathroom, then bent down. He was hit by the smell of stale urine.

"It's kind of embarrassing," the man said. "Sometimes I get all tensed up and then I can't do a thing."

Terry muttered his sympathy. He got the man's fly open and found the rubber condom. It was bunched up near the end of the penis. He rolled it back up the shaft as best he could, but it didn't seem to fit. Not only that, but the flaccid penile tissue didn't offer enough resistance to be able to get the adhesive to stick.

"It's not working."

The man looked down. He had greasy hair and bad teeth. "I was afraid of that. I usually put it on when I've got an erection. Sometimes I have to wait all day."

Terry fidgeted.

"Direct stimulation sometimes works. Even though I don't feel much, my penis seems to know."

"You're asking me to rub it?"

"If you could. I'll try to relax."

Terry felt trapped by pity and goodwill. Inexorably, as though gripped by a spell, his hand closed around the shriveled organ.

The man shut his eyes. Slowly, the tension left his arms and the tone of his penis increased. Terry rubbed and squeezed, silently cajoling the organ while his eyes darted nervously from the man's crotch to the bathroom door. After a minute, which seemed like an hour, the tissue was as firm as the white of a boiled egg. Terry tried to fasten the condom, but it was not quite time. He drew a breath, in mortal fear that the man would next suggest that he use his mouth.

Thirty seconds more, and the penis felt ready. Terry stopped rubbing, and with both hands began to roll the condom out. Just as he had it stretched and in position, the bathroom door burst open. A wild-eyed man staggered in, threw up once on the floor, then started laughing uncontrollably.

In seconds the man in the wheelchair defervesced. Terry was left holding a memory. He did what he could with the condom, then quickly washed his hands. Mumbling an apology, he rushed from the room.

Later, he found out that the laughing man had just inhaled a maskful of compressed nitrous oxide. His name was Theodore Zachary, and people called him Zack.

The two of them met again a few weeks later under more normal conditions. Terry had fallen asleep in an afternoon lecture class and begun to snore. Zack, who happened to be sitting next to him, got him awake just as the lecturer turned on the lights to investigate the disruption. Discovering nothing in the hundred innocent faces staring back at him, the speaker made a snide remark and resumed his lecture. The lights were dimmed, and another dull graph was projected on the screen. A moment later, Terry's head was lolling dangerously to the side. His breathing became stertorous. Suddenly, he was jolted by a sharp jab to the ribs and before he knew it, Zack was pulling him out of his seat. They made it out the door without being seen, then collapsed in the hall in nervous laughter. It was the beginning of a friendship.

Much of what they had in common centered around their irreverence for authority. In anatomy they dressed a skeleton in leather jacket, slouch hat and jeans. They lit a cigar in its teeth and had it smoking when the venerable, esteemed professor entered to impart his wisdom. In physiology they tested the effect a few drops of MDA had on the brain waves of a decorticate cat. And in neuroanatomy they hid a tiny short-wave speaker in one of the ventricles of a brain, which, upon the arrival of the dissecting team, began to cry out "Help me! Help me!" Lots of fun for the boys. Pranks to ease the strain. And on the weekends they partied.

They had to blow it off somehow, and the wild, drugged-out bashes that happened nearly every Saturday night the first two years were the thing. Anywhere from five to fifty people would show up, dance, get crazy, put the make on each other. There was always pot and alcohol, and from week to week other special goodies. Ludes were the thing for a

while, then amyl, fairy dust, ecstasy. Sometimes
they'd mix up a big punch, color it green for nature
or red for blood and drop in whatever they happened to have on hand. Good vibes, fun times. There
was always something going down.

By the third year they had less time to play, and by
the fourth, in the face of ever-mounting work and
pressure for professional conformity, the parties had
become a memory. One night, after months of not
seeing each other, the two of them met at a bar.
Zack looked awful, heavy-faced, unshaved, dull-
eyed. Terry had seen the look in some of the interns
and residents and wondered if he himself looked any
better. They covered the usual litany of outrage and
complaint, during which Zack was uncharacteristi-
cally subdued. At length Terry asked if something
was wrong. His friend wouldn't meet his eyes.

"I'm fucked up."

"What do you mean?"

"I mean I'm fucked up. I feel like shit."

"They're running you ragged, huh? Me too."

"I haven't been to the hospital in a week."

"You on break?"

He made a noise. "You could say that. I stopped
going. It didn't seem important."

Terry frowned. "What are you telling me?"

"I met a girl. A nurse. We had a thing. Then she
left."

"It happens, Zack."

"Not like this."

"Like what?"

He played with his drink. "Like for two months
every minute was her. Every second. I hardly slept.

Didn't eat. Didn't need to because she fed me. She made the hunger then fed it. And even then I couldn't get enough. The hunger never stopped." He paused. "You know hunger, Terry?"

Terry wanted to say yes but found himself shaking his head.

"You get filled up, then emptied a million times a day. When you're full, it's bliss, and when you're empty, you might as well be dead. I'm empty now. Empty as a pit."

"C'mon, buddy. It's not that bad."

Zack covered his face with his hands.

Terry had seen his friend up, down, drained by work and daunted by women, but never like this. Something was missing, something that had always been his in abundance. Perspective. Resilience.

"You scare me, Zack."

"I scare myself."

"This isn't you. You're strong. You've got to bounce back."

"I can't."

"You can." He had a sudden idea. "I've got it. A party. We'll throw a party."

"I don't think so. Not now."

"Sure now. It's just the thing to snap you out of this funk. Who knows, maybe you'll even meet someone."

Zack shook his head.

"C'mon, buddy. No one can whip you if you don't want to be whipped."

"It's my fault. I know."

"Who's talking fault? We're talking party. A jump down, turn around, get down party." Terry pumped it up, hoping something would spill over. "Some booze, a little weed, maybe something else to lively up the gang. We'll do a Halloween thing. Costumes, prizes. Burn the house down."

Zack was thoughtful. "It's been a long time."

"There you go." In the air he framed a marquee. "The Zack and Terry show. Midnight to dawn. Be there or nowhere."

Another minute and he got Zack to agree. They shook hands. A party was born.

On the twenty-ninth, two days before the event, the hosts convened on the seventh floor of the medical sciences building, a tall concrete and glass structure of beakers, rats and Nobel prize dreams that housed the experimental labs. Earlier that week Terry had noticed a couple of free-standing tanks of nitrous oxide chained to a cart. It had crossed his mind, which by then was exclusively occupied with the coming festivities, that a tank of N_2O might be just the ticket to send the party into orbit. Zack, sucked up in the wake of his friend's enthusiasm, didn't argue. It was close to one in the morning when they arrived, working their way cautiously around the perimeter corridor, door after door of pungent chemical smells and radiation warning stickers. Researchers were notorious for the hours they kept, rushing in at a moment's notice to sacrifice a mouse or cleave a gene. Fortunately, they also tended to be oblivious to the world at large. Through an open doorway they saw a woman at a sink who paid them no attention. Overhead they heard the muffled cries of dogs. The cart was where Terry remembered it, the two tanks still inside, both of them full. They arrived without incident, quietly undid the chain and rolled one of the tanks, which weighed close to eighty pounds, to the floor. Zack grabbed the base, Terry the top, they lifted and started down the hall. Their plan was to take it by elevator to the basement, where there was an exit door about twenty yards to the rear that opened onto a side street where they had parked a van. The elevator came, and once inside they let out a collective sigh. It had been easy, and with big grins they counted down the numbers. Four . . . three . . . two . . . one. B, thought Terry, for blast-off. Big time. B for bonanza.

The elevator stopped at one.

The doors opened, and a security guard on routine rounds stepped in. He had a boring job and welcomed the chance for human contact. He nodded cordially to the boys. He looked at the tank. Slowly, his mind slipped into gear.

B, thought Terry, for bummer. Bad planning. B for busted.

The guard called the cops, who were too busy to come. Two medical students caught with a substance that wasn't even controlled aroused their interest about as much as a wife calling her husband names. They told him to issue a citation and lay it on thick. Ethics, the public trust, stuff like that. The guard, piqued at being slighted by the boys in blue, played it heavy. He took fingerprints and photographs. He promised to send a report to their dean. Before sending them home, he said if he ever caught them again, he'd bust them to kingdom come.

They got back to Terry's apartment around four, feeling pretty edgy. Half a Quaalude later, things looked a little better. Terry figured that the guard, himself probably no stranger to recreational drugs, wouldn't be a chump. Zack at first didn't seem to care, but later he got morose. He said they were probably meant to be caught. He asked for another lude. Terry found one, split it, and by the time the sun peeked its pretty little face above the horizon, the champs were down for the count.

The night of the party Zack called to say he felt too shitty to come. Terry had to go over and drag him bodily back to his apartment. Once inside, he took Zack to the small study next to his bedroom.

"I've got a surprise for you."

On the desk was a pile of uninflated balloons and next to them a green cylinder identical to the one they had tried to heist. A thin vinyl tube was connected to a nozzle at the top, and attached to it was a translucent plastic mask. Zack was nonplussed.

"Where'd you get it?"

"I figured this was going to be our last fling. I didn't want it to be a dud."

"It's nitrous?"

"He who laughs last," said Terry, grinning. He undid the mask, replacing it with a balloon. "You want to take a trial run?"

"I don't think so."

"C'mon, buddy. Don't be glum. Not tonight."

"Maybe later."

"We'll put you in charge. How's that?" He slapped the tank. "No tickets necessary."

Zack toyed with the mask. "There're tickets and then there're tickets."

Terry laughed. "There you go."

The party started slow, but by ten-thirty the place was jammed. There were devils, vampires, belly dancers and the usual retinue of greasers and mad surgeons. Terry dressed as a werewolf, gluing tufts of hair on his cheeks and chin and limning his eyes with red makeup. Zack shocked everyone by shaving his head. That was the extent of his costume, and it was plenty. Looming in the crowd, his pale skull an opaque message, he was the scariest one there.

At eleven Zack started handing out the balloons. Each person got one, whose end had to be pinched immediately to keep the gas from exiting. This was also the way to safely regulate the amount of each inhalation: if someone started to get too much, his fingers would automatically relax and the balloon would fly away. The high lasted only a few seconds, which was another reason for the balloons. They made the drug portable. By midnight the apartment was filled with these multicolored spheres of good-will, and Zack came out of the study. Terry tried to get his attention, when all of a sudden his friend's face froze. Terry followed his gaze to a woman dressed as a cat. She had a black body suit, painted whiskers, furry ears on a headband. She was dancing with a cowboy. Zack made his way over, and the two of them had words. A minute later when Terry looked back, Zack was gone.

Terry pushed through the crowd to the woman, who was no longer dancing. He introduced himself.

"Andrea," she said in return.

"You're Zack's friend."

"I thought so. Apparently I was wrong."

"You dumped him."

"We had a thing. It ended." She gave him a look. "You his guardian?"

"His friend."

"Zack's a nice guy. Maybe a little sensitive."

"Something wrong with sensitivity?"

"Look, I'm sorry. I'll leave." She turned to go, but Terry grabbed her arm.

"You don't have to do that."

"I didn't come to cause trouble."

"Why did you come?"

"I heard you guys throw a good party. C'mon, you knew that." Her eyes twinkled. "You're legends."

She had a way about her. Terry asked her to dance. Later they had a smoke. She was really quite nice, and idly, Terry wondered how it would feel to have that hunger.

By then Zack had returned to the study and had shut the door. There was still enough gas for four or five deliveries, but instead of using a balloon, he reattached the green plastic mask to the end of the vinyl tube. Then he put the mask over his nose and mouth and tightened the elastic band around the back of his head. It felt funny touching his hairless scalp. He sat for a minute or two, thinking if there was anything left for him to do. From the other room came music and occasional bursts of laughter. He sighed and opened the valve.

It was a relief when the gas entered, and for a moment he felt like laughing. He turned the flow all the way up. The room receded. The voices outside spun away. Night grew, the world turned on a pin, and then it was gone.

Andrea was at the funeral, and afterward, she and Terry fell into a brief affair. The Dean's Committee instigated an investigation of the death. They had the guard's report and couldn't understand why anyone would go back after being caught once. Terry couldn't explain. He was living in a state of disbelief. He didn't have the spirit to fight.

In the end he was not expelled. He was suspended, with reenrollment contingent upon his completing a counseling program. He tried but couldn't get it to work. The feelings were there but not the words to talk about them. After half a year he quit and didn't bother trying to reenroll in school. It was easier to look for another line of work.

Terry's walk through uncharted territory ended at a barbwire-topped fence, on the other side of which some kids were playing basketball. They showed him a place to get through, and minutes later he was strolling down the paved path of Riverside Park. On his left flowed the Hudson, stirred by spring wind. On his right was grass, and beyond it, cigarette butts and concrete. His dilemma was this: why stop walking? He wasn't hungry, nor was he tired. The only thing that kept him rooted to this spot, to this city of dubious purpose, were the memories. And if he could leave them behind, like the skin of a snake, a torn garment, a disproved theorem, he would not

have to suffer. He would not have to learn, or
change, could simply walk away. Leave Frankie and
Zack and all the rest. Never stop, never think, never
plan or remember. If he could walk.

7

Caring For Yourself [6]

Andrea Galang, Miss Pacific Coast USA, has a problem. Her beauty queen consultants, grooming her for the upcoming Miss USA contest, have suggested she have a tiny lump removed from the tip of her nose. Her personal adviser, a former Miss America contestant herself, agrees.

"Trust them," she says. "Why be 98 percent perfect when you can be 100 percent perfect?"

This is a question that is difficult for Andrea to answer. She plays with her nose, pushing the tip one way then the other. The flaw there is virtually imperceptible and the surgery is minor, but still she is wavering.

"It's always been a part of me," she says. "But then, they say they'd just have to shave a little bit off."

Practice and preparation and dedication to perfection are what makes a winner. That means, according to Andrea's adviser, a young woman has to be willing to change.

"If you don't, you stifle yourself. Beauty is America's landscape. Revlon and L'Oreal color the hills. Jean Naté flavors the air. Lauren, Miyake, Ungaro and all the rest shape the paths. Pay attention to the terrain and be flexible. If augmentation is what you need, augment. If reduction, then reduce. Wanting to feel good about yourself is a universal desire. Minor discomfort is a trifling price to pay for success."

Frankie paced the apartment, unwilling to spend another day trapped inside. He felt angry and abandoned. A dozen times he went to the front door and a dozen times came back. Desperate for release, he was too frightened to go. The phone didn't help. It had him by the throat.

He wanted to rip it out to keep from hearing another alien voice, an unknown friend, the mother again, caging him with familiarity. The prospect of never knowing enough to be able to say "wrong number" enraged him, and yet what could he do? He was at its mercy, would have to listen to anyone, anything, for a clue. It could come that way, on the phone. Like blackmail. Someone could whisper a price, a spot. Do this, and we'll give you back your body. Your identity. If he left the apartment he might miss it. Or worse, he might miss a call telling him that the whole thing was a joke, a trick, and if he just closed his eyes and said the magic word, everything would return to normal. It could happen like that too. A voice over the phone. A messenger. Manna from the heavens.

He spent the day watching TV. The game shows and ads worked on him, and there was no liquor left in the house to dull his sense of helplessness and confusion. From time to time he looked out the window, locking eyes once briefly with one of the women in the sewing factory, perhaps the same one as before. She gave no sign of recognition, and the next time he looked she was gone. With some consternation he noticed that the light outside had changed. It was dusk. Shadows were dissolving. He had spent another day inside.

Without thinking, he went to the closet and put on a pair of shoes. His tee shirt had taken on a smell, and he replaced it with a long-sleeved blouse from one of the hangers. On top of this he threw on a quilted jacket with big plastic buttons that fastened on the wrong side. He found some money, a map of Manhattan and a key ring in the top drawer of the bureau, all of which he stuffed in a pocket. From a dog-eared phone book in the living room he copied down Virgo's address, then went to the front door and made sure the keys fit. He paused.

Don't stop, he warned himself. Don't think. Go.

The phone rang. Faintly. Once, twice. He dashed into the living room and grabbed the receiver. The line gave him a dial tone, yet the ringing continued. He didn't understand. He traced the sound down the hall to the bedroom, but when he entered it stopped. A strange voice started to talk. It was hallucinatory. There was no one in the room. In a minute the voice was replaced by another, a woman's, extolling the virtues of microwave cooking. Finally, he got it. Angry at himself and embarrassed, he yanked the TV plug from its socket. Then he went to the front door, threw it open and cut himself loose.

The street was a hive, a frenzied world of unimaginable activity, and Frankie's first impulse was to flee. He was certain at any moment he would be discovered and subjected to ridicule, or worse. It was the fate of the alien, and he shrank into a doorway, grimly preparing himself for catastrophe.

Minutes passed and nothing happened. Perhaps he had overreacted. Screwing up his courage, he stepped onto the sidewalk, hugging close to the building's wall. People walked by without paying him the least attention. It was amazing. But then a man in a stocking cap tried to sell him some jewelry. His eyes cruised over Frankie while he dangled a gold necklace in his face. Frankie was petrified and at the same time had an urge to punch him. When the man reached in his pocket for something else, Frankie fled into the street, where he was nearly hit by a car. The driver screamed out the window and leaned on his horn, and in seconds every car behind was honking too. Frankie stumbled to the other side of the street, accidentally bumping a woman carrying a heavy plastic bag. Stalks of celery, greens and the head of a plucked chicken stuck over the top. The woman scowled, and Frankie hurried away. He fought through the crowd that was swarming the produce market and a few buildings up came to the entrance of the sewing factory. Groups of women were on their way out, chattering to each other in a language he did not understand. He had a fleeting impulse to follow one home, insinuate himself into her life, be acknowledged and taken care of. But no one gave him the least notice, and he passed on. Near the end of the block was an Italian butcher shop, where a squat, gray-haired woman was skinning a lamb. Next to it was a jewelry shop, and next to that, a bakery. A man with greasy arms came out carrying a pink box tied with string. A turbaned woman holding a tiny dog hurried in.

Frankie halted. He had traveled less than a block, and already he felt hopelessly lost. His fear of being singled out had not materialized, but now he had another worry. It was pure chaos out here. Bedlam. Another few moments and he might easily be swallowed.

At the corner he took out his map, which he studied for what seemed like hours. At last he came to a decision and headed off down the block. Half an hour later he was back where he had started. He was afraid to ask for help, afraid his voice would give him away. He tried again. Chance rewarded him, and he found a subway station but guessed wrong on which train to take. He ended up in Brooklyn, where he finally broke down and asked a subway attendant for directions. It turned out to be no big deal, except for the part of standing body to body with complete strangers in the packed car. Someone grabbed his ass, and he stiffened but was too embarrassed to say anything. When it happened again, he managed to move away. At last his stop came, and he hurried out of the station to the street. He was frazzled and needed to recuperate, and he ducked into the first place he could find, a fast-food joint where he ordered a burger and soda. Surprisingly, no one hesitated when he spoke, no one whispered furtively, no one gawked. His breasts and wide hips aroused no particular comment, nor did the pitch of his voice, nor his clothes. No one, in fact, seemed much to care one way or another what he was or did. You think you're a man but you look like a woman? Fine. New York's a big place. Plenty of room for everybody. By the time he got to Virgo's he felt, if not comfortable, at least somewhat less conspicuous. Then he caught sight of the naked woman on the bar's marquee. His self-consciousness returned, and he hugged himself, pulling the edges of his jacket tight. He glanced around. Marshaling his forces, he went inside.

The early evening crowd was there in force, and the bar was thick with smoke and the smell of beer. A young woman danced on a platform to music whose bass line vibrated in Frankie's chest, while the men at the bar whooped and thrust paper bills at her pelvis. Frankie's first impulse was to turn and run. He did not like the noise, and he felt threatened anew by the chaos. Already he was conscious of men staring at him. One, on his way out, made a point of bumping into him. Standing only inches away, the man apologized profusely. He put a hand on Frankie's shoulder. Frankie shook it off. The man said something that Frankie didn't hear, and his face took on a look of feigned injury.

To get away from him Frankie went deeper into the bar. He wanted a drink. The floor was thick with bodies, but miraculously a line opened for him as he went forward. An obviously drunk man made a blunt proposal of a sexual favor. Frankie stopped and slowly turned. The man was a head taller than him and leered down through bloodshot eyes.

"I got fifty bucks," he said, fumbling in his pocket and producing a crumpled-up bill. "Wha'dya say?"

"Fuck you," replied Frankie.

"Now there's an idea." He waved the bill in Frankie's face. "C'mon, sweetmeat, I've seen you here before. You're no virgin."

"What I am, mister, is none of your business."

The man took a long drag on the beer in his hand, then put the empty bottle on the bar. Smiling, he reached again into his pocket. "Another fifty then." He held up both bills. "A hundred bucks is enough to buy any pussy. Anytime, anyplace."

Frankie felt a sudden and uncontrollable surge of pure aggression, a blind impulse to do something nasty to this man, to drive him into the ground, overwhelm him with superior strength and power. His hands bunched into fists. "I'm going to bust your face, buddy, you don't leave me alone."

The man laughed and made fists of his own. They were twice as big as Frankie's. He laughed again.

"Look," said Frankie, taking in the man's size and obvious advantage. "I'm not what you think I am. I'm not a woman. I'm a man. Just leave me alone."

The man raised his eyebrows and looked Frankie over. A lewd smile played across his face. "Is that right? Well shit, I'll pay to see that."

"I'm not lying," said Frankie.

The man smoothed out the bills but did not put them away. "A hundred bucks says you are."

Frankie felt trapped. The desire to attack and vanquish was opposed by another force, a deeper instinct that seemed to be pulling him away, urging him to cower and flee. He looked around, hoping to find a friendly face. Other men were watching, some with wet-lipped, salacious grins. He turned back to the man, who seemed to have grown larger. His mouth gaped sickeningly, as if anticipating a meal. He was still holding the money.

Impulsively, Frankie grabbed the bills, silencing the inner cry for retreat, and crumpled them in his palm. As though a bystander, he watched the fingers of his other hand take the bills and hold them in the air. The crumpled paper looked like an ugly flower, and in one deft and sudden motion he stuffed it in the man's mouth.

By the time the man recovered from the shock, Frankie had pushed his way to the end of the bar. Frantically searching for somewhere to hide, he caught sight of a door at the back with an EXIT sign above it. Over his shoulder he saw the man scanning the room, his face flushed and furious. Frankie wasted no time. Yanking the door open, he rushed inside.

He found himself in a short hall, at the end of which stood a heavy metal door with a bar release. To the side was a second door with a STAFF ONLY sign. It gave when he tried the knob, and quickly, he stepped inside.

The room was long and narrow, with a concrete floor and tall, raftered ceiling. At least half of it was taken up by stacks of liquor and beer. In the other half were a couple of folding chairs and a mirror. Next to the mirror was a rack of clothes.

Frankie was shaking, and it didn't take him long to figure out what to do about it. He tore off the top of one of the cases and pulled out a bottle of Wild

Turkey. The liquor burned going down, but it felt warm in his stomach. He took another slug.

A few minutes later there was a noise at the door. In a panic Frankie backed against a wall and grabbed the neck of the bottle, which he was prepared to shatter and use as a weapon. The door swung open, and a young woman, naked save for a tiny g-string, entered the room. Her face registered only mild surprise upon seeing someone already there.

"Hi," she said.

Frankie tried to hide the bottle behind his back, but the woman came over and took it from him.

"I could use a drink."

She was tall, slender to the point of starvation, and shaved clean. The roots of her flaxen hair were black, her eyes green, her breasts veined blue. Frankie stared as she straddled one of the chairs and tilted the bottle to her lips. He had never seen a naked woman before.

"So I heard you were sick."

He did not reply.

"No? Wrong?" She handed the bottle back.

"I'm all right," he said. "I'm better."

"You want to get high?" The girl leaned over to the clothes rack, which held some coats and street clothes, as well as half a dozen cheap lamé dresses. From a pocket of one of the coats she pulled out a thin joint.

"Got a light?"

Frankie reached in his pockets and came up empty. The girl stuck a finger in her g-string and peered down.

"Nothing here either."

"There," said Frankie, pointing to the plastic counter in front of the mirror. There was a matchbook, which he handed to her.

She lit up and inhaled deeply, shutting her eyes and holding it. Her exhalation a few seconds later gave the impression she was blowing off demons. Frankie was interested. He held out his hand for the joint.

After they'd smoked it down, the girl got up and took one of the dresses from the rack. She held it against her sinuous body and struck a model's pose.

"What do you think? Is it me?"

Frankie gave it some thought. "Who are you?"

"Ah," she said. "That question." She closed her eyes. "Tonight . . . tonight I'm a debutante. It's the ball." She twirled once on her toes. "The contracts are being handed out, they're on tiny dance cards the girls wear on their wrists. Which boy's on mine? Is it Jack Denning? He's going to Princeton. Or Tom Harvey? Going to Yale to be a lawyer. Who does Christie get? Who takes her home and lays her in the back of Daddy's car?"

The gown slipped to the floor, and the girl's hands dropped down to cover her breasts. It was meant to be a tease, but it came across as painfully shy and sad. When she opened her eyes, she found Frankie staring at her.

"Your turn," she said self-consciously.

He looked away, not knowing what to say. Surrounding him were stacks of liquor, a cracked mirror, dresses hanging on a rack made of pipe. They made a story, but he didn't know the words. Gradually, he became aware of a pain in one of his knuckles, and when he looked down saw that he was digging at the skin, almost to the point of drawing blood. The mannerism seemed so natural, so automatic. Immediately, he stopped.

"I'm looking for Cox," he said.

There was a pause, and then the girl giggled. "Big ones or little ones?"

"Cox," he repeated. "The guy who works here. Have you seen him?"

"He's not here." She giggled more while picking up the dress and stepping into it. It was a spangled red halter dress that barely reached her thighs. "Angel Face is protecting the ladies tonight."

"When's he coming back?"

"Mr. Cox," she said, giving his name a heavy accent, "does not honor me with his schedule." She bent in front of the mirror and arranged her hair. "You two have something on?"

"I have to talk to him."

"Lipstick," she muttered, pulling a tube from a clutch purse that was in the other pocket of her coat. "Definitely lipstick."

Frankie watched while she applied it, sucking her lips against one another to spread it evenly. It turned them a deep and glistening red, nearly the shade of the dress.

"So," the girl said. "How do I look?"

"Fine. Lovely."

"Full of love," she said gaily. "Yes. Definitely."

"There was a man out there," Frankie said quickly, before she left. "We had a little run-in."

"Yeah. I saw."

"Is he still out there?"

She shrugged. "I don't know. Maybe he got himself thrown out."

"Do you think you could find out? Come back and tell me?"

"It'd be tough to get back once I'm out, Frankie. You know how it is. Why don't you just go out the back."

"The back?"

"Look, I gotta go." She was already halfway out the door. "I wouldn't want to miss the chance of getting to know one of these fine gentlemen now, would I?"

She left, and Frankie had an urge to go after her. He did not want to be alone. He had another drink, after which he found himself staring in the mirror. Looking back was a face not quite as strange as the one he had seen that first time in the apartment. He played with the dark waves of hair and drew his finger along the cheek. He pursed the lips. A companion? It had to be the drugs working. Lovely, he had told the girl. Maybe he was lovely too.

He left the bar by way of the door at the end of the hall, which led into an alley off the street. Retracing his path to the Forty-ninth Street station, he took the train downtown. It was close to nine when he got home.

Through the door he heard music as he worked the keys in the locks, and when he got inside he was hit with the same smell he'd just left in the back room with the girl. He followed it to the living room, expecting to see Terry. Instead, standing beside the sofa was a very large black man. Frankie froze.

"Where's Terry?"

"Taking care of some business."

With one eye on the man, Frankie called down the hall. A muffled response came from the bedroom, and a moment later Terry materialized, carrying a paper bag. He handed it to Marcus and flopped on the couch.

"How you like the weed?"

Marcus didn't reply. He was watching Frankie, whose reaction, familiar enough from some folks, had taken him by surprise. It set in motion certain subtle changes of behavior.

"*Excellante*," he said, slumping a little to minimize his height. He had a smoldering number in hand that he offered to Frankie, who shook her head. Marcus took another drag.

"Sit down, you guys," said Terry. "You're making me nervous."

Frankie flashed him a look but did not budge. Marcus nodded to himself and joined him on the couch.

"So," Terry said to Frankie. "What's happening?"

"Cox wasn't there." He wanted to say more, but the presence of the stranger made him tight-lipped. It came to him how he'd been looking forward to getting back to the apartment, to the safety and solace of its constrained yet familiar world. Now this man made him feel newly invaded. It put him back on guard.

Marcus had suspicions of his own. No matter that Frankie was an old friend, some things were older than friends. Like staying alert. Like not giving anything away. People could turn at any moment. He'd seen it hundreds of times.

He sat on the couch with his heels tucked back, his hands open at his sides. His expression was both distant and poised, nonchalant and vigilant, a face behind which almost anything could have been going on.

For a time nothing was said. Frankie stood in the doorway, arms folded, trying to decide whether to stay or go. Terry hummed nervously to himself. He hadn't told Marcus about Frankie, and now he regretted it. He had the feeling that something was about to go down, something beyond his control. He didn't like it, and he went over to Frankie.

"Be cool," he whispered. "Marcus doesn't know."

"Who is he?"

"A friend." To make things look natural, he laced an arm around her waist. Frankie tried to twist away, but Terry held her tight.

"Try not to make a scene. How about a smile?"

"I don't want to smile. Tell him to go."

"He just got here."

"Tell him."

Marcus looked up, and Terry made a face.

"She's got a headache," he said lamely. "Maybe you should go lie down, honey."

Frankie said nothing, but Marcus seemed to come alive. He made a space between his knees.

"C'mere," he said.

Frankie didn't move.

"C'mon." He gestured imperiously. "I got fingers that'll pull the pain right out."

Frankie wasn't going anywhere. He crossed his arms and stood firm.

"Go on," said Terry with a grin. "Maybe he'll pull out some other stuff too."

When he saw the reaction his offer was receiving, Marcus stood up and went over himself. Frankie shrank at his touch, a reaction Marcus did not fail to note. He placed one of his enormous hands on the small of Frankie's back and the other gently on a wrist. In full command, he escorted his charge to the couch.

Under the steady pressure of the man's palms on his shoulders, Frankie sat on the floor between his legs. He was less frightened than angry, oppressed and temporarily overcome by what he felt to be a conspiracy between the two men. The muscles at the back of his neck tensed up, pressing on the nerves that wound through his scalp. If he didn't have a headache before, he was getting one now.

Marcus placed his hands on Frankie's head, spreading his fingers until they touched in front and back. With his thumbs tight against the notch at the base of the skull, he began to make tiny circles on the cheeks and temples with his fingertips.

Despite himself, Frankie found it soothing. His eyes, which he depended on to warn him of danger, began to get heavy. When Marcus shifted his work to the knot of muscles over his jaw, he gave a yelp but did not move away. Something in him seemed to settle deeper into the floor. He gave a sigh.

Terry said something from across the room that Frankie didn't hear. Marcus had his palms over his ears, and his strong fingers were laced over the dome of Frankie's head. He'd press, then release, press, release, and at the release Frankie would feel a sudden lightening, as though his head were expanding into space. Next, the fingers moved to his neck, searching out the bones of his spine. Marcus found a tender spot and Frankie arched in pain. Marcus softened his attack, working the knot until the pain began to dissipate. He moved lower.

"Take off your coat," he said.

Frankie obeyed, not wanting him to stop. Marcus kneaded the long muscles that ran along the ridge from neck to shoulder, digging in with his fingers and rolling them in his hands. Frankie felt that part of his body dissolving, as though Marcus were removing the bones. The soft tissues that remained were getting softer. The muscles were turning to jelly. Another sigh, and he slumped against the couch.

When Marcus finally stopped, Frankie barely noticed. He was miles away in a place where awareness was an annoyance. It took some time for him to return.

"Thank you," he murmured, his voice mostly breath.

"Headache gone?"

He nodded and opened his eyes. The room seemed brighter. It was also emptier.

"Where's Terry?"

"Went to get some beer."

Frankie nodded again, undisturbed by Terry's absence. With an effort he got up, then went and sat in the armchair across from the couch.

"Where did you learn to do that?"

"That?" Marcus lifted his arms and cocked his wrists down, pointing with both forefingers to where Frankie had been sitting. He sounded incredulous. "That?"

Frankie was afraid he had said something wrong. Marcus's eyes got big.

"That was a small job. The minor tune-up. Change the oil, check the brakes, send you home. No money down, pay as you go. That I do blindfolded, hands behind my back. The big job, now the BIG job, the one they fly in my ship for, champagne, armed commandos, that one, now that one . . ." His head was sideways, grinning, and his hands twisted the air as though he were sculpting clay. "It lay you up for a week. Check you in and check you out. You understand? Flat as a gnat. Gone. Like they look at you and say, 'she dead.' And you be thinking the same, 'cuz you try to find your bones and they gone. I got 'em right here." He held out his hands. "Right here. And that's where I keep 'em, till you ready to come back. And when you ready . . ." He snapped his fingers. "You come. 'Cuz where you are, you see it. Your mind's right there, and everything be clear as glass right in front of your eyes. That's the big job."

Frankie tried to follow what he was saying. He got the general idea that Marcus was making a joke, but he had a sense that something else was being said too. He began to like the man, and he apologized for his earlier behavior.

"I was frightened."

Marcus didn't reply.

"I mean, when I first came in. I didn't know who you were."

Marcus's eyes narrowed and he studied Frankie, a man poring over a riddle. He had questions that pride kept him from asking.

"You see," said Frankie, "I lost my memory."

The fatuous simplicity of the statement, as though he were talking about some key he had misplaced, frustrated him. It told the truth and missed it completely. But he didn't know how else to say it, how to describe something that didn't exist.

"I don't remember anything."

He glanced to Marcus for some sign of understanding, but his face was impossible to read. Moments passed, during which Frankie wished that he hadn't spoken. He felt stupid and embarrassed. Then Marcus broke the silence.

"I knew a man like that," he said. He pointed a finger at his temple and made at pulling a trigger with his thumb. "Took a bullet right here. Blew off a good part of his head. They figured him for dead, but we got him out. When I saw him in the hospital, he didn't remember nothing. He could talk but it didn't make sense. He had eyes too, working eyes, but he couldn't see right. You could tell that by the way he kept twisting his head when he was looking at you, like he was trying to get something back on that had come loose."

He stopped, making a gun again with his hand. From his mouth came the sound of a muffled shot as he sent an imaginary bullet into the wall. "Man's whole life blown away by one little bullet. One wrong move shuts him down." He cut Frankie a look. "You understand what I'm saying?"

"No guns," said Frankie. "It's not like that." All at

once he wanted to stop the masquerade and tell. It was crazy, but maybe this man would understand. He seemed a little crazy too.

"I woke up one day and my mind was gone. Everything except one thing. One thing I still knew."

Marcus nodded, as though he were already in on the secret. Frankie leaned forward and cleared his throat.

"I'm not Frankie, Marcus. I look like her, I talk like her, but I'm not her." He took a breath, exhaled. "I'm a man. I know it sounds crazy, but it's the truth. I don't know how, or why, but that's what I am. Inside. Inside I'm a man."

Marcus took the news with surprising equanimity. At first he grinned, but he quickly wiped the look from his face when he saw that Frankie was serious. Then he became cautious, working the angles of the confession, trying to see if Frankie was trying to put something over on him.

"A man," he said.

Frankie nodded.

Marcus stood up, drew himself to his full height, which was huge, and puffed out his chest. Fisting his hands and flexing the muscles of his arms, he said again, loudly, "A MAN?"

Frankie was a little intimidated but held his ground. He stayed perched on the edge of the chair and fisted his own hands. "Here," he said, laying the fists on his belly, his chest, finally his head. "Yes. A man."

Marcus looked down at him, frowned slightly and relaxed his pose. He bent to examine Frankie's face, looking long and hard into his eyes.

"Maybe you need the big job."

Frankie smiled. "Maybe I do."

Marcus found the roach and fired it up, pacing as he smoked. He had a tight black beard, nappy like the hair on his head, and he rubbed it as he paced.

"One time a lady came to Aunt Orphah," he said. "Summertime. Heat so thick you wanted to peel it off, jump out of your skin into something cool, like one of them slow, lazy rivers. Except they got blood-suckers live in the water, suck your blood you stay in too long.

"Aunt Orphah, she had me in the kitchen working some root. She was at the stove when this lady come in. Young-looking girl with a pretty face, except something's wrong. Eyes be all tired like she missing sleep, and troubled, like there's something else too. She's trailing three kids dressed up like they going to church. She goes up to Aunt Orphah and starts talking in a low voice, looking down the whole time at the floor and scraping her feet. She got a problem, she say. It's her man, he be stepping out on her, her and the kids. Giving her fits and bad thoughts.

" 'You a doctor,' she tell Orphah. 'Help me get him back.' She fumbles in her dress and holds out a dollar bill.

"Orphah looks the girl over, then sits her down. The kids stand in a line next to her, watching with big eyes.

" 'You want him back,' says Orphah, 'you got to make him want to come back.'

" 'I treat him good,' the girl says. 'Ain't no reason for him to go out on me.'

" 'I'm talking 'bout something different,' says

Orphah. 'You possessed by the man. What you got to do is turn the tables. You got to stop his headway.'

"Orphah cuts me a look and wipes her hands on her apron. Then she turn back to the girl.

" 'First thing is you got to get the man worried. You take a pair of his socks—don't wash 'em—and cut the toes out and wear 'em up under each of your arms. You do that for a week and he be worried to death. Won't know more'n half the time what he's doing. After another week he be looking for something to take down the pressure. And that's when you turn the trick.

" 'You get you a sharp knife. Go down to the hardware store and buy one and then get yourself a piece of steel, don't matter what shape it's in, jus' so that it's steel. You take that steel and you name it yourself. You drive it down in the middle of his track, his right track, and then you take that sharp knife that's never been used, good and sharp, and you speak to it. You tell it, 'I want you to cut his headway. I want you to stop him 'cuz I know that you can.' You lay your mind into that knife. You tell it, 'don't let him get out of the house 'less there's satisfaction with me.' And then you make a whack right across his left track jus' as hard as she can cut. Take that knife then and bury it right under the eave of the house with the blade down. Cover it over with dirt and lay a board or a brick on top so the sun won't never hit it. And that man he never will go away from that house not unless you say it.'

"By now the girl be nodding, and that troubled look in her eyes, it be halfway gone. And Orphah ask do she understand and the girl say yes, she do. Then

Orphah takes the dollar bill and smooths it out, taking plenty of time so the girl can see. She folds it
three times, two sideways and one across, and then
she puts it away. The girl lets out a sigh like she's
been holding her breath a long time, then gets up
and thanks Orphah and leaves with the kids. When
she's gone, Aunt Orphah asks me have I been paying
attention. I tell her I have.

" 'Good. This here ain't no rootwork. It's pure
conjuration. You leave off other people's heads and
they won't go bothering yours. And if they do, you
jus' get your nature right and they can't do nothing
'bout it.' "

Marcus paused. For a moment another memory
seemed to intercede. He glanced at Frankie.

"I try to hold what Aunt Orphah said in mind." He
tapped his forehead. "Right here at the front."

"What happened to the girl?"

"She was all right."

"You saw her again?"

"Didn't have to. Aunt Orphah knows her business.
She knows it good."

He nodded to himself and started pacing again.
Two steps took him from one wall to the other, and
Frankie got the feeling that he was too big for the
room. It occurred to him that this was a man who'd
led a fettered life. He was drawn by this, as well as
another quality he couldn't quite name, an openness
maybe, a field of vision that could admit even
Frankie's own strange truth. He waited for some further word, something beyond the story to show that
Marcus did, in fact, believe.

Minutes passed. Marcus seemed lost in a world of

his own. Just as Frankie was about to say something, there was a noise in the hall. Seconds later Terry burst into the room, a paper bag crooked under one arm, a pizza box balanced on the other.

"Who's hungry?"

Marcus stopped his pacing. "I should be getting home."

"One beer," said Terry, pulling out a six-pack and tossing him a can. "And a slice of pie. Then you go."

Marcus stared at his feet.

"Stay," offered Frankie. "Like the man said."

"I miss anything good?"

Frankie shrugged. Terry glanced at Marcus.

"You guys talk?"

Marcus took a draw on the beer. He knew better than to get involved in family business.

"What'd she tell you?"

"Moms had a saying," he said. "Don't stick your nose out else it might get nipped."

"You're among friends, man."

Marcus nodded. "Yeah. That's just what I was thinking."

"What are you two whispering?" asked Frankie.

"The olives," remarked Terry, peeling one off his pizza with a flourish. "Nature's little circles. Her zeros. They're a sign of peace, you know that? Little black holes of truce and harmony."

"What are you talking about?"

"Don't be thick, Frankie. I'm talking about the olive branch. The goddamned olive branch." He turned to Marcus. "We got some heavy shit going down here. Heads going off all over the place."

"I can't ignore it," said Frankie.

"You make it too hard," replied Terry.

Marcus finished his beer and picked up the paper bag. "I'll catch you folks later."

His departure was followed by an uneasy silence. Terry wanted to reach out but was unwilling to risk being rebuffed. He was tired of all the craziness. Frankie worried that Marcus hadn't taken him seriously. He felt the isolation creeping in again. He, too, wanted to make contact.

"I had a rough time at the bar," he told Terry.

"Cox is a rough guy."

"I didn't see him. I told you that. A guy tried to pick me up. It got ugly."

Terry showed signs of interest, and Frankie told him what had happened. When he came to the part about stuffing the money in the guy's mouth, Terry laughed.

"You got balls, Frankie. If nothing else, you do have balls."

"Maybe if I did, jerks like that would leave me alone."

"He'd bother someone else. But it is an idea." He got a look on his face. "Hold on a minute."

He went to the hall and squatted down. On the lowest shelves were his medical books, anatomy, pathology, medicine, surgery. He found the text on urology and brought it to the living room, where he leafed through the pages until he came to the section on plastic surgery and prosthetics. There was a nice illustration of an artificial scrotum and penis constructed from a full thickness flap of skin from the inner thigh. The different stages of the operation were depicted to the side, as well as various sizes and shapes of polyurethane and silicone testes. He showed the drawings to Frankie, who was not amused.

"But say you had a dick," persisted Terry. "Maybe one of those inflatable jobs. And a big hairy scrotum. The next time some guy came on to you, you could whip it out and wave it in his face. He'd probably pass out on the spot."

"I'll leave that thrill to you."

"Don't be nasty now."

"It happens again, I'll kick him in the nuts."

"There you go. Now you're thinking like a woman."

"You'd do the same thing, some guy had you backed against a wall."

"Would I?" He tried to picture it. "I don't know. It'd be tough to go after the jewels."

"Maybe you haven't had the right threat."

"Maybe not." Involuntarily, he cupped his genitals. "It hurts even to think about it."

Frankie motioned toward the book. "How come you know so much about this stuff anyway?"

"What stuff?"

"That." He pointed at the page. "All those books you've got."

"I'm interested. Fascinated, you might say."

"That's what you do? It's your job?"

Terry shrugged. "I went to medical school."

"C'mon."

"Hard to imagine, isn't it?"

"You were going to be a doctor?"

"The idea crossed my mind. It was years ago."

"What happened?"

"I decided to sell books instead."

Frankie didn't know whether to believe him. He asked again.

"It's history," said Terry. "What say we talk about you. There's a question I've been wanting to ask. Just what is it you plan to do once we locate this guy you're so hot to find? We nail him, then what?"

"I assume something will happen."

"Yeah? Like what?"

Frankie frowned. It wasn't a fair question. "We'll just have to see."

"Not even a clue?"

"You losing faith? Already?"

Terry laughed. "It's water in my hands."

"Don't. Something's going to happen. I'm not sure what, but it will. It has to."

"That's fine, just so long as when it's over, it's over. I want you back, Frankie. I need you, the way a man needs a woman." He hesitated. "You understand what I'm saying? I can wait, but not forever."

"I need to talk to Cox."

"Forget Cox. Think about me."

"I want it to be over as much as you do. More."

Terry saw her sad, determined eyes, her sweet lips. It ached having her so close.

"There're worse men than me, Frankie. I could love you if you'd give me half a chance. A quarter."

"You refuse to understand. It's not about that."

"Tell me what's so bad about being a woman."

"It's not what I am."

"But you could be. You could if you wanted."

Frankie sighed. "Do me a favor and call the bar.

Find out when Cox is going to be there. The sooner we get this over with, the better."

"Cox is a worm. The man has a bezoar for a brain."

"Then maybe I should let you talk." She got the number from information, dialed it, and when someone answered, pushed the phone at Terry, who had to shout to be heard.

"Day after tomorrow," he said after hanging up. Frankie thanked him.

"I have one other favor to ask," she said. "You think I could use the bed for a night?"

The simple courtesy of the request caught Terry off guard. It seemed to come from another life. "Take it."

She started out of the room, then stopped when Terry called her name.

"What?"

"You remember what I told you, Frankie. I can take a licking, but I'm not a fool. I want you to keep that in mind."

"I'm counting on it," said Frankie.

"Do," he muttered as she disappeared down the hall, trailing his bafflement and desire in wake. "Make sure you do."

8

Two days later they went out to eat. It was a warm, breezy afternoon, and Terry wore a tee shirt under his leather jacket. Frankie had on a bulky sweater that hung below his waist, disguising his shape. He had resigned himself to wearing women's clothes, which, at least in the eyes of the world, seemed to make him less alien and therefore less noticeable. He was also starting to get a handle on his new body's balance, which initially had seemed so unnatural and precarious. The first day or two he had felt literally in danger of falling over and was constantly realigning himself, tilting his pelvis, pulling back his shoulders, locking his knees, all of which left him permanently tense and sore. Since discovering that the body seemed to do just fine when left alone, he tried not making conscious adjustments, and for the most part he was successful. Occasionally, however, there were lapses. One occurred on the curb as they left the apartment and another a few blocks later. The first time he caught himself, but the second he stumbled inadvertently into Terry's arms. They separated instantly, each with a muttered apology. Terry's was less than genuine, for in truth he felt like ripping Frankie's clothes off. He had woken with a hard-on, which he had kept on and off all morning. With the indiscriminate and implacable appetite of a man in heat he was ready to grab whatever flesh he could find.

He took Frankie to a restaurant on MacDougal, and because of the nice weather they sat outside. A group of preschoolers tethered to loops in a long rope made their way down the opposite sidewalk. Frankie ordered a sandwich, Terry the chef's salad. Before the waitress left, he told her to sprinkle a little saltpeter on it.

The girl, who looked to be barely out of high school, dutifully wrote down his request. "Additions are fifty cents extra."

"This is more like subtraction," said Terry.

She smiled uncertainly, a look he returned with a wink.

"Cute girl," he observed after she'd gone.

"Why did you order that?"

"What, you too? Saltpeter, man! Keeps down lust and the dreaded sin of Onan."

"I don't understand. What is it?"

"And here I was thinking you were a man." He grinned maliciously. "It keeps the bone soft, or so they say. You eat it, and it goes to your prick. Your peter. Like pouring salt on a bird's tail to keep it from flying. Salt-peter."

"Does it work?"

"The more intelligent question," he said, leaning

across the table and whispering so that Frankie had to lean close to hear, "the one you should be asking is, why would a man ever choose to use such a thing?"

Before Frankie had a chance to unravel that one, the waitress returned.

"I'm sorry, but the chef says we don't have any saltpeter." She lowered her voice. "Frankly, I don't think he knows what it is."

"Then bring me yohimbine," Terry commanded.

"I don't think we have that either."

"Stop badgering her," said Frankie.

"I'm not badgering." He caught the waitress's eye. "Terry Connor," he said, extending a hand. "What's your name?"

"Linda."

"You're a good waitress, Linda. I like you. If I weren't with my mother here, I'd ask you out."

Innocent she might have been, but the waitress was no dummy. With a practiced smile she said she'd be back as soon as their order was ready, then turned and left.

Frankie glared at Terry. "You're cruel."

"Try desperate."

"Look. I don't like this any more than you do."

"Then stop. You can. Anytime."

"I want to. Believe me." He twisted his napkin. "Look. I'm sorry. That's the best I can do."

Terry didn't reply.

"So what's yohimbine?"

"Nothing."

"You want me to leave? I can."

"It's a tree. From Africa. The bark contains an

alkaloid with sympathomimetic and hypotensive properties.''

"Of course. Now I understand.''

"It's an aphrodisiac, Frankie. Turns a fella into a love machine. Or maybe he falls in love with the next person he meets. I'm not sure. Up to now I've never had to find out.''

"You think you need some of that?''

"One of us does.''

The waitress brought their order, they ate, then Terry got the bill. He flirted with the girl again before leaving a generous tip. Out on the street he told Frankie he had some business to attend to.

"I want to go to Virgo's,'' said Frankie.

"Be my guest.''

"I could use some help.''

"I've already been for you once.''

"Please. I'm asking.''

The voice snagged him, but it was the eyes that reeled him in.

"All right, but I have an errand first. We'll go after that. Cox you'll have to deal with yourself.''

"You've made that clear. When will you be home?''

"When I am. An hour. Maybe two.''

"I'll be there.''

They faced each other awkwardly, Terry feeling the urge rise again, but different from before. He wanted to grab Frankie and shake some sense into her head. Teach her a lesson. Dice in a cup, he thought with grim amusement. Turning on his heel, he left her standing there.

It was close to five when he reached the Metro

building. The street was teeming with activity, cabs pulling in and out, double-parked, lined in the yard to gas up. He took the stairs two at a time but at the second floor was forced to slow down. There was heavy traffic near the office, and he had to step around one knot of drivers and through another in order to get in the door. Inside was a larger crowd, some handing in their way-bills, others laying out the cash for the next shift. The boss was doing his best to keep up.

Terry hung back at first, listening for a shouted name, a dropped word, something to identify the man he was after. But the scene was too crazy, and after a while he joined the crowd jostling toward the counter. A minute later he got the boss's attention.

"Remember me?"

The white-lipped man glanced up, then returned to his business. "What do you want?"

"My girlfriend lost her ring. You said to come back."

"Nothing's been turned in."

"You said I could look myself."

"I said that?" He was counting money. "I must be crazy."

"You said you'd let me talk to the driver. Mr. Daggoo."

"Hey, Castillo," he yelled toward the door. "You owe me ten bucks."

"I gave you fifty," shouted back a man in a Met's cap.

"Fifty today. Ten from last week."

"I ain't got ten," the man said dolefully, pulling

his pockets inside out, then lifting his hands in resignation. "I'll bring it to you tomorrow."

"Tomorrow it's ten," he scowled. "The day after it's fifteen."

"Muy generoso, amigo." The man tipped his cap and went down the stairs. Simultaneously, the phone rang. It went ignored.

"I need your help," said Terry.

"I'm ten bucks down." He took a slug of antacid and started to initial the way-bills.

"The ring," he went on doggedly, "it's really important to her. It's kind of like an heirloom."

"It musta cost a lot. Me, I'm not a rich man."

Terry was about to say he didn't seem too healthy either, when he began to get the drift. He crumpled up the five in his pocket and palmed it across the counter. The man took it smoothly, glancing at the denomination before secreting it away.

"Now I'm just five down."

Terry frowned but handed him another. He took it without changing his expression.

"John D.," he said to a man who had just paid his fifty. "Hold on a second."

The man stopped near the door and came back. He was half a foot shorter than Terry with a dark complexion and a well-trimmed pencil-thin moustache. He looked to be in his mid-fifties.

"Whatchu got?"

"Man here wants a word with you."

Daggoo looked for a message in his boss's face, then turned to Terry.

"Who are you?"

"Is there somewhere we can talk?"

"Talk here."

"Someplace a little more private."

The man studied him. Without replying, he turned and walked out the door. Terry followed him downstairs and through the gate into the lot. He moved in a tight, compact fashion; though short, he did not in any way seem slight. In the lot he stopped beside an old Chevy Impala. One of the windows was cracked a space, and a snarling Doberman kept trying to force its muzzle through. When Terry came up, the dog started to bark. It barred its teeth and snapped at him through the glass.

"Big dog," Terry said, determined not to sound frightened. He noted that Daggoo made no attempt to calm the animal. He tried to put it out of his mind.

"I'm trying to locate a couple of men. They were fares of yours a few nights ago. From a bar called Virgo's."

Daggoo studied his nails.

"You know it?"

"I've been driving thirty years," he said. "Not much I don't know."

"You remember these guys?"

Daggoo looked at him. "What guys?"

"Late forties, early fifties. Dressed in suits. One was pretty sloshed. It was about 2 A.M. the morning of the first."

"The morning of the first."

"Yeah. They took a cab. I'm trying to find out where they went."

"Trying to find out, are you?"

"They took something," said Terry. "Stole it from my girlfriend. It's important we get it back." He realized it sounded weak, but he had decided from the start that he was not about to tell Frankie's side of the story. Better a little weak, he thought, than ridiculous.

Daggoo leaned against the car and folded his arms. The Doberman continued to bark.

"Really I just want to talk to them, but I don't know where they live. I was hoping you could remember where you let them off."

"You don't know where they live."

Terry suddenly got the sense that, despite their apparent conversation, the two of them were not talking at all.

"It's a lot to ask, I know. I'm willing to pay."

"Willing to pay, are you?"

"Please," Terry said in exasperation. "This isn't a joke."

Daggoo studied him. He was not a man with an active imagination. "Sounds to me like police business."

"Believe me, it's not."

"It's like that, is it?"

"No," Terry said. "It's not like that. You wouldn't believe me if I told you."

Daggoo smoothed his moustache. "How much money you got?"

Terry reached in his pocket and drew out two tens. He handed them to Daggoo.

"Quiet, Major," the man barked to his dog. Instantly, the animal became still. "Sit." It curled up on the front seat.

"I need another twenty," he said.

Briefly, Terry considered bluffing, then gave Daggoo his last ten.

"It's all I got."

Without comment Daggoo pocketed the money. "Some fares you forget in a minute, some you remember. Fiftieth and Broadway. Virgo's, right?"

Terry nodded.

"One of the guys could hardly walk. His friend and I, we had to squeeze him in the cab. Had to get him out too. But by then he was walking better." He picked some food out of a tooth. "Upper West Side's where I took 'em. Seventy-second near the park. Place called the Alvey."

"They both got out there?"

Daggoo nodded. "The one guy was walking, but he wasn't all too good at it. The other guy kept an arm around him."

"Did you get a look at either of them?"

"The drunk one had dark hair. I think he's the one who lived there. Both of them were dressed good. Tipped cheap."

"You hear any names?"

The driver shook his head and checked his watch. "I'm losing money talking to you."

"I gave you thirty bucks."

Daggoo gave him a narrow look, as though the transaction had no bearing on their present situation.

"The Alvey," Terry repeated, trying to evoke some further response. Daggoo didn't bite. He said something to the dog and started across the yard. Terry followed him to a cab, wanting to know more but not exactly sure what to ask. The driver slid into a cab, turned on the engine and adjusted the rearview mirror. He rolled down the window.

On impulse Terry leaned on the sill and bent down until he was face to face with the man. "Will you take me there?"

"You got the money?"

Terry fished in his pockets. "I got some change. You took the rest."

"Cost five, six dollars to get there."

"C'mon," said Terry. "Stop being such a hard ass."

It was not a diplomatic comment. Daggoo put the car in gear and without changing expression, stepped on the accelerator. Terry was spun off as the cab shot forward. He swore after it, causing a few heads to turn. He didn't care. Straightening himself, he chanced to catch sight of the boss staring down from one of the second-floor windows. Terry flipped him the bird. Then he left.

He got to the Alvey on foot, the long trek allowing plenty of time to fuel his indignation and anger. Principally these were directed at Frankie, but others, including the driver, his boss and various strangers on the way, were targets too. There were moments he felt on the verge of explosion and might well have lost it were it not that he was nearly at the end of the chase. Jones, who lived at the Alvey. He savored the name and address. Once Terry had him, Frankie would be forced to end the charade. One way or another things would be set right.

The place itself took him by surprise. For some reason he had expected a small apartment building, two or three stories, a few expensive units. The Alvey was nothing of the kind. It was at least thirty stories high, with an elaborate stone facade topped by an ornate cornice. There was a gray curbside awning on which the building's name was written in elegant script. Standing beside one of its brass poles was a doorman dressed in green. He wore a military hat and a coat that sported epaulets fringed in yellow. His pants matched the coat, with a braid of yellow cord down the side of the leg. He was looking disinterestedly down the block as Terry crossed the street.

"Evening."

The man nodded noncommittally, and Terry searched for something additional to say.

"Is this the Alvey?" In addition to being on the awning, the name was etched in a brass plaque next to the door.

"This is it," the man replied evenly.

"It's a big place."

The man glanced at Terry. "Something I can do for you?"

"I'm looking for a man."

"Plenty of men here. Women too."

"His name is Jones."

The doorman gave the matter some thought before gesturing to the lobby. "Best you talk to Mr. Hoke."

He let Terry in with a key, then introduced him to the evening manager, an ex-policeman with a streak of suspiciousness. He was not about to share information concerning his residents, especially not with someone who wore jeans and a tee shirt and needed a shave. He had little patience for Terry's pleas, and a hastily concocted version of the lost ring story served only to cement his distrust. Five minutes after being introduced, he told Terry to get lost. When Terry begged for help one last time, the manager came around the counter and pushed him toward the door. Terry shook free.

"Get your hands off me."

"You got ten seconds to get out of my sight."

"Fuck you."

"Five."

"Fuck your family too."

The man pushed, and Terry twisted around. He was about to push back, when a hand grabbed his arm.

"Get rid of this asshole," the manager told the doorman. "Before I take the pleasure of adjusting his attitude."

The doorman stepped between the two of them and eased Terry out. He was firm but not violent, removing him to a spot several yards beyond the entrance before releasing him.

"I should call the cops," fumed Terry. "The fuckin' asshole should be locked up."

"You go home now."

"All I'm trying to do is help my girlfriend." He kicked a tire. "That's a fuckin' crime? That gives some jerk the right to lay his hands on me?"

The doorman brushed the wrinkles out of his jacket. "You go home now. Get yourself straightened out."

"Fuck him. Fuck everyone."

He cursed his way down the block, past another apartment building, past the Dakota, pissing on the world and all its miserable inhabitants. First the cab boss, then Daggoo, now this asshole. They were shitheads, all of them. He could see herding them into a room and chaining them up. Making them beg a little. Extracting his revenge.

It was Frankie's fault really. She was the one who'd made him play the fool, who'd sent him out to be humiliated. The blame lay on her. She should be the one to pay.

9

Survival Value

Charles Baudelaire, French poet and essayist of the mid-nineteenth century, was a keen observer of the contemporary scene. He had strong opinions and was not timid in expressing them. Near the end of his life he made an entry in one of his journals. The section was titled "Of Airs in Women":

The charming airs, those in which beauty consists, are:

The blasé,
The bored,
The empty-headed,
The impudent,
The frigid,
The introspective,
The imperious,
The capricious,
The naughty,
The ailing,

The feline—a blend of childishness, nonchalance and malice.[7]

At the time of this entry Baudelaire was suffering an extreme medical condition. The syphilis he had contracted as a youth had progressed to his brain, where it was cutting great swaths of intemperance. His mental discipline and perspicacity were failing. His judgment was riddled with error. One, then, can hardly accept his proclamations during that period as anything more than idiosyncratic and subjective.

Fortunately, a recent article in the Journal of Personality and Social Psychology *offers a more scientific view.[8] The article describes two experiments on the sociobiology of female facial beauty. In the first, seventy-five U.S. undergraduate males were asked to judge fifty photographs of females based on their estimates of the physical attractiveness of each female. About half the photographs were taken from a women's college yearbook and half from the yearbook section of a Miss Universe international beauty pageant program. Concurrent with the collection of these attractiveness ratings, precise measurements of the size, shape and distance between various facial features were made by the research team using a micrometer accurate to 0.05 millimeters.*

In the second experiment, a different group of men were asked to evaluate sixteen of the aforementioned photographs in terms of personal characteristics of the women photographed. On a six-point scale they recorded their judgments in the following categories: (1) very bright—very dull; (2) very sociable—very unsociable; (3) very assertive—very submissive; (4) very modest—very vain; (5) very sterile—very fertile; (6) have very few medical problems—have many medical problems. Subjects in the study also indicated which one of the sixteen photographed women they would choose for each of a number of actions. Three concerned monetary investment: loaning five hundred dollars for car repairs; giving a birthday present worth one hundred dollars; cosigning a loan of ten thousand dollars to start a business. Three involved various levels of self-sacrifice: helping to load furniture for a move across town; donating a pint of blood; donating a kidney. Three involved physical risk: swimming to rescue the woman one-half mile from shore; saving her from the second story of a burning building; jumping on a live hand grenade. The final three scenarios related to courtship and reproduction: which woman would they select for a dinner date; for sexual intercourse; for raising children.

Results confirmed previous studies, as well as the author's initial hypotheses. Males were most attracted to females possessing large and widely spaced eyes, small noses and small chins. These facial features are the same possessed by neonates (infants in the first few months of life). They provoke in males protective, comforting and affectionate responses. Men were also attracted to women with the mature features of wide cheekbones and narrow cheeks, as well as large pupils, eyebrows set high on the forehead and big smiles. Attractive females were seen as being smarter, more sociable and more assertive, with less likelihood of medical problems and more likelihood of extramarital affairs. They were seen as poor subjects for monetary investment. The neonatal features *of wide smile and dilated pupils were the best predictors of fertility, perhaps because a large smile suggested friendliness and receptivity and the dilated pupils conveyed sexual arousal. The combination of mature and neonatal features was posited to act as a signal that the female was at an optimal age for mating.*

The author concludes that attractive females, who in other studies have been rated as higher in leadership and dominance characteristics, are more likely to be chosen for self-sacrificial and physically risky actions, as well as for a job, dating, sex and child rearing. Such results lead him to suggest that "the possession of attractive facial features may be of survival value for adults."[9]

After lunch Frankie went home and waited for Terry. He fanned through some magazines without paying attention. He watched TV. Every few minutes he got up and checked the clock.

An hour went by, then another. He paced the front room. The kitchen clock read half-past six. Ten minutes later it was twenty to seven. He waited another fifteen minutes, then put on a coat and left.

He took the subway to Virgo's, arriving about a quarter to eight. The bar, as usual, was smoky and loud, the men up front shouting lewd and encouraging suggestions to the dancer on the platform. The girl looked even younger than the one he had met, and she seemed to be doing what she could to accommodate the prurient mood. Before he himself became the target of someone's attention, Frankie went to the bar and caught the bartender's eye. The

...had silver hair and broken capillaries on his ...eeks. He worked his way over.

"Nice to see you back." He stopped himself. "What I mean is, I'm glad you're okay."

"You're Ted?"

He gave her a look. "Was when I came in."

"Just checking," Frankie said lightly, making it into a joke. "People change so fast these days."

"That's something an old man would say. Fact is, it's true."

"As true when you're young as when you're old."

"Is that right?" He chuckled. "Take a few days off and you come back telling an old man his business."

"You got any whiskey, Ted?"

"Is this a bar?" He poured a shot, then left to take an order. Frankie threw it down, and when Ted got back asked for another.

"I'm looking for Cox," he said.

"Should be around. You didn't see him on the way in?"

"Uh-uh."

Ted stood on his tiptoes and looked over the heads of the men at the bar. "There. Next to the door."

Frankie was too short to see. He tossed the drink down, then headed off to find Cox.

It wasn't hard. Just inside the door was a man whose chest and shoulders were a good foot broader than anyone else's in the room. He was wearing a bright tie and a tailored jacket that was tight all around. His hair was short, his thick moustache trim. His half-smile never changed.

"Frankie," he said on seeing her. "I was just missing you. It's good to have you back."

"You're Cox?"

He laughed. "How about I buy you a drink?"

He escorted her to the bar, where he ordered a shot for each of them.

"You get yourself some rest?"

Frankie shrugged. "I was starting to go stir crazy."

"Yeah," said Cox. "I've been that route." He played with his drink. "We're in kind of a fix here, Frankie girl. Rosalina didn't show." He motioned toward the platform. "Shawna's the only one we got. We could use some help."

Frankie nodded.

"I know it'd be appreciated."

"You're asking me?"

Cox looked around. "There someone I'm missing?"

He was incredulous. "Forget it. I came to talk, Cox. That's the only thing that got me back."

"What's with the Cox?" He cupped a hand on the back of her neck. "It's Jerry to you, Frankie. To all the ladies."

"Jerry. All right. Look, Jerry. Maybe we could go in back. What I have to say is sort of private."

"Sure thing." Leaving the whiskey untouched, he put an arm around Frankie's shoulder and led the way to the rear of the bar. With Cox as escort they cut effortlessly through the crowd, men who otherwise would have pawed Frankie mercilessly. For this alone he was grateful, and, despite Terry's warnings, he found himself warming to the man.

In the back room Frankie took one of the chairs.

The liquor was having its effect, making him feel less like a spring ready to snap. He took off his coat.

"I need your help, Jerry. It's about the other night."

Cox shut the door, then leaned against it.

"You remember when I fainted? There was a guy at the bar. He passed out just about the same time."

"You were drunk."

"Yeah, maybe. The guy was drunk too. I think he slipped me something."

Cox laughed. "That's from the movies."

"I want to find him, Jerry. I want to pay him back."

"Yeah? What are you going to pay him?"

"I don't know. First I have to find him."

Cox weighed this. "So where do I come in?"

"You're the man up front. You know who goes in and out."

"So?"

"So would you recognize this guy if he came back? Would you call me if he does?"

"Call you?"

"Yeah. I want to talk to the asshole."

Cox considered the proposition. There was an angle he wasn't getting, but maybe it didn't matter. So what that he hadn't a clue what Frankie was talking about, he could still parlay a deal.

"How about a little snort?" he said, stalling for time. He took his works from a pocket, cut out eight lines and quickly sucked up four. He held out the tiny glass pipe to Frankie, who stared at it.

"Go on," he said. "It's top grade."

"What is it?"

"Wha'dya think?" He rubbed his nose. "Pure and sweet. Go ahead."

He waved the pipe with an insistence that gave Frankie the feeling that something was at stake, and he accepted the offer, sniffing up the crystals like he had seen Cox do. They burned his nose, which proceeded to go numb. A minute later his whole body was tingling.

"Good stuff, huh?" Cox went behind the stacks of liquor and brought out a bottle of Johnnie Walker. He took a nip and handed it to Frankie.

"Compliments of the house."

It was surprising how the liquor tasted on top of the coke. Almost like he was swallowing water. He took a couple of mouthfuls and put the bottle down. He was beginning to get loose.

"What I was thinking," said Cox, his voice rapid and oddly persuasive, "was this. You need something and I need something. We're friends, right? We should be able to accommodate each other."

Frankie found himself liking Cox, even though he wasn't sure what he was talking about. He felt good, and nodded in agreement.

"I keep an eye out for this guy. Definitely. As soon as he comes in, you're the first to know."

"He took something of mine," Frankie confessed. "Or I took something of his. I don't know. Something happened. Whatever it is, it's not right. You know what I mean?"

"Sure I do. We find the guy, we work it out." He put his hands on Frankie's chair and looked down at her. "Now the other part, you got to help me."

"Sure, Jerry."

"You got to dance, Frankie." He checked his watch. "In five minutes you got to go on."

Frankie laughed at the joke, but when he looked up, Cox wasn't smiling.

"I told you before I didn't come here to dance."

"That was then. This is now. We got a deal, right?"

"You didn't tell me."

"Don't make it hard, Frankie girl."

"But I'm not a dancer." Even to himself the voice sounded thin.

"Who told you that? You're the best, little lady. The absolute best."

He lifted Frankie easily by the arms and stood her up. "You need help dressing?"

"I am dressed." He felt like giggling. "This is silly."

Cox unbuttoned his jacket. "My job's to look out for people. Your job's to dance. Now lift up your arms. Don't make me ask twice."

Frankie ignored the command, but his resistance when Cox pulled the sweater off and dropped it to the floor was slight. His defenses had been dulled by the alcohol, and the cocaine had done something else. He felt freer, less willful, as though he had been relieved of certain proscriptions. Still, though, he was a man. He was no naked dancer.

He staggered to one of the walls and leaned against it, folding his arms resolutely across his chest. "I am open to suggestion," he said drunkenly. "Not coercion."

"I suggest you take off the rest of your clothes and get into this." Cox held up a g-string he'd taken from a hanger.

"That's not what I had in mind."

Cox looked at his watch. "Three minutes."

Frankie shrunk against the wall, dull-wittedly but desperately trying to think. The drugs made it hard. Strangely, too, they made it seem less important.

Cox pried his arms apart, then tore off the blouse, popping several buttons in the process. He smiled when he saw the unfettered breasts.

"You make it easy," he said, keeping Frankie pinned against the wall with a shoulder. "Now the pants."

Frankie grabbed at them, but Cox easily shoved his hands aside. He quickly got them down to the ankles, then told him to sit. When he didn't obey, Cox forced him to the floor. He yanked off the boots and socks, tossing them across the room, then finished with the pants.

"Undies too, sweetheart."

By this point Frankie was offering little resistance. He was there with only a tiny part of his mind. The rest was numb.

Cox replaced the underpants with the g-string and told Frankie to stand up.

This time he obeyed. Cox checked his watch.

"Under three minutes," he said proudly, barely winded. "Not bad for a stiff."

"I'm cold," Frankie muttered.

"Have another drink." He handed her the bottle, then stepped back. "You look good, baby. Once you get on stage, you'll warm right up."

Just then the door opened, and Shawna, the other dancer, came in. "Forty bucks," she said, waving the money. "Sure as hell beats working at Burger King."

"Show time," Cox said brightly. He handed Shawna the bottle and told her to pick up the clothes. Then, placing an arm around Frankie's bare back, he led her onstage.

Frankie remembered the rest of the evening only in fragments. Fact merged with fantasy in one hallucinatory nightmare. The bar was a cage full of animals; the music, knives in the brain. He had to be helped up onstage. Someone put high-heeled shoes on his feet. When he tried to move, he fell, and the shoes were removed. The faces at the bar were suffused with blood, leering and screeching as though they had yet to be fed the meat of the meal. He turned his back, trying to hide. Cox yelled at him to move, squeezed his heel until the pain made him jump. His upper body started to sway, the effect of nausea and vertigo. He took a step to the side to steady himself. There were shouts of encouragement. He took another step, wanting to die.

In the mirror he glimpsed himself. He had not seen the woman like this before. She was something to look at, and he touched the glass, then himself. His face, his lips, his breasts. He took a step forward but was stopped by a cold force the length of his body. He frowned and tried again.

Terry had entered the bar a few minutes before, feeling tired and irritable. He had phoned Frankie to tell her he had changed his mind about coming home, but there had been no answer. Now he was ready to lay into her not only for the accumulated humiliations of his day but also for her unwilling-

ness to wait as she had promised. He scanned the
room, assuming she was talking somewhere with
Cox. He didn't bother to look onstage. When he finally did and saw her there, he was stunned. He saw
Cox caress her heel, saw her start to move. He was
puzzled, but when she started to sway in time to the
music and show her stuff, he found himself grinning. This was more like it. Life, it appeared, was
returning to normal.

Up onstage, Frankie was reeling. Unable to disappear into the mirror, he stumbled around until he
faced the bar. He saw a face he recognized. The man
was smiling, waving, blowing him a kiss.

"Terry," he whispered, touching his lips to be sure
he was speaking. The nightmare loosened its grip.
He took a step forward, then another. He was being
rescued, and in his dream there was a doorway, beyond which stretched a gilded staircase. But that
night at Virgo's there was only air. One more step
and he was off the platform, hanging for a split-
second in mid-air before plunging downward, taking bottles and glasses with him. He landed with a
sickening thud on the floor, where he lay in a heap.
By some miracle none of the cuts was deep. Later,
hands lifted him and covered him with a coat.
Someone called his name. The last thing he remembered were the words, "you'll be all right." Had he
the strength he would have laughed. Roared. As it
was, he lay back, closed his eyes and departed.

10

Terry made himself a cup of coffee and tried to think straight. His relief at having Frankie back to her old self was tempered by his anger that she had done it for Cox and not him. He kept seeing the man's hand on her ankle and his smile when she started to move. He couldn't get it out of his mind. For a week she'd been acting crazy, denying him the merest hint of intimacy. And here she was putting out for Cox, performing for a shit of a man, a cretin, a brute. The thought enraged him.

He downed his coffee and marched to the bedroom, throwing open the door. The room was bright with sunlight, and a panel lay across Frankie's sleeping face. There was a bruise on her cheek where she had struck the floor, and part of her lip was swollen. Running like a worm down her calf was a line of dried blood. Surveying the damage, Terry had a change of heart. Anger took a backseat to compassion, and he knelt by the bed and tenderly stroked her cheek. He covered her leg with the blanket, then stood by the window and waited for her to wake up.

An hour passed, and the sunlight left the room. Frankie stirred and pulled the covers tighter. She moaned and opened her eyes.

"God."

"Not here," said Terry. Frankie turned to the sound.

"You."

"You're alive, I take it."

"Don't say that. This isn't life. It can't be."

"It's life, Frankie. I'm sorry."

She groaned and sat up, tugging the sheet around herself. "How long have you been here?"

"The sun was on your face when I came in. You looked like an angel. Wounded, but angelic."

"I feel like shit."

Terry shrugged. He had ceased being surprised by Frankie's mouth. "At least you've reverted to your old self."

"Yeah? What's that?"

"The woman I love."

Frankie gave him a look. Terry was smiling.

"I'm sorry to disappoint you, but I'm not the woman you love. I'm the same as I was. Nothing's changed."

"You danced. I saw you. You're a woman, Frankie. Make life simple and say it."

"I'm a man."

"The fuck you are."

Frankie closed his eyes and slumped against the wall. Images from the previous night played across his mind, some more substantial than others, all of them dreadful. Cox's face loomed up, smug and invincible. He shuddered.

"You shouldn't have gone," Terry was saying. "I told you. You should have listened."

"You're right."

"How could you dance for that shithead?"

"He made me."

"Of course he made you. What did you expect?"

"He seemed so nice at first. Someone to trust. Then he changed."

"What is it with you? All of a sudden you're stupid? I warned you, didn't I? Didn't I tell you not to mess with him?"

"I had to talk to him. We agreed to that."

"Sure we did. And what did I tell you? Wait at home, I said. I'll go with you. Did you hear me say that? Did you even think of using your fuckin' brain?"

"It got dark. I got tired of waiting."

"You got tired." Terry started to pace. "You piss me off, Frankie. I have to watch you every second now? That's what I have to do?"

"You didn't come, so I left. That's all I'm saying."

"So now it's my fault, is that it?"

"I didn't say that."

"You want to know who's to blame? Go look in the mirror. You can turn it on and you can turn it off, Frankie girl. Whatever happened there you brought on yourself."

"That's not true."

"You got drunk with the man." Terry was hot. "Whose fault was that? You danced. You let him take your clothes off."

"He tore them off."

"You won't even let me touch you. Not a finger. Not even to help."

"He ripped off my shirt and threw me down. I felt like a piece of garbage. He thought it was funny."

"You humiliated yourself. You humiliated me."

Frankie stared at him.

"You put out for Cox. I'll tell you something. You can put out for me."

Frankie stood up, cinching the sheet around his chest and tucking it in. "You want to rip my clothes off? Is that it?" He planted his hands on his hips. "Go ahead."

Terry paused, but only a moment. With the same hand that moments before had caressed Frankie's cheek he tore the sheet away. Frankie flinched but held his ground.

"There. Satisfied?"

Terry slapped her.

"Good, Terry. Fabulous. Now you're really a man."

He slapped her again. Frankie raised a hand in defense, but Terry struck it down.

"You've flipped out good this time." His eyes darted over the naked body before him as he rubbed his hand. "What the hell am I going to do with you? You're making me crazy."

"Leave me alone."

"I wish I could leave you alone. But I can't trust you. You're out of control. You need help."

Frankie picked up the sheet and covered himself. He was shaking. Part of him wanted to hit Terry back and another part wanted to surrender. He told him to go away.

"I love you, babe. Believe me. I just want this to be over. I want it to stop."

Terry went to the bureau and pulled an envelope from one of the drawers. Inside was a bottle of pills, two of which he thrust at Frankie.

"They'll help calm you down. You'll sleep. It's the best thing."

Frankie took the pills. The promise of sleep, of flight from danger and insanity, was hard to resist. Terry brought a glass of water and helped Frankie back in bed. Gently he arranged the covers. He apologized for slapping her and got Frankie to acknowledge how tempers could run hot. Guys sometimes did things they weren't too proud of, but in the end everything usually turned out okay. He promised Frankie it wouldn't happen again.

"We've got better things to do than fight," he said. "You've got to rest. I've got to find that man. As long as I know you're home and safe. That's the most important thing. Safety. You've been hurt enough."

Frankie had to agree. He appreciated Terry's belated kindness. He knew about anger, and what Terry had said before was right. Sometimes a man just had to get it out of his system. Frankie was not exactly sure what he had done to become the target, but then again he wasn't sure about a lot of things. This wasn't his world, and he didn't know the rules. When he tried to understand, he got confused and angry. The pills, thankfully, helped. They took the edge off, dampening the pain in his leg, cooling his burning cheek. He began to drift, and life became less intolerable. It was a matter of letting go. That was the way to ride. Low in the saddle, no resistance. It was so much easier. From that vantage the country flattened out, and the choices dropped away. No questions, no problems, just glide on through.

An hour later, with Frankie safely tucked in and asleep, Terry left the apartment to take another crack at the boys at the Alvey. There was a new doorman but the same manager, who was as close-lipped and tight-assed as before. It wasn't worth it. This chase had him by the balls, and with Frankie finally cooling out at home, he was inclined to give it up. In the back of his mind was the persistent belief that if he waited long enough, she would drop the whole thing altogether.

For a few days it seemed that way. Frankie was content to stay at home and drift in the sea of Terry's pills. He took to taking them two and three times a day, which Terry did not discourage. He liked knowing that Frankie was taking care of herself, and he liked knowing where she was. He brought her videos and flowers. He cooked. In the hours after work he sometimes read to her, poetry and stories he thought she would like. He took pleasure in watching her fall asleep to the sound of his voice.

One day the pills ran out and Frankie's mood took a dive. He demanded to know what Terry had been doing to find the man. Terry told him about the Alvey and then, unable to contain himself, confessed that he hadn't been back to the hotel since early that week. Frankie erupted. His nerves were frayed enough as it was; he didn't need this on top of everything.

"You knew and you didn't tell me? What the hell have you been doing all this time?"

"Taking care of you, baby. You didn't notice?"

"I'm going there myself." He stormed into the closet and began pulling out clothes.

"You're in no shape to leave."

"I'm rotting here. I need a break."

"It's not safe." He grabbed the clothes from her hands to keep her from dressing. "I want you to stay here."

Frankie yanked them back. "What do you care?"

"I worry about you, that's what. There're a thousand Jerry Coxes out there. I don't want you to get hurt."

"That's funny coming from you."

"You watch your mouth."

Frankie almost laughed. "What you're saying is you've got my best interests at heart. You're looking out for me. I should appreciate the concern."

"I'm saying I'll take care of it."

"When?"

"Tonight. After work. Maybe I'll have better luck at night."

"I feel like screaming," said Frankie. "I want to break something."

"It's the pills. You're crashing."

"Get me more."

"I don't think so."

"Please." He was shaking.

"We'll see. Try a hot bath." Terry got ready to leave for work. "Be good, Frankie. Stay home. If things get bad, remember I'll be back. Just keep that thought pinned right up front. Your man Terry'll be back to take care of everything."

After work Terry killed a couple of hours at a movie. His plan was to give the evening manager plenty of time to go home, and it was close to 3 A.M. when he arrived at the Alvey. He was carrying a book package he'd made up at Suter's, and to his palpable relief there was no doorman to intercept him. The lobby doors were locked, but inside was a night clerk he'd not seen before. Terry held up the package, and after a brief inspection through the glass the man buzzed him in.

"I'm looking for the manager," said Terry.

"Mr. Hoke leaves at midnight. Mr. Thompson won't be here until seven. Perhaps I can be of assistance." The clerk had an olive complexion and spoke with an Indian accent.

"I have a package to deliver. A book."

"Is it not late in the day, or should I say early, for delivery of books?"

"I got held up."

The man gave him a look.

"No, no. Not like that. Delayed."

"I see. Of course." He held out his hand. "I will take the book."

"One thing," said Terry, keeping a grip on the package. "We got the address and the last name of the party, but we're not sure of the first. A Mr. Jones?"

"There is a Mr. Jones in residence." He checked the register. "Mr. Phillip Jones." He frowned. "But the man is in the hospital. I was here the night he was taken. Why would he order himself a book?"

"Maybe someone else did," Terry said quickly. "Do you know what hospital?"

"That I do not. But I will see that he gets it."

Again he reached for the package, and this time Terry handed it to him. Thanking the clerk for his kindness, he left and headed home. It had been easy, ridiculously so. That's how life could be, he realized, when people trusted one another. It's how it should be, would be, once Frankie snapped out of her little snit and came to her senses.

She was asleep when he got home, but from the looks of things it hadn't been easy. The covers were all twisted, her hair tangled, her body curled into a tight ball. There was an unhealthy smell too, and Terry cracked open a window for fresh air. He laid a blanket on her and quietly left the room.

Locating the man wasn't hard. Terry got a page full of hospitals from the phone book and went down the list. There was a Brenda Jones at Lenox Hill, a Horwick Jones at Columbia-Presbyterian, a Phillip Jones at NYU and another at Park Memorial. The one at NYU was a fifteen-year-old boy. The other, the one at Park Memorial, was their man.

11

"You do like I tell you," said Marcus. He had a beer in his hand, and Terry had another. "Come up the back stairs at eleven. That's when the nurses all go in their little room and report to each other. Then they hand out the jobs for the night. No one's out on the floor 'less there's a reason."

They were sitting on the fold-out couch in the front room of Marcus's apartment in Harlem. Frankie was in a wooden armchair, which, together with the couch, was aimed at the focal point of the room, a large wooden cabinet that housed a TV and stereo. Hidden in one of its compartments was a tape deck, and on top of the cabinet twenty or thirty cassettes were arranged neatly in a holder. In an alcove on the opposite side of the room was a small kitchen, beside which stood a tall metal garbage hamper identical to ones used in the hospital where Marcus worked. The room was immaculate. It was two in the afternoon the following day. Charles

Bronson week, and the TV was tuned to *Death Wish 3*.

"As soon as I knock on that door, you count to twenty. Then you come out. The room's halfway down the hall."

"What are you going to be doing?" Frankie asked.

"What I'm always doing." He had a slug of beer. "Will you look at that."

On the screen Bronson was blowing away enemies with a handgun that would have stopped an elephant.

"The man's got a weapon," Marcus said in admiration. "A definite weapon."

"And a vengeful heart," said Terry. "Not to mention good taste in women."

"He knows how to protect his own," said Marcus.

Frankie was having trouble paying attention. He had slept all night and most of the morning, but he was still tired. His skin crawled. His muscles twitched. The TV didn't help.

"You have a gun?" he asked Marcus.

"I got two," he said proudly. "A twenty-two pistol and an Overlander Rossi."

"What's that?"

"What's that?" A gleam came into his eye. "It's a twelve-gauge three-inch magnum sawed-off shotgun with two twenty-inch barrels."

"Is that good?"

"Depends on which side of the trigger you're on. Puts out a ten-foot spray of shot six feet in every direction. It'll take out five men just as quick as one. And it don't matter what side of the door they on. I been robbed twice. Won't be no third time."

Bronson's anger again erupted into violence, while his leading lady huddled in a corner, her own fury evincing in herself fear and helplessness. Marcus offered to show his gun, but Frankie demurred. Instead, he asked about Marcus's aunt.

"She's taking a nap." There was one other room in the apartment, which was usually Marcus's bedroom. He had given it to her. "She gets tired easy."

"How old is she?"

"She old. Does fine, 'cept she needs her rest. Ain't used to the big city. All the hurry up. Down there in Larkeeville they got a saying ain't nothing faster getting caught than a rabbit on the run. Aunt Orphah, she ain't never been caught. And she getting slower all the time."

"I'd like to meet her."

"She be going home in another few days. Done all the visiting she come to do. You got something in mind?"

Frankie started to reply, but Terry broke in.

"We're winging this one. One step at a time. We go, we meet this guy, we work it out. Then we get on with things." He shot Frankie a glance. "I've got faith in my lady. Call it a man's intuition. I just know it's going to shake out fine."

Marcus finished his beer and fired up a roach that was sitting in an ashtray. When he'd smoked it down and a commercial came on, he got up and ran it under cold water, then popped it in his mouth. He cleaned the ashtray and sat back down.

"This thing," he said to Frankie, "it still eating at you?"

Frankie glanced at Terry, nodded.

"You fightin' it?"

"Some of the time. Mostly I feel lost."

"It's not always good to fight," said Terry. "I'm trying to teach her."

"The man's right," said Marcus. "Only a fool fights hisself."

"I'm not a fool."

"But it's a fact. It takes two to tangle. One goes home, you might as well pack up too."

On screen Bronson had a half-naked woman draped like a rag over one arm, a shotgun in the other. Frankie felt cornered, and without thinking, he stood up and punched off the tube.

"Go ahead and get your guns," he told Marcus. "Pass 'em around. Maybe then the two of you'll get the picture. One cock to another."

Terry laughed, but Marcus, who took any threat, no matter how preposterous, seriously, became instantly alert. He glued his eyes on Frankie, willing her to look back.

"You sit down now," he ordered. "No one's gonna hurt no one around here."

Frankie set his fists on his hips. "I want an apology."

"Do like the man says," said Terry.

"You too."

"You're crazy, babe." Terry cut her a look, but the face he got back made him hold up his arms in surrender. "Hey, you want it, you got it. Everyone's friends here. No need to make a scene."

Frankie turned to Marcus. "Now you."

Marcus hadn't moved, but now he spread his huge hands on the edge of the sofa and pushed himself up.

He was a large man, and up close he seemed to fill the room. Frankie was dwarfed, but he held his ground.

Marcus said nothing. He was disturbed by Frankie's outburst but didn't feel responsible. That and his pride kept him from apologizing. On the other hand, he had a strong sense of justice and knew what it was like to be humiliated.

"Look here," he said, pulling open his shirt and taking out a tiny leather pouch attached to his neck by a string. "You see this?"

"I see it," said Frankie. "So what?"

"It's my gris-gris. I got everything in it I need to keep safe." With one of his big fingers he touched his forehead. "To keep the mind in control, you understand what I'm saying? Otherwise you slip down where they want you to be, running around crazy with all the others who just as soon be that way. You gotta keep track of things. Even when you asleep, you gotta keep one eye open."

"What's in the bag?" asked Frankie.

"Once I used to act the fool. I didn't think it then, but it didn't make it any less a fact. After a while I got myself in a jam. It was just a matter of time. I ain't saying who or what, but every time I went and did something it was like someone else doing it. Ended up in jail one time, didn't even know how I got there. Got let out and was back a week later. When I got out the second time Moms sent me down to Larkeeville. That's where her folks was. I guess she figured I needed a shake-up." His expression turned inward, and his voice took on a new tone and cadence.

"It's pure country down there. After the first week I was more crazy than I'd been before. You know what it's like when you're waiting for something to happen, and the harder you wait the longer it takes? I was waiting to leave, and the more I wanted to go the less I went. So finally Aunt Carol, that's who I was staying with, took me to visit Aunt Orphah. She lived in town in a house with my cousin. When we got there, she was just finishing up with one of her customers. I got introduced, and Aunt Orphah made me stand there while she looked me over. She did it the way a person might do to something he was buying, ending up right in my eyes like a fork stuck in each one. Then she invited us in for some biscuits and asked about Moms and the rest of the family up north. At the end she asked about me and I said a few things, but not much. She looked at me again like she had before, then got up and left the room. When she came back, she was carrying this bag in her hand.

" 'You got an evil spirit pressing down on your brain pan,' she told me. 'It making you act crazy. That's why you wanta go off every time. Something doing you harm, and you have to drive it off. Otherwise it set in deeper and deeper till it drag you past helping.'

"Then she handed me the bag and told me what I had to do to protect myself. And I did as she told, and by the end of that month I was a different man. Whatever it was that possessed me got pushed out, so that when I did things I could tell what it was I was doing. The pressure dropped off, and all of sudden I started seeing what it was I was supposed to be seeing. And that's why I keep it here . . ." He patted his chest and gave Frankie a meaningful look. "Ain't had no trouble since."

"Why were you in jail?" asked Terry.

"For running with the wrong crowd. There's plenty of people willing to oblige if you want to play the fool."

"What's in your bag?" Frankie asked again. He was placated by Marcus's story, which he accepted as a form of apology. "What's your gris-gris?"

He reached out to touch the pouch, causing Marcus to stow it quickly back inside his shirt.

"Different things," he said. "What exactly is a private matter. You let it out, it loses its power. It might even get used against you."

"You think your aunt can help me make one?"

"She can tell if you need it. If you don't mind her looking through you first. She got the keenest sight of anyone I know."

"It'll take more than that," said Terry. He was growing impatient. "Besides, after tonight we won't need sight. We won't need sound, we won't need words, we won't need nothing but touch and feel. Skin to skin. Ain't I right, babe?"

Frankie felt a chill. "I wish I knew what to do. What to expect."

"You do what you have to," said Terry. "Whatever that is. Get it done. I don't plan on going back."

"You don't have to go at all. Watch TV. Stay home. Do whatever you want."

"Listen to that," said Terry, cracking a smile. "Damned if I don't love you." He pushed up his sleeve. "I got a quarter to three, Marcus. You?"

"It's two forty-eight."

He adjusted his watch. "All right then. We got our plan, and we're synchronized." He gave Marcus a big grin. "I'd say the commandos are ready for action."

At twenty to eleven Frankie and Terry walked through the sliding glass doors that led to Park Memorial's emergency room. Other than the rear entrance next to the loading docks it was the only way into the hospital at that time of night. The waiting room was brimming with its usual assemblage of humanity and the varying degrees of its suffering. Boredom mingled with impatience: anguish, with deep sleep. When the triage nurse's attention was diverted by a man who for no apparent reason began cursing at the top of his lungs, Terry grabbed Frankie's arm and pulled her into an adjoining corridor. They found the back stairwell without being seen and climbed to the eighth floor. At the landing they stopped to get their breath.

"I wish I had a drink," said Frankie.

"I got a jay. You want a smoke?"

Before he could answer, there was a knock at the door. Terry counted to twenty, then peeked outside. Marcus was where he said he'd be, mopping the floor. About ten feet on either side of him were knee-high yellow and black "Wet Floor" barriers. Terry caught his eye, and after looking up and down the hall, Marcus nodded back. Terry pulled Frankie out, and the two of them hurried to Room 816. Frankie made it inside, but just as Terry was about to follow, a nurse came around the corner carrying a medication tray. Terry had the presence of mind to move away from the door, so that by the time she noticed him, he was standing a few feet down the hall. He girded himself as she approached.

"May I help you?"

He shook his head dumbly. "I'm fine."

"If you're here to see someone, you'll have to come back in the morning. Visiting hours were over two hours ago." She was in her forties, hair cut short, eyes alert and suspicious.

"I'm not here to visit."

"Hey, Shirley," said Marcus, sidling over with his mop. "What's happening?"

She glanced at him. "What are you doing up here this time of night?"

"Same as always. Mopping and popping. Cleaning and dreaming."

"You best save your dreaming for home, Marcus Parks."

"Shirley," he said, leaning closer and gesturing with his head. "The brother here's a friend of mine."

She looked from him to Terry and frowned. "What you two be up to?"

"We got a little private business. No harm to no one. Be done before you finish handing out the pills."

"Private business best be done privately," she said.

"Sure you're right," replied Marcus, slapping the mop on the floor while making no pretense at cleaning. Shirley eyed Terry.

"You know Marcus here?"

He nodded. "Like he said. We're friends."

"Friends or not, this here's a hospital."

"I'm sorry I broke the rules," he said contritely.

"You get everyone in trouble you play games like this." The comment was aimed at Marcus, and it was accompanied by a look of chastisement. Then she glanced down the hall.

"You two do what you mean to," she said, moving off with her tray, "but you best do it quick. One of the other nurses sees you, she won't be so understanding."

She disappeared into one of the rooms, and Terry breathed a sigh of relief.

"Thanks," he told Marcus.

"You better move. Shirley see you going into that room, she call the guard for sure."

Terry crossed to 816 and slid noiselessly inside. The room was much dimmer than the hall, and it took him a minute to adjust. The only light was from a stretch lamp attached to the head of the bed. It was pointed against the wall, presumably to keep from blinding the man whose head was on a pillow beneath it. He appeared to be asleep.

Frankie was on the other side of the bed, hands clenched on the partially raised side railing, knuckles white.

"How's it going?" asked Terry.

"He doesn't answer."

Terry stepped up and pinched the man's leg. There was no response. "He's out, Frankie. Either asleep or comatose."

Frankie jostled the man's shoulder. "Talk to me."

"He doesn't hear."

"He hears all right. Don't you?" Frankie's voice was strained, and he pushed harder.

"That's not going to help."

All of a sudden Frankie leaned over the railing and started shaking the man. Terry rushed over.

"Stop. You'll hurt him."

"I have to wake him up." The bedsprings squealed. "I need answers." He tried to pull the man up from the bed, but he was in restraint. He felt like screaming. "Don't pretend you're not a part of this. Say something. Anything. Help me."

"He's out of it, Frankie. He doesn't even know you're here."

"He knows." He grabbed the man's mouth. "Say it. Say who you are."

Terry peeled Frankie's fingers off his face. "You've got to calm down."

"I can't."

"It doesn't help what you're doing."

Frankie made fists of his hands, knowing Terry was right. Reluctantly, he left the bedside and stood in a corner, where he did what he could to control himself. He tried to put anger and desperation aside. He tried to cut loose the dread. A drink would have helped. Or a pill. He closed his eyes, pretending.

Five minutes later he came back to the bed and tried again. The man had yet to move. Even his eyes were still.

Cautiously, Frankie touched his forehead, his nose and lips. He felt the faint whisper of the man's breath and tried to match its rhythm with his own. He strained for contact. With all his will he tried to get inside.

Minutes passed. Nothing happened. Frankie grew calmer, but there was no connection with the man. No mingling of spirits, no sharing of minds. He kept trying, but it was no use. At length he stepped back from the bed.

"Well?" asked Terry.

Frankie shook his head.

"Talk to me."

"Nothing."

"What does that mean?"

"Nothing happened."

"Nothing?"

"No."

"We're done then? We can leave?"

"Leave?" He frowned. "Go ahead."

"Together," said Terry. "We walk out together."

Frankie turned back to the man. He seemed to be at peace, but Frankie doubted he was. He himself was still at war. "I'm not done."

"Don't say that. Don't even pretend."

"I'm sorry. I don't know what else to say."

"You want words? I'll give you words. You say 'It's over, Terry. I'm through with this bullshit. I'm coming home. Now. And not just that, but I'm gonna act right.' That's what you say."

"I wish I could. Honestly I do."

"You don't have to wish, Frankie. You don't have to think. All you got to do is what I say. Here . . ." He wrapped a hand around Frankie's jaw and moved it up and down. "You don't even have to move your mouth. Just make the sounds."

Frankie pushed him off. "Stop it."

"No, babe. You got it wrong. You're the one who's

got to stop." He started angrily for the door, then stopped. A moment later he gave a little chuckle, then turned and sauntered back to the man's bedside.

"What if Mr. Jones here happened to cash it in. That'd be the end, wouldn't it? No more dicking poor Terry around."

"He's not going to die," said Frankie. Suddenly, his eyes grew wide. "You wouldn't."

"Who's to say? I never got far enough in school to take the oath. Besides, the man's walking a fine line. He's half dead already."

"He's all I have. Why would you do that?"

"Because I love you, babe. Why else?"

"Don't. Please don't."

"Come home. Stop dicking me around."

Frankie gave a shudder and gripped the rail. "If I do, you'll leave him alone?"

"He's already out of my mind."

"Promise me."

"What do I care for an old man?" He dismissed him with a flip of the wrist. "Sure I promise. It's you I want."

Frankie sighed. "All right. I'll come."

12

A day later, after Terry left for work, Frankie went to see Aunt Orphah. The woman had woken from her nap a half-hour earlier and was sitting in the straight-backed wooden arm-chair in the living room. It was Marcus's day off, and after introducing the two of them, he put Frankie on the end of the couch nearest Orphah. He took the other.

"Thank you for seeing me," Frankie told Orphah. "I know it's short notice."

Orphah sat quietly with her hands in her lap, of-fering no reply. Frankie felt suddenly very foolish.

"There's a problem." He fidgeted, while Orphah took the opportunity to adjust her dentures, wiping her mouth afterward with a handkerchief. Frankie glanced at Marcus, then back at the woman.

"I need help."

Orphah inclined her head slightly and extended her hands, turning them palms up, as though preparing to receive a bowl of soup. "Give me your hands, chile."

Frankie obeyed.

"You ain't no cotton picker," Orphah muttered after what seemed a long time. Her own hands were rough-skinned, the fingers bony and arthritic.

"Cold hands," she went on. "Blood shivers."

Frankie quickly drew them back and blew into his palms. Then he rubbed them together before returning them to Orphah. The old lady smiled.

"Some folks say cold hands make a warm heart. You're hot inside, chile. Burnin' up." She cocked her head to the side.

"Son, fetch the lady a cup of tea."

Marcus dutifully got off the couch and went to the kitchen to put up some water to boil. Frankie didn't understand why he needed something warm if he was already too hot.

"You gots to feed a fire," said Orphah. "Else how you 'spect anything to burn? A person cain't see a fire, how's she to put it out?"

Aged and dark as a raisin, the woman projected an authority that brooked no contradiction. Her face was dominated by incredibly thick glasses, distorting her eyes to such a degree that they were barely visible. Her head was wrapped in a green scarf that matched a loose-fitting polyester suit. On one finger she wore a simple gold ring, and around her neck hung a little pouch of leather.

The water boiled, and Marcus made a cup of tea for Frankie. For Orphah he poured out a can of Coke. He put the glass in her hand and handed the cup to Frankie, then returned to his seat on the couch.

"You drink that up now," Orphah told Frankie, who sipped it until it cooled off, then gulped it down as fast as he could.

"I'm done," he said, laying the cup on the floor. Marcus immediately picked it up and brought it to the kitchen.

"You're like Marcus here 'fore he got fixed up." Orphah shook her head in gentle remonstrance. "Believin' the faster you do a thing the quicker it's done."

"City ain't country, Aunt Orphah," said Marcus. "You don't act quick sometimes, someone get over on you."

"What you rather have, them gettin' over on you or inside yo' head?"

Marcus knew enough not to reply. Frankie didn't.

"Neither," he said.

"Course neither," Orphah replied, sipping her Coke. Between sips she licked her lips. "An okra don't show its seeds through its skin. A person's nature takes time to rise."

She motioned to Frankie with a hand. "Come and sit beside me, chile. Tell me what's troublin' yo' mind."

Frankie did as she asked, kneeling beside the chair. He glanced at Marcus, who nodded his encouragement. Gathering his courage, he told his story.

By the time he was done, Orphah seemed to have fallen asleep. Her chin was on her chest, and her glasses had slipped an inch or two down her nose.

Frankie still had trouble seeing her eyes behind the thick lenses, but he assumed they were closed. He was surprised, then, when she moved, quite rapidly it seemed, and snatched one of his hands in hers.

She held it for a time, pressing it firmly between her palms before letting it go. Then she sat up in the chair.

"There's a power at work here. A trick." She seemed to take fresh stock of Frankie. "Whether it be evil or not I cain't fo' sure say."

"It's evil," Frankie assured her.

"One thing fo' definite sure. You got a highly nervous condition. This trick it's driving your nature from where it should be. Driving it right into the top of your head. You got a heightened pressure on your brain pan. Sooner or later, the trick's gonna kill it. Either that, or make you to be hysterical."

"I'm possessed," said Frankie. "Or dispossessed. Can a person be both?"

"Someone laid down a powerful spell," Orphah replied, nodding to herself. "Powerful spell indeed. You say you seen this man? This one who grabbed up your spirit?"

"The night before last. I didn't recognize him, but the truth is I don't recognize anybody. I don't remember anything from before."

"And the man? He seen it was you?"

"He was asleep. Terry thinks maybe it's a coma. What happens if he doesn't come out of it? What happens if he dies?"

"Too much pressure on the brain pan," muttered Orphah, after which she lapsed into a lengthy silence. Marcus sat with his hands on his knees, seemingly content to wait forever, but as the minutes wore on, Frankie grew impatient. The tea had filled his bladder, and his back hurt. Fear of the man's death crowded his thinking, filling him with dreadful visions of being stranded without solace or hope. He felt an urgency to be at the hospital, to shore up the man's life, to keep him from slipping away.

Just as he was ready to get up, Orphah showed signs of life. She cleared her throat and adjusted her glasses. Then she finished what remained of her Coke.

"There's only one way to fight off a trick," she said. "And that's with a stronger one. I'm gonna tell you what you need do.

"First off, you get yourself a little piece of red flannel. And a spool of thread. Black thread. Then you go get a lock of the man's hair. You can take it from here," she rubbed a wisp of her own that peeked out from the scarf, "but it be best if you get it down by his privates. You plait that hair, jus' make a little plait of it and then you wet it down. You understan'?"

"She means urinate on it," said Marcus.

"Jus' enough to make it damp. After that, you go cut the man's fingernails. His toenails too, if he let you. You let them fall on a piece of paper you've writ your name down on nine times. Then you fold up that paper tight."

"Which name?" Frankie asked. "My name or his?"

Orphah considered this. "Perhaps you best mark an X. Just like them that don't know how to write. That way there won't be no mistake. You put that paper in the flannel alongside his hair, and then you gather up some dust from your house. Lay it on top, then fold everything up and tie it with the thread. Tie it tight and make a loop to fit round your neck. Now you got your gris-gris.''

"That's it?" Frankie asked. Except for the part about the nails it didn't seem so terribly hard.

"It is 'less you want to hear the rest." Orphah turned to Marcus. "Fetch me some water, son."

When she had the glass and had taken a sip, she went on. "Once you got your gris-gris, then you got to set it to work. 'Cuz it's not what it is but what you git out of it. You understan'? It's what you git out of knowing it, which is something not to be given. Lissen here. You go to this man who's holdin' you, go to him in his sleep. Nine nights you go, an' you stay with him."

"All night? I have to stay all night?"

"Don't matter how long, long as you thinkin' on him while you there. You bend your mind to him, press it so he knows. Nine nights. An' on the morning after the last night, you take your charm an' you bury it."

"Where am I supposed to do that?"

"Dig a little hole right outside your door. A small one's all you need. Jus' enough to cover it."

Frankie looked puzzled.

"She lives in an apartment building, Auntie," said Marcus. "Ain't no dirt like they got down South."

"You got to bury it, son. Cain't hold the spell 'less it stay covered."

"How about a park?" asked Frankie. "Or a lot? Will any ground do?"

"Long as it stays under. You don't want that power to git disturbed."

He nodded slowly. "I think I understand. Kind of like a grave."

"Rest in peace," Orphah muttered quickly, touching her bosom where her own gris-gris hung.

"And after that?"

"What after? You do like I say an' the troubling spirit don't never bother you again. You git your nature back right where it belong."

Frankie looked to Marcus, who was nodding.

"A person don't live in a house what's not his own," said Orphah. "He carries it with him. You git the pressure off and your nature back. Your own free nature."

She let out a sigh and made to get out of the chair. Marcus was instantly at her side.

"I still got a touch of fatigue," she said. "Perhaps I best lie down another few minutes."

Marcus helped her up, and Frankie handed her her cane. On an impulse he gave her a hug, a display of gratitude Orphah took in stride. When she had left the room, Frankie headed straight for the bathroom. The visceral relief he experienced there seemed an extension of the hope engendered by his meeting with Orphah. It was as though a great impediment had been removed. The woman had given him something to do, something real. He was determined to succeed.

He arrived at the hospital at eight-twenty, ten minutes before visiting hours were over. He took the elevator to the eighth floor, where a handful of visi-

tors were waiting to go down. One of the nurses at
the station pointed to the clock as he passed.

"You're a little late."

"I'll only be a few minutes."

Without waiting for a reply, he hurried down the
corridor to Room 816. He paused at the door, feeling in a pocket for the scissors and nail clipper. In
the other he fingered the piece of flannel he'd cut
from a skirt that was hanging in the bedroom closet.
He tried to compose himself. Drawing a breath, he
opened the door.

He was ready to make some excuse if a visitor
were there, but the room was empty save for the
man. The curtains around his bed were drawn back
and the lamp was off. By the faint city light that
entered the small window in the far wall, he appeared, as before, to be asleep. His face looked paler
than it had, his eyes just a bit more sunken. Before
he lost his nerve, Frankie took out the scissors and
moved to the head of the bed. With a trembling hand
he reached over the rail and lifted a tuft of hair near
the man's temple. It felt greasy and in need of a
shampoo. Frankie tried not to tug on it for fear of
harming the man. Holding his breath, he snipped
the hair off.

The sound of the scissors seemed deafening, but
the man did not stir. In repose he seemed already to
have been laid to rest. Emboldened, Frankie took
another snip. And a third. He was building up courage for the task that followed.

He placed the hair on the piece of flannel, which
he had laid on the bed, then called the man's name.
He jiggled his shoulder. When there was no re-

sponse, he carefully took the edge of the bedcovers in his hands and peeled it down. The man was still in restraint. A heavy canvas jacket was wrapped around his torso and tied to either side of the bed. Fortunately, it sat high enough on his chest that it did not interfere with the task at hand. Frankie had worried that he would have to remove the man's pants, but the hospital-issue pajamas made it unnecessary. There was a big slit in the fabric right over his crotch, and even in the dimness of the room Frankie could make out the dark mat of his pubic hair.

He was not thrilled at the prospect of handling the man's penis, but even less did he want by accident to nick it. Gingerly, he pulled the organ out. There was a condom around it, connected by a tube to a bag on the side of the bed. The penis itself was as limp as grass.

Laying it to the side, he took some of the curly pubic hair above it between thumb and finger. It was coarser than the hair on his head and less greasy. He snipped a piece off and added it to the other hair. The man made no protest, and Frankie took another snip before turning his attention to the feet.

They were clean and well cared for, though providentially, the nails were in need of a trim. Frankie debated briefly whether to take a piece of each one and decided that a few would do. He took out the clipper and the piece of paper with the nine Xs, then cut a slender crescent from the big and little toenail of each foot, letting them fall on the paper. He did the same with the man's fingernails then folded the paper tightly, placing it on the flannel beside the piles of hair. Then he folded the flannel and put it in his pocket. And sighed. It was done.

The man moved.

He made a sound in his throat and turned toward the window. His lips convulsed, and one of his hands spasmed into a claw. Frankie froze, petrified. An instant later it was over. The man's hand collapsed to the bed, his guttural groan ended, his face returned to its previous emptiness. Repose, or something like it, settled over his body. It was as though someone had turned a switch.

Frankie let out his breath and backed away. He was about to leave, when a harrowing thought occurred to him. He inched back to the bedside and placed a hand in front of the man's mouth and nose, holding it there until he felt breath. With a sigh of relief he turned and left.

On the way home a thought kept nagging at him. He had assumed that once he got his rightful body back, everything would be as it was. But after tonight he had doubts. What if he recovered the body in its present state? The man was sick and quite possibly brain-damaged. What if the spell worked and Frankie were consigned for the rest of his life to this creature that needed to be kept forever in restraint? What then? Luck might well transform him into little more than an animal. Which captivity would be worse?

When he got home, he went to the kitchen and laid out his store. Reasoning from what Orphah had said, that there was something of power in both head and pubic hair, he decided to use them together. He twisted the strands around one another, weaving as best he could a little plait, which he tied at either end with the thread. Then he took it into the bathroom and wet it down as he'd been told. He brought it back to the table and placed it beside the scrap of paper with the nails, then reached down under the stove and got a big ball of dust. When everything was together, he made a pouch of the flannel, the neck of which he tied securely with thread. Finally, he added a loop of thread large enough to fit over his head.

He lifted the pouch. It was nearly weightless. He wondered briefly if there were some prayer or incantation he was supposed to use. Orphah had mentioned nothing, and he couldn't think of anything himself. So he put it on.

Nothing happened, and it occurred to him that maybe the pouch was supposed to be in contact with his skin. He unbuttoned the top buttons of his blouse and slipped it beneath the neckline. The flannel was soft, the moisture of the wetted hair not having made its way through the fabric. He tucked the sack between his breasts.

He waited, but still nothing happened. There was no great movement in his mind, no thundering change of perspective. In their absence he worried that he had done something wrong. He went over the contents once again, then tried the pouch in various positions. He forced the earlier doubts from his mind. Like a sick patient he expected a fast cure. He was ready to be done.

After a while he gave up and went to bed. He was

worried that Terry would notice the pouch when he got home, and he didn't want to be awake. He lay on his back, playing with the sack and trying to recall Orphah's words. In person, her advice had seemed so specific, but in retrospect it was amorphous and vague. He had to guess, improvise, and he didn't trust himself. He wanted someone to hold his hand.

And maybe that was the point, he had to stretch beyond himself. To get he had to give. To gain power he had to exert power. Or else it was just the opposite, which was the same. Like a magnet that attracts and repels. The image was so clear, the way things are on the verge of sleep. A magnet. His freedom.

13

 It took Terry exactly a day to find out what Frankie was up to.

"So it's voodoo now? Mumbo-jumbo? Halloween? What the fuck, Frankie. I thought this was over."

"It's your own friend," said Frankie. "You don't trust your own friend?"

"Marcus does what he wants. This stuff runs in his blood. What you are is a spoiled white girl from New England. Trust me. Sorcery isn't your thing. The only trick you need to learn is the one that makes you act right."

"That's what she promised. Nine nights, she said, and you'll have your nature back. For you that means the girl. And I'll tell you something. I wish her the best of luck."

"There you go again. This ain't no crap shoot, Frankie. It's all you. You say it's over, it's over. Luck or no luck."

"Nine more days I'm asking. Then it's finished. Done with. After that you can do what you want."

They were in the kitchen, Frankie in a bathrobe,

Terry bare-chested. He had expected things to chill out after their scene in the hospital, had taken Frankie at her word and been ready to open his heart. And now this. The woman had no sense, no decency, no love. She lived to jerk him around. He felt this as a physical thing, a rebuke of his spirit, his manhood. He slapped the table, cursing her.

"I've waited long enough, witch. Long enough for any man." He swept a dish to the floor, then grabbed a fork.

Frankie stood his ground, but the abuse was hard to take. He felt trapped, on the one hand by the man's anger, on the other by the feeling that he had caused it. He didn't want things to escalate and asked Terry to stop. Swallowing his pride, he apologized.

"Here." He took off the pouch and held it out. "If it bothers you so much."

"You're what bothers me. Not some pissed-on sac." He brandished the fork like a dagger, harboring thoughts of embedding it somewhere.

"You're scaring me."

"Good. Maybe that'll drive some sense into your head."

Frankie hugged his bathrobe tighter.

"God, you make me crazy. Fucked up and crazy."

"I'm sorry. I wish I could be different."

"Be different then. Stop fucking with me."

"I'm trying. Believe me. I'm desperate too."

"This desperate?" Terry raised the fork above his head, the expression on his face twisted and chilling.

"Don't," whispered Frankie.

He stared at her blindly, then slowly turned his

gaze to his outstretched hand. A frown crossed his face, as though he couldn't quite place where the fork had come from. A moment later he let it slip from his grasp, and it clattered to the table. The sound seemed to fracture him.

"Don't leave me," he said. "Please. Don't go."

Frankie was nonplussed.

"You get me all worked up, then all of a sudden something snaps. I do things I don't want to. It's not me. It's someone else. I'd never hurt you, Frankie. You know that. Never."

Frankie nodded uncertainly. "I'm sorry."

"Say you'll stay. Please. Say you will."

"Where else would I go?"

"This thing is so hard. So damned hard." He was on the verge of tears. "I see you, I hear your voice, and I can't believe it's not you. But then how you act, what you say, it doesn't make sense. If you wanted to leave, you'd leave, wouldn't you? You wouldn't stay just to jerk me around. We've had our problems, but I've never done anything to deserve that. You wouldn't hurt me on purpose. I know you that much. You wouldn't."

"Nine nights," said Frankie. "That's all I ask."

"Nine? Then it's done? You promise? It's over?"

"Yes."

Terry heaved a sigh. "Maybe some things have to run their course. That's what they taught us in school. Like a skin rash. Or the flu. It takes a certain time for them to pass."

"I don't think I've got the flu."

"Or bad luck. Maybe that's what this is. A run of bad luck."

"Very bad."

"I seem to be a magnet for that." He told her to put the pouch back on. "You do what the lady told you. If nine nights is what it takes, take nine. Love is patience. I'll wait."

The next evening Frankie got to the hospital early. Again he was the only visitor in the room. The man was as he had come to expect, motionless, wan, oblivious. Frankie sat in a chair and watched him. He tried to concentrate, to focus his mind upon something the nature of which was vague at best. It was grueling work, and after what seemed hours he had to stop. The man had given no evidence of any change, nor had Frankie felt anything different from what he had started with. When he checked the time, he saw that he had been there all of twenty minutes. He gave it another five then left, feeling inept and frustrated.

When he got home, Terry was cooking dinner. He had gotten Sal to cover for him and left work early, picking up fresh fish and vegetables at Ling Fat's near Spring. He gave Frankie a warm smile and told her to wash up if she needed to. The food was just about ready.

At dinner he asked about her day. Nothing much to it, replied Frankie. TV in the afternoon, then the hospital.

"And?"

"Nothing. Same as before."

"What did you do?"

"I sat with him and tried to think. Don't ask me

about what. I alternated between feeling silly and feeling ridiculous.''

"It's only the first day.''

"I didn't even last an hour.''

"You're breaking new ground, Frankie. Give it time.''

He sighed. "What did you do today?''

"I worked. Sold some books. Thought of you.''

"You like books.''

"I guess. It's a job.''

"How long have you been there?''

"I don't know. Two, three years.''

"And us . . .'' Frankie had trouble with the word. "How long have we been together?''

Terry smiled. "Going on two, babe.''

"What about before?''

"Before, the world was dark. The garden was bare. Empty and bare.''

"You were in medical school.''

"Who told you that?''

"You did.''

Terry hesitated, took a bite of fish.

"You were going to be a doctor?''

"That was the thought. It didn't work out.''

"What happened?''

"It was one of those things. Now I sell books. It's easier on the nerves.''

Frankie was silent a moment. "I wonder what I did.''

"You danced, babe. Like a dream.''

"I don't mean that. Before.'' He sighed and fingered his pouch. "I wonder if I'll ever find out.''

Terry wanted to touch her. He hated to see her so forlorn.

"I've got an idea. How about I call in sick and go with you tomorrow. For support."

"I don't think so."

"C'mon. You could use a shoulder. Let me help."

"What help? I don't even know what to do myself."

"It never hurt to have a friend."

"I wouldn't know." He stopped himself. "I'm sorry. You're being kind."

"I am kind. C'mon, babe. Say yes."

"Supposing I do? What happens if I change my mind? You going to blow a fuse?"

Terry held up a hand. "One word and I'm gone. I swear."

He seemed so earnest and eager to please, so different from before that Frankie chose to bury his doubts. He made Terry promise once more. Then he agreed to take him along.

The man in the hospital now had a slender feeding tube taped to his nose. He seemed with each visit to be drawing further away from the land of the living, and if it had been hard reaching him the first night, by the third the task seemed all but impossible. Frankie tried everything. He stood beside his bed, whispered to him, held his hand, touched his brow. At times he got angry and wanted to harm the man, but mostly he felt depressed. Terry initially was a boost, encouraging him and shoring up his confidence, but by their second night together Frankie had grown weary of his company. He was always hovering nearby, at his elbow, by his side, close behind in the shadows. He didn't speak, but Frankie could feel the urgency of his presence. Soon he became more concerned with pleasing Terry than in reaching the man, and once he realized this, he knew their arrangement had to stop. He had to do this thing alone. In his heart he had known it from the beginning.

Terry took the news well. True to his word, he agreed not to come again. To his way of thinking they were already a third of the way home. There were only six nights left.

On day four Frankie tried a different approach. He arrived early, but at the end of visiting hours hid in the small bathroom attached to the room. He had decided to try a longer stint, and midnight was an hour that held a certain sway in his mind. The evening before, Terry had showed him the chart at the foot of the bed where the nurses recorded the man's vital signs. They checked him at set times, twice a shift. One was due a little after nine, the next not until one. Frankie waited.

The nurse came on time, checked the man's pulse, his blood pressure and urine output. She lifted his lids and shone a light in his eyes, then made sure the feeding tube was secure. Tonight, in addition to the tube down his nose the man had an IV in his arm. She checked this as well, then logged everything in the chart before leaving. Frankie gave himself five minutes. Then he came out.

The man was clearly worse than before. His cheeks were more hollow, his skin more sallow, the bones in his hands and arms more prominent. As

Frankie had lost his own identity and spirit, his substance, so too did the man seem to be losing his. In a curious way this awoke in Frankie a sense of kinship, of belonging, the first he had experienced since coming. He touched the man's temple, thinking that perhaps his mind, as ruined as it seemed, was running in parallel with his own. He willed himself inside.

Three hours later he woke to someone jiggling his arm. It was the one o'clock nurse, a young woman barely out of school. He had fallen asleep in the chair by the man's bed. She was telling him he had to leave.

He made up a story and did as she said, having no wish to cause a stir. When he got outside, he tried to piece together what had happened. He remembered being on the verge of something, then getting very drowsy. Vaguely, he recalled curling up in the chair for a nap.

He fingered his pouch, trying in vain to retrieve what had been in his mind. The harder he tried, the more it eluded him. The flannel sack itself was no help at all. In contrast to what he had been led to believe, it felt devoid of life, nothing more than a collection of hair, paper and piss. In no way could he imagine it holding a man's vital force. And his soul? It was a joke.

Terry had plenty of questions when he got home, but Frankie was in no mood to talk. He pretended a headache and went to bed, staying there through the morning feigning sleep, and when that became impossible, another headache. Terry allowed how it was probably that time of month, a new disturbance for Frankie to worry about. He felt overwhelmed, and when Terry brought him a couple of codeines for the pain, he didn't argue. He had been drugless for nearly a week, and the pills put him to sleep for real. When he woke up mid-afternoon, Terry was gone.

He felt better, and after some food, better still. He took a shower, and then, recalling Terry's comment, felt cautiously down below with a finger. When it came back as clear and colorless as rain, he was immensely relieved, grateful beyond words to be spared yet another mysterious assault on his manhood. He got out and dressed, then killed time watching the seamstresses across the street. He envied the simplicity of their tasks, the seeming clarity of their lives. Terry called at four and again at six. He didn't try to hide his worry about Frankie's own health, and he leaned on her to take a break. When she refused, he got mad, but a moment later backed off. He said he had a present for her and couldn't wait to see her. He wished her luck.

That night at the hospital Frankie ran into Marcus. He was mopping the floor outside the emergency room where someone had lost dinner. One of the evening supervisors was watching him work.

Frankie, who had spoken to no one but Terry for days, was glad to see him and went up to talk. Marcus acknowledged his greeting with a glance but kept right on working. He didn't speak. His supervisor, a chubby man in a short-sleeved white shirt and tie, sauntered over.

"Something I can do for you, ma'am?"

Marcus shot Frankie a look.

"I . . . I was looking for the bathroom."

"Right around the corner."

Frankie followed his finger, trying hard to think of something else to say. He looked at the floor where Marcus was mopping. "Is it clean?"

"Is what clean?"

"The bathroom."

"Sure it's clean."

"I'm sorry," said Frankie. "I know you do a good job. It's just the last time I was here, there was someone in there. You know, a drunken person. A woman. She was quite rude and not only that, she made an unpleasant mess."

"We're not the Ritz, lady. We get all kinds."

"Of course you do." He looked to Marcus for support, but his friend's face was opaque. He turned back to the supervisor. "I was wondering if maybe you could peek in there and see if it's all right."

"You want me to check the ladies' room for you?"

"I'd be so relieved . . ." He squinted at the man's name tag. "Fred. It would be a favor to me."

Incredulous, the man tried to figure out if this was a put-on, but when he looked at Frankie, all he got back was a pretty girl with a smile. He shrugged.

"What the hell. Wait here."

When he was out of sight, Marcus stopped mopping and broke into a grin.

"You got old Fred slippin', and you got him slidin'."

"I need to talk to you."

"The man loves to watch me work. Waiting for a mistake. Fact is, I don't make no mistakes."

"It's the fifth night, Marcus. After tonight I'll be more than half done. Nothing's happened."

"You got your gris-gris?"

Frankie showed him. "But nothing's changed. I'm still the same. And not just that, the man's getting worse. He's dying. I know it. I'm scared."

"Nothing wrong with being scared."

"It worked for you, didn't it? That's what you said. Your gris-gris. You weren't joking?"

Marcus patted his chest. "It still be working. You do like Aunt Orphah said. The woman knows her business."

"I need to see her again."

Marcus shook his head. "Can't."

"Please."

"She gone back to Larkeeville. I put her on the train day before yesterday."

Frankie's face fell. "I'm doing something wrong. I know it. Tell me what to do."

"You do just like she say. You keep faith and the rest, it'll take care of itself." He smiled and nodded down the hall toward his supervisor, who was returning. "Just like me and the man. You take care of you, don't go bother worrying 'bout no one else."

With a gleam in his eye the supervisor assured Frankie that the bathroom was clean, and he made a point of walking her down. Frankie thanked him and disappeared inside. Ten minutes later when he came out, the two men were gone.

There was a new device when he got to Room 816. It was attached to the man's chest. A jagged green line played across a screen, its shape changing subtly from moment to moment. Frankie figured it was something for the man's heart, which added to his uneasiness.

Near nine he hid in the bathroom, and when the nurse had finished her business, he came out and sat by the man's bed. He was determined to make something happen, though not at all sure how. It occurred to him that maybe he was pushing too hard. With his own eyes he had seen people respond to force by becoming more recalcitrant and unyielding. It had happened in the bar and more than once with Terry. Opposition had made things worse. Was the solution then that he become less willful? It was difficult to imagine, for a means that did not require the force of his will seemed tantamount to resignation.

Close to midnight he was startled by sounds outside the door. He hadn't expected anyone for another hour and leaped out of his chair for the bathroom. Into the room came the nurse from the night before, and this time she had a doctor in tow. He looked barely older than she did and wore a short white coat with a stethoscope draped around the collar. While the nurse checked the man's vitals, the doctor listened to his heart and lungs, felt his belly and shone a penlight in his eyes.

"How's his I and O?" he asked. The nurse checked the clipboard.

"Hundred cc difference. Not too bad."

"He looks all right."

"You've got to be kidding."

"What I mean is, he's stable. Nothing's going to happen tonight."

"Carla says he's already checked out. He's going to need a miracle."

"C'mere." He put his hands around her waist. "This is the miracle I need."

The nurse squirmed away, but on the second embrace she stayed. She laced her arms around the baby-faced doctor's neck and the two of them kissed. He slid his hands down to her butt, then she got hers on his. They ground up against each other for a few moments, kissed again, then separated.

The doctor fixed his tie. The nurse straightened her hair. She checked the man's IV site and fluffed up his pillow. Then they left.

Frankie crept out of the bathroom. He was shaken by what he had seen, both its fervor and impropriety. What had possessed them? He felt defensive on behalf of the man as well as himself. His life was already enough the voyeur's. He didn't need it shoved in his face.

He fled the room and slipped down the back stairs without being seen. On Second he caught a bus downtown, keeping his face pressed against the window to avoid the eyes of strangers. He got off at Houston and hurried home. Terry was watching television when he came in.

"Hey, babe. What's the good word?"

Frankie said nothing, and Terry turned off the TV and patted the couch.

"Come on over and talk."

"I can't keep up with this," muttered Frankie. He sat an arm's distance away, his head in his hands. "I feel pummeled. It's getting to me."

"What happened?"

Reluctantly, Frankie told him. Terry's grin grew, and his laughter had the ring of vindication.

"Sex and death. The same old shit. That boy could have been me."

"I didn't think it was funny."

"Sure it's funny. What'd the guy in bed do?"

"Nothing. Just like always. It's been five days. Every night it's the same."

Terry hadn't stopped grinning. "Doesn't sound the same to me."

"You know what I mean. Between him and me. I'm not feeling anything."

"I can't believe that, Frankie. How about when those two were going at it? You didn't get a twinge of interest? Not even a flutter?"

"I was afraid of being caught. My heart was pounding."

"Sure it was. Mine pounds every time you walk in the door. That's what a woman like you does to a man."

Frankie ignored this. "I saw Marcus. He tried to be nice. He said to keep at it. Have faith."

"You do what Marcus says. And listen to me. Something is happening. There's no doubt in my mind." Before Frankie could react, Terry had grabbed her hands and pressed them to his heart. "Can't you feel it? Right here. It's happening, Frankie. I swear. Tell me I'm wrong. Tell me you're not feeling something too."

Frankie was unable to respond. He tried to pull away, but Terry held him tight.

"It's my heart, Frankie. My soul." His voice was taut. "Don't break it."

Frankie had to look away. A moment later Terry loosened his grip and broke into a laugh.

"Hey, lighten up, Terry. Right? I got you something today. What the hell did I do with it?" He rummaged in his pockets until he produced a tiny box. He gave it to Frankie. Inside were a pair of earrings. Two little dangling cupids.

"Go ahead, put 'em on."

Frankie didn't like the idea, but he was too drained to resist. Besides, a gift was a gift. He'd gotten precious few.

He went to the bathroom mirror and managed to get the earrings through the holes in his ears. The cupids danced merrily, aiming their arrows alternately into thin air and at his skull. Terry smiled when he came out, commenting casually on Frankie's good looks. He drew an imaginary bow and turned it on himself.

"The hunter," he said. "The lioness. De Leon, you pierce my heart."

Frankie arrived at the hospital early the next evening. He was tremulous but resolute, and as soon as the 9 P.M. nurse finished her business, he hurried from the bathroom to the man's bedside. He had been witness to one act of dubious propriety, and the lengthening days of his vigil had stretched the limits of his own. Quietly, he lowered the bed railing, then folded back the thin hospital sheet. Pushing aside the various tubes and wires, he got into bed.

The man had an inoffensive smell, except for his mouth, which was rank. The restraint covered his gown, which reached to mid-thigh. His legs were thin as rails. Frankie lay next to him for what seemed like hours. He himself was rigid as a board. He tried to relax, tried closing his eyes and willing something to happen, but nothing did. He could barely stand it. He shifted position, then shifted again. The second time, his motion tripped the heart monitor, which started to beep. He froze, hoping it would stop. When it didn't, he panicked. Jumping off the bed, he yanked up the man's covers and bolted to the bathroom. Moments later a nurse and orderly rushed in. Once they had assured themselves that the man was all right, the nurse chewed out the orderly for not keeping the railing up. She watched while he locked it in place, and then the two of them left.

Frankie made it out of the hospital in a cold sweat. He felt foolhardy, but worse, he felt worthless. Fate was taunting him and he couldn't stand up. His very existence was at stake, and he could do nothing.

When he got home, he told Terry he was through. The whole thing was a joke, a sham. He'd had enough.

Terry wouldn't hear of it.

"You got to hang in there, girl. Three more nights. The lady said nine, you got to give it nine. You quit after six, it's like playing half the game. The last three innings is when the shit happens. It's probably happening now. Didn't I tell you that? You just got to let it take hold. Like a drug, like a song, anything, it takes time to take hold."

He became the cheerleader. Seeming to draw fuel from Frankie's hopelessness, he called two and three times a day from work, bubbling with confidence and enthusiasm. Dropping all pretense, he fantasized openly about life on the other side of their ordeal. He brought Frankie a copy of *The Joy of Sex*, and when she threw it on the floor, he laughed and said she was right, she didn't need a book. The next day he came home with a bottle of perfume.

The man in the hospital changed little over the next day or two, although the proliferation of machines and plastic IV bags brought a new and menacing feel to the room. Frankie stopped sneaking around and came now only during visiting hours, doing what he could to reach out, trying to stave off despair. From time to time he experienced a flicker of promise, here and there a glimmer of hope. The moments were fleeting, but at least he was out of hiding. If nothing else, the final path had brought him into the open.

The ninth day arrived, and Terry couldn't contain his excitement. He was up early to straighten the apartment, then went out for flowers. He had made sure to get the day off, and a half-hour before it was time to go to the hospital, he was out on the street flagging down a cab. Frankie came down the stairs slowly. He was dressed in black slacks and a Loden coat, and his face suffered the look of someone bearing a grim sentence. On this the last day he was immune to Terry's buoyancy, felt, in fact, that it violated the gravity of the occasion. At the hospital when Terry bounded out of the taxi and toward the entrance, Frankie told him to stop.

"Don't come with me."

"Frankie . . ."

"No. I know you mean well, but don't. I have to do this alone."

Terry started to argue, then stopped. He held up his hands.

"Hey. You're the boss. You tell me what to do."

"Wait for me. Will you do that?"

Terry gave a big grin. "Babe, you come down that elevator I'll be the first one you see. The only one. You and me. Like always."

Frankie turned away and with a sense of foreboding entered the hospital. He waited with a throng of visitors for the elevator, rode it up, then exited and walked down the hall as if in a dream. A nurse he didn't recognize was replacing an IV when he came into the room. She made small talk that he didn't hear, calibrated the drip, then left. Frankie stood at the foot of the man's bed. He tried to think of a prayer, an invocation, something to ease his apprehension. He took the pouch from around his neck, cradled it in his palms and closed his eyes. He took a deep breath. And another. Some of the tension went out of his body. His hands tingled, and his spirit, remarkably, began to lighten.

The heart monitor sounded. Two short beeps, then silence, then a cascade of beeps that didn't stop. Frankie felt a quickening of his pulse, and then the door of the room was thrown open. A nurse rushed in, checked the man's pulse, then hit a button on the wall that started blinking red. In moments there were two more nurses in the room, one of whom told Frankie to leave. Instead, he backed into a corner and made himself small. The overhead lights in the room were now on, the man's bed railings were down and his clothes were off. One of the nurses ran out and came back in wheeling a stainless steel cart with lots of drawers and a machine on top with paddles. Two doctors rushed in, then a man carrying a bag full of tubes. He went immediately to the head of the bed, pulled the patient's chin up, stuck a metal guide in his mouth and shoved a tube down his throat. Then he attached a black bag to the tube and started pumping in air. A nurse smeared paste on the man's chest, and a moment later one of the doctors grabbed the two paddles and yelled for everyone to stand back. Positioning them over the paste, he pushed a button. The man's body jerked, then came to rest. For an instant the clamor in the room ceased. All eyes were on the heart monitor, whose green line looked like the scribbles of a lunatic. The shock from the paddles sent it into a different pattern, but only for a moment. Then the jagged, disorderly scribbles returned.

They shocked him again, stuck an IV below his collarbone, drew blood, and shocked him a third time. They gave him vial after vial of medicine. One of the doctors suggested cracking the man's chest, but they settled on sticking a long, skinny needle through his ribs into his heart. Someone asked if anyone knew his HIV status. Someone else, after learning of his comatose condition, wanted to know just what they were saving him for anyway.

The team kept at it for close to an hour, long after the man's heart had stopped beating. The room was hot and thick with the smell of medicine and sweat. There was blood on the sheets, plastic casings and tubes everywhere. At last one of the nurses turned to the doctor who had taken charge and asked if they could call it. It was not really a question.

Up to this point Frankie had gone virtually unnoticed, but as people started to file out of the room, a nurse he recognized came and took him outside.

"I'm sorry," she said. "We did what we could."

Frankie was in a state of shock and didn't reply. The nurse led him to a room down the hall.

"To some it seems harsh. I know. Sometimes it's better not to see." She paused in the doorway. "Give us a moment to clean up. Then you can come back if you want."

She left Frankie alone. He still had the pouch in his hand and in his mind the image of the man's gray and inert body. Dazedly, he wandered into the hall and down the back stairs. He felt ravaged and numb. He wanted to fall asleep and never wake up.

Terry met him in the lobby, took one look at his face and hugged him tight.

"It's over," he said. "Done. You let Terry take care of things now. Everything's going to be all right."

He took her outside and hailed a cab, but as they were ready to get in, Frankie halted.

"No," he said, struggling out of his torpor. "I need to walk. I have to bury this."

Terry looked at Frankie's closed fist and frowned. Rolling his eyes, he apologized to the cabdriver, who with an insult drove off. Terry was not pleased.

"You're dragging this thing out."

"I have to bury it. That's the last thing."

"And where are you going to bury something in the middle of fuckin' Manhattan?"

Frankie shook his head, and Terry swore.

"You come with me."

He led her to Stuyvesant Square, which was locked, then down Third to Bowery, setting a brisk pace. He kept an arm around her shoulder, and once or twice let it slip down to her ass. Each time Frankie flipped it off. Terry tried conversation, but the lady wasn't talking. He bided his time by whistling.

Frankie barely heard. He was in a world apart, a nightmare of fear and dread. He felt that he was suffocating and knew that he had to get the pouch in the ground. The task consumed him. It kept his panic temporarily at bay.

They got to Roosevelt Park, a slim and poorly lit slit of concrete and ravaged earth, and found a tree. The soil was damp, and while Terry stood lookout, Frankie crouched down and dug a hole with his fingernails. When he got deep enough, he dangled the pouch above the hole and closed his eyes. It felt even more weightless than it had before. With a final silent and desperate entreaty he dropped the sack in the hole and covered it with dirt. Then he stood up, tamped it down and waited.

After a few minutes Terry tugged him away, saying it wasn't safe to stay there too long. They started home.

"Well?"

Frankie said nothing.

"It must be a relief."

"Nothing happened."

Terry laughed. "Sure it did. You stayed your nine, you buried the thing. It's over. Finished. You're

Frankie again. Fuckin' Frankie de Leon. Thank the Lord for that."

"I'm not."

"Don't start with it, Frankie. I'm not asking this time, I'm telling. You look here." He pointed to his mouth. "You listen. You're not a man, you're not a dyke, you're not some weird transvestite queen. You're Frankie de Leon. It's time to get that into your head."

"I don't know what I am," muttered Frankie. "Something was supposed to happen. She promised."

"Something did, babe. And now you're coming home with me." He took her hand so she couldn't let go. "It's been a long time. Maybe we should get a little something to celebrate with."

He stopped in a store and got a pint of whiskey, waiting until they got home to crack the seal.

"So," he said, tossing down two quick ones. "Tell me how good it feels. How happy you are. I want to hear."

Frankie tried to keep a grip on himself. It wasn't easy. Terry kept the pressure on.

"Tell me how thrilled you are to be a woman. My woman. How much you've missed me." He puckered his lips. "Me and my kisses. My sweet kisses. Tell me."

"I can't," said Frankie, his voice barely audible.

"Sure you can." Terry took another hit. "Tell you what, I'll help you out. You just repeat after me." He got full in Frankie's face. "I'm through with this shit. I'm done fuckin' my man around. I'm gonna act right and show him what love is." He cut her a shit-faced grin. "You start with that. The rest we'll make up as we go along."

Frankie swallowed and shook his head. Terry grabbed her jaw.

"Say it."

"I can't. It didn't work. What she said, all those nights . . . it's no different. It's worse. It's a nightmare." He started to cry. The nights of waiting, of worry and pent-up hope burst on him like a storm. He hugged himself and sobbed in despair.

Terry had his own storm to contend with. It rose up and slapped him in the face, and while he was reeling from the punch, it slapped him again. He was enraged at Frankie's helplessness and her denial of him.

"I've had enough of this shit," he shouted. "I want what's mine. Now, not later."

He grabbed her, but Frankie twisted away. He came after her again.

"I'm a man, bitch. Not some dog. Not some cur you throw out that comes crawling back. It's time you learned who's boss. Past time. Way past."

Frankie couldn't hold him off. He was too big and strong. He pulled off her coat and then her blouse. She tried to run, but there was nowhere to go. He dragged her into the bedroom, got her pants down and then his own. Frankie pleaded with him, but he was in a world beyond pleas. Pinning her to the bed, he pulled out his cock and raped her.

And later, when it was over, and his anger and pride and manhood were still not assuaged, he raped her again.

14

Someone was buzzing the door. It came to Terry in a dream, which he tried to ignore. He had a massive hangover and didn't want to move. Light hurt his eyes, and sound was worse. He covered his head and dug into the sofa, where he had fallen asleep. The buzzing stopped. A moment later the pounding began.

With a groan he rolled to a sitting position, buttoned his jeans and pulled on a tee shirt he found on the floor. Raking his hair with a hand, he staggered to the door.

There was a well-dressed woman outside with graying chestnut hair and powder on her face. She wore an ankle-length coat, black kid gloves and a gold brooch on her lapel. Slung over one arm was a purse; over the other, a Bonwit Teller shopping bag. She was not happy.

"Don't you people believe in answering the door?" She tried to see around him. "I'm here to see my daughter."

A wave of nausea rose in Terry's throat. "She's asleep," he croaked.

"At one-thirty in the afternoon?"

He shrunk beneath the woman's stern and disapproving gaze, knowing full well why she had come. He must have been too far gone to have heard the call. Guiltily, he asked what had been said.

"We had a date," said Mrs. De Leon. "Apparently she forgot. Apparently I'm not important enough. I want to see her."

Terry swung the door open and, muttering an apology for how things looked, ushered her into the living room. He told her to make herself at home and said he'd get her daughter. He made a point of avoiding her eyes.

Frankie was curled in a ball on the mattress, face turned to the wall, eyes open and unblinking. At the sound of the door opening he shuddered and clutched the covers tighter around himself. Terry stopped at the foot of the bed.

"Your mother's here. She wants to see you."

Frankie made no response, and Terry knelt down.

"I was drunk, Frankie. Out of my mind. That wasn't me last night. It was a crazy person."

Frankie cringed.

"If you knew how bad I felt. How sorry I am." He reached out to touch her. "I would never hurt you, Frankie."

"I'm bleeding."

"Where? I didn't do anything like that." He noticed some crumpled, pink-stained tissue on the floor. "It's your period."

"I want to be alone."

"Please forgive me." There were tears in his eyes. "I want to be good to you. That's all I want. Let me try. Let me be good."

He hugged her mournfully, getting nothing in return. Eventually, he stood up and left the room.

"She's not feeling so hot," he told Mrs. De Leon. "Maybe you should come back another time."

The woman was instantly alert. "What's the matter? I want to see her."

"She feels lousy. She's having her period."

"I'm her mother," she replied, spearing him with a glance. She stood up, clutching her purse firmly under her arm. Then she called down the hall.

"Francesca? It's your mother. Make yourself presentable. I'm coming in."

She marched to the room, knocked once and opened the door. One look at her daughter and she knew something was wrong. Frankie wouldn't speak, and when she trembled and tried to hide beneath the covers, Mrs. De Leon momentarily lost her temper. She barked at Frankie for her stubbornness and intractability. She accused her of being thoughtless. Then she steadied herself.

"We're leaving." She pulled some clothes from the closet and threw them on the bed. "Get dressed. I'm taking you to a doctor."

"Please, go away."

"Do you need help?" With an effort she crouched down and pulled the bedsheets off Frankie's legs. "I did this for you when you were a baby, I can do it now."

"No," pleaded Frankie, ashamed beyond words.

He tried to cover his nakedness with his hands. "Please."

"Then do it yourself," commanded Mrs. De Leon. She stood up. "I'll tell your boyfriend we're going."

She found Terry waiting where she had left him. He offered her coffee, which she refused.

"I'm taking Francesca home."

The news came as no great surprise. Feebly, Terry asked if Frankie had agreed to go. Mrs. De Leon gave him a withering look.

"I know a sick child when I see one." She grabbed her shopping bag. "Now if you'll excuse me."

She went down the hall and stood at the bedroom door, tapping a foot impatiently. Terry was too ashamed to argue, and Frankie, too numb and battered to resist. Under Mrs. De Leon's imperious gaze he pulled on dress, coat and shoes and surrendered to his fate.

Circuits

Human males secrete a scent, a complex molecule found in greatest concentration in the small of the back, the crotch and armpit. Under certain conditions this scent exerts striking effects on the behavior of the human female.

The optimum period between menstrual cycles for procreation in the human species is 29.5 days. All else being equal, women whose menses occur at this interval will be the most successful at breeding young. When the male scent is experimentally dabbed on the upper lip of females, the female olfactory apparatus is stimulated, resulting in neurologic changes deep within the brain. Chief among these is a regulation of menstruation toward a 29.5 day period. Those women who are most receptive to the male odor will thus tend to cycle in such a way as to optimize their reproductive capability. Those men, therefore, who produce the most potent and penetrating scents will tend to see their seed take root and flourish.

Such is the situation now, but recent findings suggest that human reproductive behavior was not always so unidirectional. Archaeologic diggings in Turkey have uncovered evidence of a race of men and women that lived some four thousand years ago in large, leaderless groups. There appear to have been few divisions among them, save once a year when the sexes would separate into couples, man joined to woman, woman to man, for the purpose of conceiving children. From information gleaned from potsherds and cave paintings, investigators hypothesize that if this union were successful, the man's penis would slowly wither.[10] Over a period of months he would grow womb, passage and breasts. When the baby was born, the two would suckle it, man and woman equally, until gradually the woman's milk dried. Her breasts then would shrivel, and the passage between her legs close. Slowly, she would grow a penis of her own. In a year the roles would reverse, and a year later reverse again. This race is now extinct, although the scientists, using biological markers, are searching the countryside for traces. Hermaphroditism, they point out, is common in the animal kingdom, and clearly, the genetic information persists in humans. Quite possibly the trigger resides in the olfactory apparatus,

*as is the case, for example, in many species of anne-
lid. Evolution notwithstanding, they postulate that
the reemergence of man's capacity in this regard may
simply be a matter of locating the proper neural cir-
cuitry and turning on the switch.*[11]

Terry called every day, sometimes twice a day, but
Frankie wasn't talking. Not to him, not to Edna, the
woman claiming to be his mother, not to anyone. He
felt dead inside, inert, blank. He stayed in bed, leaving only when forced by Edna to see the doctor, a
family friend on the staff of Yale-New Haven who
ordered tests, a scan, and referred Frankie to a psychiatrist. The psychiatrist recommended hospitalization, at which point Edna balked. Her daughter
wasn't so sick that a few weeks of rest, fresh air and
motherhood would do any harm. The psychiatrist
cautioned her regarding severe depression and the
possibility of self-inflicted injury. He prescribed
some pills and made a follow-up appointment. Edna
took her daughter home.

A week passed, then another. The pills made
Frankie feel, if possible, even deader. He stopped
taking them, at first secretly, then openly. Edna was
concerned, but the psychiatrist saw it in another
light. The freeze that had gripped Frankie was starting to thaw. He warned Edna to be prepared.

A few days later Frankie had his first bout of tears.
They took him by surprise, with a force that was
frightening. He couldn't believe such hurt and helplessness existed. Hour after hour, day after day he
cried. He felt under constant attack, and it took
nothing at all to set him off. He was afraid of the

phone, the radio, the television. He shrank from
Edna. When he thought he could not possibly weep
more, when his throat was raw and his chest hollow
as a cask, another bout would begin. Over and over
he prayed for the numbness to return, for the death
to revisit his heart.

It went on like this for seven days, a week that
stretched into a lifetime. Then one day, in the midst
of brutalizing himself for the thousandth time, he
heard a new voice. It was too meek and timid to take
seriously at first, but over time it grew bolder. It
wasn't his fault, the voice said. Someone else was to
blame. Cox, for slapping him around, for giving him
drugs and forcing him onstage. Marcus, for steering
him to an old and foolish lady. Orphah herself, for
promising to help and not coming through. And the
man in the hospital, for lacking the will to reach out,
for giving him nothing, for dying. He thought of all
the people who'd cheated and misled him, who'd
stood in his way, adding to his misery. His anger
grew.

He was in the kitchen one morning, staring darkly
out a window when the phone rang. Without thinking, he picked it up. The voice, small and subdued,
was unmistakable. Frankie listened a moment, then
exploded. The accumulation of bitterness and rage
spewed forth in a torrent of invective and abuse. He
shouted like a madman. A fury. Mercilessly, he spat
his bile.

Terry sat at home and listened. It was the first time
since the rape that Frankie had spoken to him, and
he was choked with emotion. He clutched the phone

as if it were a lifeline. Tears of shame and relief ran down his cheeks.

Frankie paused for breath, and Terry took the moment to mutter an apology. To his own ears it was feeble and pathetic; to Frankie's, it was worth less than dirt. He told Terry to shove it and hung up. That night, he had his first good meal in weeks.

Terry continued to call, and Edna, with Frankie's blessing, continued to put him off. But as her daughter started to come around, eating better, dressing herself, speaking in more than monosyllables, Edna began to ride her a little. Without knowing specifically about the rape, she understood enough to know that the man was no good for her daughter. She told Frankie to get rid of him, the sooner the better.

"And do what?" asked Frankie.

"Stay here," said Edna. "Get your strength back. Find someone nice."

Frankie gave a mordant laugh. Nice was not in his book. Far from having spent itself, his wrath had sent out roots, deepening, spreading, changing to a form occult and malignant. Before Terry had called, Frankie's anger had been unfocused. Now it had a target. While fate may have been what robbed him of his manhood, Terry was its instrument. His was the face of the enemy, and Frankie vowed in his heart to avenge himself.

The next time Terry called, pleading for another chance, Frankie took the phone.

"Terry. I haven't heard from you in weeks."

"I've been calling every day."

"Have you?"

"I want you back, Frankie. What happened won't happen again. I swear it."

"Edna says I should get rid of you. The sooner the better."

"Edna has her own ideas. She doesn't like me. You know that. No man's good enough for her daughter."

"But you are?"

"You used to think so."

"Have you raped me before?"

Terry was silent.

"No answer? Maybe you don't remember. Or you're not quite sure. Which is it, Terry?"

"You're being cruel."

Frankie laughed contemptuously. "So you want me back. Like old times. You'll be good to me. Treat me right."

"I've been trying, Frankie. I need help. You have to give me a chance."

"You've had chances."

"Another. Give me one more."

"Say you want me."

"I want you. You know I do."

"Beg."

There was silence.

"No? You want me but not enough to beg?"

Terry drew his breath. "This is my punishment?"

"Think of it as your reward."

"I can't do that. I can't beg."

"I'm sorry."

"I made a mistake, Frankie. I'll admit that as long as I live. You have my regret, my guilt, my sorrow. Leave me my pride."

"Your pride." He savored the thought. "I like that. I'm glad, Terry. A man deserves his pride. You be sure to keep it safe." He paused, weighing his next words. They were not half as hard as he had imagined.

"All right. I'll come."

"You will?"

"I'm anxious to see you. I'm eager. Come and get me, Terry. Take me home."

15

Now the bustier conquers the night with a flutter of tier-drops. Black silk faille whispers across a dance floor, signaling the new allure. Spare, small, strapless, to bare your shoulders, snug your waist. Then the brief, leggy skirt splurges into a trio of tiers.

Soft as cashmere, brave as makeup. Pure was never so pretty. Or so unabashedly colorful. One hundred and fifty-eight exuberant new colors for your lips, eyes, cheeks and nails. Because while your skin wants nothing but purity, your mind may be on something else.

Frankie returned to the apartment a month to the day after having been spirited away. It was late spring, and there was an urban sweetness to the air. The Chinese souvenir shop was doing a brisk business, and the sidewalk fruit stand was spilling over with customers. Frankie threaded his way past the crowded bins and waited down the block for Terry to catch up. They entered the walkup and had reached the third floor when Frankie stopped and asked if Terry wouldn't mind going back down and getting him an apple. The red ones had looked especially good. Terry hesitated a moment, then smiled to himself and loped down the stairs. Five minutes later he was back, breathing hard. Frankie thanked him.

"No problem," said Terry, buffing it up before handing it over. He opened the apartment door for Frankie, who entered first, stiffening slightly as he passed the bedroom on his way down the hall. The place had a stale smell, especially in contrast to what he had gotten used to at Edna's. It was also a mess. There were dishes in the sink, books on the floor, clothes piled on the couch. A grease-stained pizza box sat on the kitchen table.

Terry followed Frankie to the living room, where he collapsed on the couch. He had been on the road for close to ten hours, fetching Frankie, braving Edna's corrosive glares and silences, bringing his woman back. He was exhausted.

"So," he said happily, stretching out his legs. "We start fresh. Ground zero. Before the fall."

"Not exactly," said Frankie.

Terry glanced at her and eked out a smile. "It was worth a try."

"There're some things I have in mind to change."

"Like me."

Frankie gave him a look. "You've apologized. Is there more?"

"Much more. You give me the chance, you'll see how much."

"Promises again?"

"Facts," he said. "Cold facts."

"I'm anxious to get started," said Frankie. "Here, for example." He gestured around the room. "You have to admit, it has a shabby feel."

"Lived in," replied Terry. "Homey."

"It's filthy."

"You stayed too long at Edna's, babe. The woman's got her hooks in."

"She begged me not to leave," Frankie said pointedly. "She pleaded. Any time I want to go back, the door's open. Wide open."

Terry got the message. He asked what changes she had in mind.

"I want it cleaner. Tidier. New curtains, a new couch, maybe a fresh coat of paint . . ." Frankie ticked off a dozen other improvements that had Terry reeling.

"Why don't we just move to Park Avenue?"

"You're making a joke."

"Where are we going to get the money? Edna? She's never given us anything in her life."

"She doesn't like you."

"The feeling's mutual." He was trying to figure things out when all at once it came to him. "Wait a minute. You've got another job. That's it, isn't it? You've been waiting to spring it on me. The big surprise."

Frankie shook his head.

"No? Then I have to explain something to you. I'm a book clerk. I make six bucks an hour. That's two-forty a week. This place costs five and a quarter a month. You haven't worked since March." He cut her a look. "You want new stuff? Figure it out, Frankie."

"I have."

"I'm on the edge of my seat."

"Get another job. Make some money."

"I have a job."

"A second one."

He started to laugh, but the look on Frankie's face sobered him fast. Getting her home apparently was not the same as having her back.

"You're going to make me work for this, aren't you?"

"Look at it like this," said Frankie. "You get another job, then I won't have to go back to the bar." His eyes shone. "Think of it as a way of protecting me from guys like yourself. Plus you make money. What more could a man want?"

It took Terry two weeks, but with Marcus's help he finally got a day job in the hospital laundry room, cleaning sheets. They were brought down in plastic sacks, double-bagged and tied to keep the waste and stench from leaking out. In his medical school days Terry had been ample witness to the sundry ways a body could unload itself, but never had he had to handle such quantities of the material, nor the soiled linens, some of which had been ripening since the day before. He was responsible for pulling the dirty and dripping sheets out of the bags and getting rid of anything that might not break down in the machines. He wore a mask to protect his face, but it didn't blunt the smell. The first time it hit him he was nearly knocked to his knees, and it was weeks before he could make it through a day without gagging.

He'd shower and scrub before leaving the hospital, and on those days he didn't have to rush off to Suter's, Frankie would make him shower again when he got home. They'd have dinner, then Terry would struggle to stay awake before crashing for good at eight or nine. On the days he worked both jobs he'd come home by twelve and be asleep by twelve-thirty. He was using the secondhand couch with all its lumps and busted springs, and at one point he raised the idea of buying a new one. Frankie, who was managing the money, seemed sympathetic to the suggestion, but when it came time for their first purchase, he ended up getting a bed frame, box springs and new mattress for himself. When Terry complained of her selfishness, Frankie took him to task.

"You want to see it that way, go ahead. On the other hand, you could be proud that you're providing for me. You could feel a sense of accomplishment. You'd rather be unhappy, that's your right. You want to get into who deserves what, I can do that too. I prefer to see that we're making progress. That there's a chance for you to get your shit together before I walk out the door."

There was a certain logic to the argument, and while not exactly pleased to be on the losing end, Terry kept his mouth shut after that. Most of the time he was too tired to argue, too exhausted to worry about where he slept. He woke at five to get to the laundry job at six, and five days a week he had to rush across town to get to the bookstore on time. On his days off Frankie let him sleep in, as long as he was out of bed by eight. There was a lot of work to do, scraping the stove, shampooing the carpets, scrubbing the bathroom. Frankie had him take down all the books in the hall and dust the shelves, then wash the windows and walls. That these labors were reserved for those precious few hours when he wasn't working, when all he wanted to do was rest, would have seemed unjust were it not for the change that seemed to have taken hold of Frankie. Her surliness was gone, her previous bizarre preoccupation with being a man seemingly forgotten. Terry took her efforts to upgrade the apartment as symbolic of a desire to improve their life together as a whole, a task he was more than willing to join in. Her physical unassailability continued to vex him, though now, at least, he understood it as his cross to bear. The sin was not forgotten, but it could be forgiven. Having her back home gave him a foothold. He would prove he was not a man to fear.

With Terry at work Frankie spent his days watching TV and plotting. There was so much to learn, such vast quantities of this new life to absorb. Having a purpose helped him focus, it kept him from getting lost in the convolutions of human behavior he observed on television. The morning soaps were the easiest to study. Emotions seemed simple; motives, for the most part, were clear. From the sum of his limited experience and these shows he developed theories about women and men. The ads taught him lessons too. He would watch for a few hours, take a break, then watch for a few more. With money from the second paycheck he had Terry buy a VCR so he could tape the shows and play back those whose lessons were particularly telling. He was an avid pupil.

At times he tired of television, and then he would open a window and sit on the sill, gazing at the traffic below or across the street at the women in the sewing factory. He began to have thoughts of going out, which he had not done alone since the rape. The apartment felt safe, but it was also a prison. Leaving would be a test of his strength.

He chose a day when Terry was doing a double. If for some reason he had a setback, an embarrassment, if something went terribly wrong and he had to run home, he didn't want Terry to see. He chose his clothes carefully, with an eye toward drawing as little attention as possible. Loose-fitting jeans, sneakers, baggy tee shirt. He found a fatigue jacket and buttoned it to the neck. Shades, hair brushed severely back and tied, no jewelry or makeup. It took an hour to prepare himself and another to build up his nerve. The TV kept drawing him back, but at last he punched it off. There was a sudden silence, followed by a vacancy of intent. For an instant he forgot what he had meant to do. When he remembered, he went to door, girded himself, then stepped through and went down the stairs. Moments later he was in the world.

It was not nearly as traumatic as he expected. After a few anxious minutes it became clear, in fact, that no one cared about him in the least. At the grocery he was jostled impersonally by a woman carrying a bag full of oranges. He bought a banana, and the man who took his money barely gave him a glance. People streamed by him on the street, chatting with one another or, more commonly, lost in worlds of their own. He wandered down the block, peering in the various store windows, getting his legs and his bearings. Everyone seemed exceptionally busy, and he drew as much attention as a fly. He went as far as Houston, then turned and walked home. Climbing the stairs he felt a sense of relief and realized he'd been tense the whole time. But he had done it. No one had harmed him, no one had gotten in his face, no one had even noticed. He was ready to try again.

He went out every day after that, broadening his scope, exulting in his freedom. He visited shops, galleries, boutiques, absorbing the largesse, his eye and ear ever attuned to his fellow travelers, most especially the women, the female clerks and shoppers, the working girls, the students, the panhandlers and hustlers. He studied their ways and manners, their nuances of style, form, posture. He watched them alone and in groups, both with other women and with men. As he grew bolder, he moved in closer, eavesdropping on conversations, drinking in subtleties of tone and behavior. There was so much to learn, and at home he'd practice, standing at the mirror, speaking to himself, walking, striking poses. He sifted through Frankie's extensive wardrobe and tried on different clothes. Skirts, dresses, blouses, stockings. He played with his hair and even tried makeup. Always at home. Always with a purpose.

The change was not lost on Terry. He was happy with Frankie in jeans and a sweatshirt but thrilled with her in stockings and skirts. As she started to dress and act more feminine, he found it easier to handle the stress and fatigue of two jobs. To see his penance have such a positive effect was a stimulant, and he worked ever harder to please her. He planned their meals and cooked the food. He did the dishes and the laundry. When the bathroom needed cleaning, he cleaned. When something needed fetching, he fetched. He tried to anticipate Frankie's thoughts and needs. He wanted her to know just what he was capable of.

One night after dinner Frankie asked him about medical school. They were sitting a couple of feet apart on the couch, Terry in jeans and a button-down shirt, Frankie in leotard, leather skirt and stockings. Terry tried to brush the question off but Frankie kept at him until he relented and told the story. Frankie sat motionless throughout, and when Terry was done, a silence filled the room.

"You must feel awful."

Terry shrugged. "I probably would have made a lousy doctor. No sympathy for the human condition. Not when it counts."

"What I mean is, being responsible for that man's death. It must haunt you."

He gave her a look. "I didn't kill Zack. He killed himself."

"The way you tell it, he needed help. He was crying for it. You didn't know?"

Terry struggled with that. "I thought I was helping. I didn't know how deep it went."

"You didn't know what you were doing."

"No." His voice was faint. "Maybe not."

"You didn't," Frankie repeated. He made a show of studying his nails, then frowned and looked up. "Or did you?"

"What's that supposed to mean?"

"The girl. The nurse. What was her name?"

"It doesn't matter."

"Andrea," said Frankie. "You wanted Andrea. You were jealous."

Vividly, Terry recalled the night of the party. Zack's shaven head and sad face. The girl in the cat suit. His own curiosity. "I wasn't jealous. I wanted to help."

"You wanted the obsession. The thrill. You wanted the girl."

"I didn't. Later maybe, after he died, but not then. I hardly knew her then."

"Would you do it again?"

"We needed each other," he said softly. "It was one of those things. We were trying to forget."

"The tank," said Frankie. "The gas. Steal it and bring it to your friend. Present the means of his death on a silver platter."

Terry cringed. "I didn't do that. It was an accident. It wasn't my fault."

"That's what you tell yourself. And what else?"

He tried to muster anger, outrage, but couldn't. The truth was that his own recriminations were worse than hers. He hung his head and hid his face. A moment later he felt a hand on his cheek.

"It must be hard," said Frankie, sliding over and taking Terry's head in his lap. "I didn't mean to open such a wound."

"Bad luck dogs me," muttered Terry. He sighed,

and gradually, the lines eased off his face. "Until now."

Frankie smiled at that. "Let's talk about something else."

"Your turn."

He started to say something, then cut himself off mid-sentence. "Maybe now's not such a good time."

"What?"

"Forget it. It's not that important."

"Tell me."

"You'll be mad."

"Mad is over. I don't know mad."

Frankie played with a strand of Terry's hair. "It's your smell. It's so strong." He hesitated. "Too strong sometimes. Do you know what I mean? It's too much for me. It makes it hard to get close."

"You're close now."

"It's not easy."

Terry regarded her, alert to hidden meaning.

"Some men wear perfume. I've seen it on TV."

"Cologne. For men they call it cologne."

"Will you try?"

"I should be insulted."

"Please. For me."

He considered. "My smell. That's what we're talking about, right? It's the smell that bothers you?"

Frankie nodded helplessly.

"It's never bothered anyone before." He turned it over in his mind. "Then again, the lioness isn't just anyone. She's back, isn't she?" He drank in the thought. "What the hell. She wants her man to smell sweet, why not?"

"And a haircut," said Frankie.

"The hair too, huh?"

"For me."

Terry laughed. "For you, babe. A shave, a haircut, cologne. You'll make a man of me yet."

Frankie smiled at that too.

A few days later he bought Terry an earring. It was a thin, silver hoop he had seen on a young woman in a store. Terry, who did not like ornamentation on his body, not the necklaces and bracelets that some men sported, certainly not earrings, initially balked at wearing it. When Frankie acted hurt, he said he'd think it over, hoping she'd let the matter drop. But she kept at him, arguing that they'd never get anywhere if he couldn't accept her gifts. It was a matter of trust, she said, of willingness to be open to new things, to be pampered and beautified. You gave up a little in order to get a lot more. If Terry couldn't see that, maybe she should look for someone who could.

The next day Terry arrived at Suter's late. He was on his way downstairs when Brenda called to him. She looked peeved.

"What's the matter? You don't say hello anymore?"

"I'm late."

"That's new? Sal's got his gadgets. Come talk to me."

"What's on your mind, Brenda?"

"Listen to that." She shook her head. "If it's an effort, don't bother. I'll talk to someone else."

He came over. "I'm sorry. I've been preoccupied."

"I've noticed. I take it the lady's back."

He nodded. "With a vengeance."

"Bad shit?"

"No, it's fine. It's great. She's opening up doors."

"I was worrying about you."

"You don't have to worry."

"I'm a friend. Friends worry."

"Things are falling into place. It's a whole new life. Her leaving, maybe that was the best thing that could have happened."

"Sometimes it's like that. It's hard to think straight when someone's in your face all the time."

"That's where I want her. Closer even. As close as humanly possible."

Brenda fanned the air. "Watch out, Frankie."

"No," said Terry. "It's not like that."

"I've got some news of my own."

"That part's over and done with."

"I met a guy."

"Believe me. It's finished."

"It just started."

"What did?"

"I'm telling you. His name's Eddie."

"Whose name?"

"This guy I met."

"A man? You met a man?"

"Bingo. One of them."

"But you don't like men."

"Sure I do. I like you."

"You know what I mean."

"I used to go out with guys. Fifteen, twenty years ago. I was even engaged once."

"Yeah?" He took a fresh look at her.

"Good Catholic boy, sweet as the baby Jesus himself. A girl's dream."

"How you've fallen."

"Thank God for that." A customer handed her a book, and she kept talking as she rang up the sale. "While you were dragging your sad-ass face all over the floor, I turned forty. You know what happens when a woman turns forty?"

"She worries about turning fifty."

"She thinks about kids. If she hasn't before. Most of my girlfriends from school, Catholic school you gotta remember, they got knocked up by the time they were twenty. Some of them are grandmothers today. It makes a person think."

"Sure. The clock's ticking."

"I could use some advice."

"I'm sure the Church would love you back."

She gave him a look. "Religion I think I can handle. I mean about men. What does a guy like? It's been a long time. I'm kind of rusty."

Terry thought about it, shrugged. "Depends on the guy. What's a woman like?"

"A woman? Attention, I guess. Affection. Security. Peace and quiet. Money."

"There you go. Ask him out to dinner. Give him a check."

She made a face.

"No? Then how about flowers?"

"Guys don't want flowers."

"Sure they do."

"You're serious?"

"Answer me this. You want the guy or you want his body?"

"I haven't made the distinction," she replied, affecting indignity.

"But you want a baby. I assume the man's got sperm."

"That's crude."

"Well what about him? What does he want?"

"I haven't asked. I would assume it's me."

"You're a catch," he told her. "Sure it's you."

Brenda took a moment to get her bearings. The conversation had moved somewhat farther afield than she had planned.

"Sperm, huh?"

"No," said Terry. "Flowers. Bring the man flowers." He started toward the stairs, then stopped and came back. "I'm curious. How does it feel to be with a man? After all this time."

"Different," she said.

"How?"

"He has a lot of hair." She smiled at some private joke. "It's exciting. We seem so . . . what? Innocent? It's fun. I'm never sure what's going to happen next."

Terry nodded, thinking of the period since Frankie had returned from Edna's. Not knowing what to expect pretty much summed it up. The woman could be kind one moment, cruel the next, engaging then aloof. He couldn't figure her moods, and it forced him to be alert. It kept him on edge.

"By the way," said Brenda. "I like your earring."

Instantly, his hand went to his ear, and he angled his head away.

"You're embarrassed."

"It looks stupid."

"C'mon. Lots of guys wear earrings. It's no big deal."

"Frankie gave it to me."

"You should be proud then."

"I never wore jewelry before."

"It's a fast-moving world, Terry. Earrings today, no telling what it'll be tomorrow."

"You don't think I look like a sissy?"

"What's a sissy?"

"Seriously."

She laughed. "The H word, huh? That's what's worrying you?"

"It's so big," he said, fingering the hoop. "Most guys wear studs or little rings."

"You're in love, right? So take what the lady gives. Be grateful. It looks fine. Don't worry about it."

"I appreciate the vote of confidence." He started off. "Just for your information, I'm not worried about the H word."

"No?"

"No." He grinned. "I'm already a hunk."

Brenda grinned back. "Sure you are, you harlot you."

Marcus's reaction was not so very different. He and Terry ran into each other at shift change the next day, Marcus on his way in, Terry out. They slapped hands.

"I ain't seen you around," said Marcus. "Where you been hidin'?"

"Same place you left me the first time. Cleaning up the shit."

"Ain't that the truth." He hung up his clothes and put on his work scrubs. "They givin' you trouble?"

Terry shook his head.

"They will. You just ride it. Do like I do." He stood stock still and hooded his eyes. "Blind, deaf and dumb. That's the way they want it. Might as well oblige." He locked his locker. "Take a walk?"

"I should be going."

"You working tonight?"

"Home. Frankie's expecting me."

"Sure she is. And what you s'pose she want more, a happy man or a harried one?" With an arm over his friend's shoulder he ushered Terry down the hall that led to the secluded courtyard. Once there, he fired up a skinny roach.

"You run too fast and you on the run. A woman see that, she find a way to use it." He loosened his limbs and took a few lazy turns around the patio. "Take my man Charles. He quick with a gun, the rest of the time he slow and easy. The women, they come to him like flies to ripe fruit."

"I'm not looking for women," said Terry. "The one I've got is just fine."

"Sure you're right." He held out the joint, but Terry shook his head.

"I really should get going."

"Fine is right," said Marcus. "You don't watch out, they put a tax on you, haul you off for rehabilitation. Make you nice and clean, like candy. Wrap you up and pop you on their pretty little tongues when they want something sweet."

He smoked down the roach, dowsed it with spit and tossed it in his mouth. Then he turned a big-toothed grin on his friend and clapped him on the shoulder.

"My man Terry. Rolling with the punches."

"I'm showing her how good a man can be. It's something I owe her. Something I promised myself."

"You go to church?" asked Marcus. Terry shook his head.

"They got a lot of words there for what a man should and shouldn't do. A lot of advice on how you s'posed to behave."

"I'm helping myself. Frankie and me, we're getting it together."

"You get it, you got it." He winked, then noticed the earring. Terry explained how it was a gift, which drew a chuckle from Marcus.

"You a marked man now. The lady, she got her hook in."

This irritated Terry. "Something wrong with that?"

"No man, it's cool. You a stud."

"You're ragging me too much, Marcus. Cut it out."

The big man frowned and looked over his shoulder, as though searching for someone to blame. He took off his scrub hat and ran a hand across his head. He regarded his friend.

"We just goofin'," he said. "Jammin'. You go ahead and show your stuff and I tell you something. Ain't no man with a higher spirit than a man in love. It's a stone fact. You do what you want and don't listen to no one tells you different. The lady love you, you go on and love her right back."

Tectonics

Things you can do right now to improve your looks[12]:

1. *Devote five minutes to stretching exercises each morning.*
2. *Stop crossing your legs.*
3. *Put a two-by-four under the top legs of your bed, so fluid won't collect (and make bags) under your eyes as you sleep.*
4. *Stop frowning (tape your forehead—when alone—to help).*
5. *Order virgin marys at cocktail parties.*
6. *Sit way back in your chair so you won't slump in the middle.*
7. *Buy a pair of cheap, vulgar rhinestone earrings; wear them with self-assurance.*
8. *Stick your face in the freezer compartment and count to one hundred just before leaving for work every morning.*
9. *Keep the electric depilatory needle handy.*
10. *Cinch your belt a notch tighter.*
11. *Hire someone of the opposite sex to fawn over you in public.*
12. *Glitter your cheeks with gold.*
13. *Wear feathers.*
14. *Scour your face with baking soda and rinse with warm milk.*
15. *Rid your mind of ugly thoughts. Work hard. Beauty comes from within. Get a rhytidectomy.*

16

That week Frankie got a call from Edna. She was coming into the city to shop and invited her daughter to meet her for lunch. Pointedly, she requested that she try not to look like a homeless person. An instant before hanging up, as though it were an afterthought, she asked how Frankie was doing.

"Fine. I'm doing fine."

"That boy. He's not giving you problems?"

"Everything's under control."

"I'm glad. But you be careful. You never know when things might take a turn for the worse."

Frankie did not reply.

"Tuesday then?" said Edna. "At noon. You won't forget?"

"No."

"Please. It's so humiliating to be stood up."

They met the following week at the Plaza as planned. Spring had retreated a step, and there was a chill in the air. Edna wore a tweed suit and gloves, and Frankie had on slacks and a baggy sweater. Edna couldn't help but comment.

"I don't understand you. You have such a nice figure. Why do you hide it?"

Frankie glanced around the restaurant self-consciously and tugged at his sweater. "I don't want to be stared at. Especially not in public."

"What's wrong with being looked at? You're an attractive woman. You should be proud."

"I'm not."

Edna made a face. "At my age, I can understand. But yours? Let the people see."

"Why?"

"Why? Because a pretty woman, a nice woman, makes the world a better place. And Lord knows, we need more of that."

Frankie had no interest in making the world a better place. Nor, based on his experience, did he have any power whatsoever in that regard.

"It's not all vanity," said Edna. "You take care of yourself, it rubs off. Believe me. It affects how you're treated."

"I've been treated like shit."

Edna bristled at both the word and the disclosure. "You told me things were better. You said they were under control."

"Now they are. They weren't before."

"You don't have to placate me. Tell me the truth."

"The truth is it's all right. I'm learning. It's an adventure."

Edna searched her daughter's face, and at length, seemingly mollified, returned to the menu. "It's there for the asking, Frankie. I've always tried to teach you that. You just have to ask."

They ate lunch, while Frankie considered the situation. Despite his self-consciousness, he was eager to learn more, to build up his store of ammunition. With both the means and the knowledge, Edna presented the perfect opportunity, and when they were done, he took her advice and asked if she'd take him shopping. The shock almost knocked her over.

They went, of course, to Bergdorf's, Edna's mainstay. She kept modestly abreast of fashion and was aware of some of the more trendy boutiques on Madison Avenue, but Bergdorf's held for her an unassailable position of elegance, tradition and style. She guided Frankie through the polished doors and across the marble floor to the elevators. A uniformed attendant was waiting inside and with a curt nod took them up. There were three other women in the elevator, all expensively dressed. Frankie hung close to Edna, who, after reaching their floor, walked briskly toward the rear wall, where a saleslady was working behind a chest-high counter. The woman stopped what she was doing and looked up.

"Mrs. De Leon. Did you forget something?"

"I've brought my daughter. Francesca, this is Nina. Nina, Francesca."

The woman came from behind the counter and shook Frankie's hand. She was in her fifties, wore a mauve sweater-dress belted at the waist and a Hermès scarf around her neck. Her grip was firm.

"It's a pleasure. Your mother and I, we've known each other for years."

"We're having an unexpected fling," said Edna happily.

"The best kind," smiled Nina. She scrutinized Frankie. "What exactly did you have in mind?"

Edna took control, suggesting something casual as a start. Nina nodded and took them to several different racks, by the end of which they'd selected three outfits: two dresses and a blouse-skirt combination. Frankie took the first, an eggshell white sleeveless gown, to the changing room and put it on. It was made of jersey cut on the bias and gathered asymmetrically at the waist, below which it fell in gentle folds to the knee. Nina adjusted it when he came out, then stepped back and took stock.

"It's meant to be worn with a bra," she told Edna, who gave Frankie a look.

"My daughter doesn't believe in them." She folded her hands rather primly and turned her attention to the dress. "I like the lines. It has an airy feel to it. Youthful."

Frankie looked in the mirror. The dress seemed very feminine. It made him look graceful, almost statuesque. He could see that appeal. The bareness of the arms, however, made him feel naked.

"It's a romantic look," said Nina. "Elegant, though not forced."

"Turn around, dear."

Frankie did as he was told, and the dress flared a little before settling back on his legs. It was very light to the touch, almost a caress.

"I feel exposed," he said.

"Well of course," said Edna. "It's a summer dress. Let's see how the other one looks."

Frankie returned to the dressing room, slipped the dress off and got into the second, a brushed cotton jacquard with boat neck, puffed sleeves and a long, flaring skirt. Sewed into the waist was a lollipop pink stretch belt. The outfit was loud, almost painfully garish.

"Walk a little," Edna told him when he came out, and he paraded for the women, feeling something like a toy.

"It's for someone fuller," said Edna. "More body."

"Again, it needs a bra. Maybe a little padding."

Edna nodded without conviction. "How does it feel, Frankie?"

"I feel silly."

"I agree. It's too obvious. And the color doesn't do you justice. Go ahead and try the other."

The last outfit was a combination. The skirt was a rosy satin, straight, short and tight. The blouse was silk, with capped sleeves and a deep vee neck. As he tucked it in, the sleek material grazed a nipple, causing him to shiver involuntarily. He frowned and waited for the sensation to subside, then went outside.

"I like the blouse," said Edna. "The skirt . . . I don't know. It's awfully leggy."

"She's lucky to have them. Walk a little, dear."

Frankie went to the mirror, turned and walked back. The skirt barely reached mid-thigh, yet its snugness restricted his movement, forcing him to take mincing, half-steps. He felt awkward and at risk.

"It's sexy," said Edna. "I'll admit that."

"Um-hm. Heels would lengthen the line even more. And maybe a string of pearls. She has a lovely neck."

"Though I have to say I'm not sure that's exactly what we want. Beauty is one thing, exhibitionism quite another."

"You have to remember where we are," said Nina. "In New York, this is what people expect. Young people especially."

"There's plenty of opportunity without being a beacon." Edna turned to her daughter. "What do you think, dear?"

Frankie was bewildered. His original purpose had become obscured not only by the clothes themselves, the array of fabric, color and style, of texture and fit, but by the two women, whose breezy commentary seemed to hide deeper meanings.

"I don't know what to think." He stared in the mirror, fingering the blouse. "Maybe I do need a bra."

"Good for you," chirped Edna. She told him to go inside and change and bring the rest of the clothes out. At the counter they sorted through the three outfits. There was broad agreement on the first, which was kept, and the second, which wasn't. Edna and Nina disagreed on the third, Edna willing to buy the blouse but not the skirt, Nina urging her to get both. Just as the saleslady was in the process of a diplomatic retreat, Frankie, who to that point had been silently trying to make sense of it all, spoke up. Perhaps it was Edna's earlier comment that the skirt looked sexy. Perhaps it was Nina's dogged persistence. Something lit in his brain, and he told Edna he wanted the skirt too. The request was rewarded with a scowl, followed by a look of maternal tolerance. In a different situation Edna would have dug in, but she was on something of a roll with her daughter and didn't want to jinx it. Feeling terribly indulgent and secretly thrilled, she bought the skirt too. Then she took Frankie by the arm and led her to the escalator.

One flight up was lingerie, its ethic heralded by a milk-skinned mannequin in black lace bra and panties. Other mannequins, in teddies, camisoles and peignoirs, were scattered like guides across the floor.

"I don't know why everything has to be sex sex sex," muttered Edna. "Just because a woman needs underclothes doesn't mean she has to flaunt herself."

Frankie had seen similar garments in other stores, but never in such profusion. He wanted to linger, but Edna kept tugging him along. All at once she stopped.

"Like that," she said, pointing to a thong brief barely wider than a rubber band. "Why would a woman ever wear something like that?"

Frankie got a chill. Bleakly, he recalled the night at Virgo's when Cox had forced the g-string on him. He had a sudden urge to flee.

Edna pulled him along until she found a saleslady, who led them to a rack of bras. She took several out, some of which had proper names. Celeste, Intima, Jubilee: Frankie had trouble paying attention. His curiosity was faltering in the face of a nameless dread. He kept glancing around, certain that he was being watched.

"Which do you like?" Edna was asking.

"I want to go."

"It's been a long afternoon, hasn't it? We're nearly done."

The saleslady held up a sheer bra with scalloped cups. "This one's just in from Paris. The underwire is programmed to return automatically to its original shape. It's a good day-to-night bra. Quite versatile."

She waited. Frankie tried to control his fear by focusing on his reason to be in the store to begin with. He thought of Terry and marshaled his strength.

"It's fine."

"There're others," said Edna, lifting a bra adorned with lace. "This one is nice."

"Fine."

"Which do you prefer?"

"It doesn't matter."

Edna glanced at the saleslady. "Well then. I guess we'll take both. You're sure of the size?"

The woman appraised Frankie with an eye that in twenty years had sized upward of a quarter million breasts and nodded confidently. She rang up the sale and handed them a bag with the merchandise inside. Edna led Frankie away.

"You must be tired," she said when they were outside. "I'll treat you to a cab home. I still have one or two more errands to run."

"Errands? This was an errand?"

"A nice one," Edna assured her.

Frankie was nonplussed. "It seemed so monumental."

"What? Buying you clothes?" Edna smiled, patting her daughter's hand. "It was fun, wasn't it? You made your mother very happy."

They walked a block or two together, Edna's mood gradually sobering until it became clear something was gnawing at her.

"If you stay with me much longer, you're going to end up hearing a piece of my mind."

Frankie wasn't ready to be alone and unconsciously slipped his arm through Edna's. The older woman took it as a cue.

"Just how long do you plan on staying with this man? It's your life, I know, but it's mine being your mother. I can't forget how you looked. I don't think I'll ever forget."

"I'm better now."

"Don't these things have patterns? Something could happen again."

Frankie had not told her about the rape, not specifically, and it was not the kind of thought that would instinctively enter Edna's mind. But there were ample other horrors for her to imagine. At first she had blamed Terry. Later, it was herself.

"I worry, Frankie. I want life to be good to you. That's what a mother hopes for. Even before she bothers to hope for herself, she wants her child to be happy."

"He hasn't hurt me again. He won't."

"How can you be sure?"

Frankie had to think about that. He considered his life to that point, the cruel tricks of fate, the up-

heaval and the violence, each incident as gratuitous
and unexpected as the next. He couldn't imagine
being harmed more than he had been. In a curious
way it made him feel invulnerable.

"Promise me if something happens, you'll call. It
doesn't have to be me. Someone. Anyone."

"Nothing's going to happen. Believe me. I'm
stronger now. He understands. I'm in control."

"Maybe you are strong, but you're mulish too.
You've always been that way." Edna faced her
daughter. She was having trouble containing her
fear. "Being stubborn isn't the same as being strong,
Frankie. Especially not when it puts you in danger."

"I'm not," he said, both because he believed it and
because he wanted to put her at ease, to reassure
this woman he had grown fond of. At the same time,
her constant intimations of weakness and danger
had the effect of eroding his self-confidence and
threatening his resolve. He did not want to become
the victim of self-doubt. It was time to get away.

"I'll be all right," he told her. Without thinking, he
leaned over and kissed her on the cheek. "You've
been a big help. Thank you."

He picked up the bags and started off. Edna
brushed away a tear.

"Please wear stockings with that skirt. And a bra.
And don't forget to hang up the blouse when you get
home or it'll wrinkle. Promise me. I love you."

Frankie rested when he got home, had a light dinner, then dressed. He wore the lace-edged bra, the
silk blouse and satin skirt. He did his hair as best he
could, then opened the latest issue of *Vogue* to an

article on makeup and spent the next hour doing his face. When he was done, he watched a tape of "Dallas" and practiced his sitting and walking. It was kind of fun. Having no recollection of a personality, he had no compunction changing it. He felt, in fact, a certain gleeful abandonment, a licentiousness that seemed to accompany his charade. The art of deception used a wide palette. Nothing, it seemed, was forbidden.

At a quarter to twelve he retired to his bedroom and waited for Terry. It wasn't long, and when he heard Terry in the hall, he called through his closed door that he'd be out in a minute.

Terry dragged himself to the living room and collapsed on the couch. He was too tired to eat, too exhausted to think. His head was already nodding off when Frankie appeared in the doorway. He blinked and shook himself awake.

"Jesus."

Frankie stood very still. He felt unexpectedly apprehensive. "I've been playing with myself a little."

Terry was dumbfounded.

"Do you like what I've done?"

"God, you're beautiful."

"I'm not."

"You're right. You're not beautiful, you're fucking gorgeous. What did I ever do to deserve you?"

"Everyone deserves someone. That seems to be the message around here."

"You're moving out of my league, babe." He shook his head. "Way out."

Frankie liked that. He lifted his chin the way he'd seen a woman on TV do and took a few measured steps. He leaned against the door frame and cocked a hip. Terry fanned himself.

"You walk around the streets like that, someone's gonna make a pass. You could start a riot."

"You think?"

"I'm serious. It's rough out there. You've got to be careful."

"Don't worry yourself."

"C'mere."

Frankie kept his distance, feigning coyness.

"C'mon, babe. Don't tell me you got all dressed up just for yourself."

"You haven't showered."

"I'll shower later."

"Fine. I'll come back."

"I'm too tired."

"I understand." He started out of the room. "It's been a long day. I'll let you get some rest."

"I'll shower," said Terry.

Frankie stopped, then smiled. "That's my boy."

For the second time that day Terry showered and shaved. He cleaned his earring with alcohol, combed his hair and put on fresh clothes. When he came out, Frankie was sitting on the couch.

"Tell me something," said Terry. "Where'd you get the money for that?"

"You're a good provider."

"Sure I am. And I know for a fact what I earn doesn't make a dent in something like that. Where'd you get it?"

"Don't underestimate yourself."

"Bullshit. Edna?"

Frankie kept his mouth shut.

"Who, Frankie?"

"No one."

"The fuck no one. Who bought you the clothes?"

"What do you care?"

"Listen to that." He came toward her. "You cheating on me, Frankie? You got someone on the side?"

"There's no one."

"Someone who swings a tad looser than old Terry. Who lives a cut above."

"Who could that be?"

He laughed harshly, mimicking her words. "Someone who doesn't shovel shit all day. Someone with a little money. A little respect."

"I don't want money, Terry."

"No? Then why the fuck you got me busting ass all day and night?"

"You're not happy? You want me to leave?"

"I want you to give me something besides words. Besides promises."

"Promises? What promises? Name one."

"Dreams then. Hopes." He faced her. "I'm not stupid, Frankie. I know you're getting back at me."

"Why would I do that?"

He hesitated, shamed by the answer. Frankie asked again.

"I'd do it to you," Terry said softly, wishing it could be different, wishing their whole relationship could be something other than what it was. "Don't," he begged. "Please don't."

"Or what? You'll hit me?" Frankie gave him his cheek. "Go ahead."

Terry stared at the smooth skin, the lips, the long, graceful neck. With a shudder he turned away.

"You see?" said Frankie. "It's not so hard being nice. Not when you put your mind to it."

On an impulse he kicked off his heels and rolled his stockings off. "You want to touch me? Here. Rub my feet. We'll see how you do."

Her toes were cold, and fleetingly, Terry thought of her heart. Taking a foot in each hand and kneeling at her side, he began to rub.

Terry's jealousy bore down. He couldn't shake the image of Frankie parading around the city in tight skirt and blouse, in any garb for that matter. To him she was irresistible, and he was certain that other men could not help but be equally enthralled. He was fretful and suspicious, and her flirtaciousness only made matters worse. He tried to lose himself at work, taking on extra tasks, skipping meals. He pulled doubles at the hospital whenever he could. He drove himself to the point of collapse.

Marcus finally pulled him aside. It was the end of swing shift, Terry's fourth double that week. Marcus took him outside behind one of the dumpsters and literally forced him to get high. Afterward, he took him to a bar, where the two of them knocked down half a dozen beers. Terry loosened up for the first time in weeks, and by the time he got home, he was swaggering like a pirate. He passed Frankie's door, which was ajar, then stopped and went back. It was 2 A.M., and she was sitting at the vanity she had bought a few weeks before, putting on lipstick. Terry swung the door open and entered.

Frankie, who but a moment before had been feeling overwhelmed by the task of impersonation, diminished by it and drained of both spirit and desire, hid his relief. Terry's entrance brought back his purpose. It reminded him of the challenge, and for the moment at least, kept him from turning back. He finished what he was doing, screwed the lipstick down and put the cap on. Then he picked up an eyebrow pencil.

"Going out?" asked Terry.

"You didn't knock."

"It's my apartment. Are you?"

"No."

"It's two in the morning. Why are you doing that?"

"This? It's something a woman does."

"You're lying."

"It takes time to look right. It doesn't just happen."

"You're seeing someone." He took a step closer. "Who?"

"You, Terry. You're the only one I'm seeing. The only one I want." He finished with the pencil, then found a long ribbon and tied it in his hair. "You have trouble believing that?"

"I want what's mine."

"And what is that? Do you even know?"

"You. I want you."

Frankie felt a wave of disgust.

"A touch," said Terry. "A kiss. Something real."

Frankie had to struggle with himself before finally extending a stiff hand. Terry took it, gently at first, luxuriating in the simple touch of flesh. He brought his lips down and kissed each finger, then did the same to the palm and wrist. He moved to the arm,

and when Frankie resisted, held her tig[...]
haled her scent and kissed the soft belly o[...]
ceps. He wanted more, but a voice told him not [...]
greedy. A different voice told him to take what was
his. He too had to struggle with himself before deciding. With a sharp tug he pulled her off the chair
and into his arms.

Frankie stiffened but did not raise a hand. In a
stern, commanding voice he ordered Terry off.

He hugged her tighter.

"I'm not asking twice."

There was a moment of indecision, then slowly the
life went out of Terry's embrace. His arms slid off
her waist. He backed away.

"I'm disappointed in you," said Frankie, wiping
his arms as though sloughing himself of dead skin.
"I thought you could be trusted."

Terry hung his head.

"Obviously I was wrong."

"All I did was hold you," he muttered. "A man
can't hold his woman?"

"A man has to earn his woman. It takes more than
a few good days."

"I wasn't hurting you."

Frankie's eyes flashed. "You could never do anything like that."

"That man's dead."

"Don't say that. I want him alive, walking, breathing. I want him here with me. I want him to watch.
To see."

"I wouldn't hurt you. I swear."

"Who then? Who would you hurt?"

"No one."

"Please, don't insult my intelligence. You know the answer to this. Who is it? Who would you hurt?"

In ignorance he shook his head, and Frankie sighed in disappointment.

"Such progress, then this. It's frustrating."

"I'm sorry."

"I should leave. Obviously it's too hard."

"No. Please." He panicked, clasping his hands tightly behind his back. "I won't touch you. I swear. Not until you say."

Frankie looked at him sadly. "I'm sorry."

"Tie them if you don't trust me."

"What?"

"My hands. Tie them."

"I couldn't do that."

"Do it. If that's what it takes."

"I wouldn't know how."

"There's rope in the kitchen."

Frankie frowned, but Terry could see he had a foot in the door. He went to the kitchen, pulled out a length of quarter-inch clothesline, cut it and hurried back to the bedroom. Frankie took it and, following instructions, began to wrap Terry's wrists. But the rope was stiff and hard to work with, and it had an institutional feel that seemed at odds with a very personal moment. Frankie searched the room for something more fitting. There was a leather belt in the bureau, stockings, a cheap bolo tie. In the mirror he happened to catch sight of the ribbon in his hair. It was blue, like his eyes, and made of silk. He pulled it out, unwrapped the cord from Terry's wrists and wound the ribbon in its place. He pulled it tight, then Terry instructed him on a good surgeon's knot.

When it was finished, Terry tried to free himself, twisting and tugging until he was sure the cuff was secure.

"Nice job," he said admiringly. "Now what?"

"You tell me."

"I sip from your hand? Eat from your palm?"

Frankie studied him, wondering at his seeming jocularity. Clearly, there was still much to learn. Hooking a finger over the ribbon, he tugged the man backward down the hall.

"For now," he said, "how about trying to act like a human."

In Lieu of Mascara

In order to excite voluptuous sensation during intercourse, savage races make use of various means . . . In Abyssinia, and on the Zanzibar coast, young girls receive instruction in certain rotary muscular movements known by the name of duk-duk, which they employ during coitus for the increase of sexual pleasure. Many Daiaks perforate the glans penis with a silver needle from above downwards; this needle is kept in place like a seton, until a permanent canal is formed through the glans: in order during coitus to stimulate the woman more powerfully, into this canal, just before coitus, various small articles are inserted, such as little rods of brass, ivory, or bamboo, or silver instruments ending in small bundles of bristles; these project from the surface of the glans, and exercise a more powerful friction on the vagina, thus increasing the sexual pleasure of the woman. Men without such an apparatus are rejected by the women, while those who have made several such canals in the glans, and can therefore insert several instruments, are especially sought after and prized by the women. Such an apparatus is known as an ampallang, and in a symbolic manner the woman indicates to a man of her choice her desire that he should make use of one; he finds in his bowl of rice a rolled-up leaf, enclosing a cigarette which represents the size of the desired ampallang. Among the Alfurs of North Celebes, in order to increase the voluptuous pleasure of the woman during intercourse, the men bind round the coronal glandis the eyelids of a goat, beset with the eyelashes, thus forming a bristly collar; in Java and in Sunda, before coitus, the men surround the penis with strips of goatskin, leaving the glans free. In China they wind round the corona glandis torn fragments of a bird's wing; these also project like bristles and increase the friction. Among the Batta of Sumatra, travelling medicine men perform an operation by means of which they insert, beneath the skin of the penis, small stones, sometimes to the number of ten, at times also angular fragments of gold or silver; these heal in beneath the skin, and increase the stimulus of coitus for the women.[13]

The next day Frankie made a friend. He heard a scratching at the window and pulled back the curtain to find a cat on the ledge. It was brindle, with a white mark on the forehead and green eyes. He let it in and poured out a saucer of milk, but the cat seemed more intent on rubbing against his leg. It purred when he stroked behind its ear, then lay on the floor and presented its belly. Frankie petted until the animal tired of the attention and with an effortless leap disappeared out the window. In the following days Frankie found ways to lure it back. He put out food, left his window open, called to it. He bought a toy mouse stuffed with catnip. The cat became a daily visitor and soon staked out a spot of its own near the radiator. Often it would curl up in his lap while the two of them watched TV. Frankie tendered the thought of shutting his window and claiming the cat for his own, but he was too sensitive to the idea of imprisonment to go through with it. The cat came and went to its own tune. There seemed little value in a friendship predicated otherwise.

There was, however, a price. As Frankie's affection for the animal grew, so too did his awareness of the emptiness and lack of companionship elsewhere. His life to that point had been one trauma after another, the only calm moments being those that presaged a storm. He had been unable to steer his thinking much beyond the question of survival, and indeed, had he been offered a gentler life, assuming he did not reject the idea outright as a sham and a lie, he would have said no. There was something about the action that kept him going, something addictive in the punches and counterpunches, the dogfight. As much as they hurt and robbed him of humanity, they also gave him reason to live. Revenge was purpose. Love was revenge.

But the cat's appearance, its instinctive affection and unbiased acceptance, challenged the necessity of that life. In the huge chunks of time he was alone, with nothing to do and no one but the cat to see, the possibility of a different kind of existence nibbled at him. One where keeping his edge was less than paramount. Where cooperation stood in place of combat, and tranquillity in place of violence. It wasn't impossible. It was water trickling down a hillside. The gathering of gravity. A stream.

To a certain degree he found companionship in television. The characters in the morning soaps were friends of a sort; the hosts of the afternoon talks, sisterly and avuncular. And there were books too, though it took time to get to know the characters, and when a story was done, the relationships were over. One or two hours a day he spent staring out the window, observing the habits of strangers, imagining what it would be like to be normal. He watched the Chinese husband and wife selling produce across the street, envying their industry and activity. He longed to reach out, but everyone seemed so preoccupied, so purposeful and ultimately remote. He was apart from the world and in desperate need of a connection. Something more than the cat, more than the TV and the passive hours at the window. If not a friend, then at least a hobby. Something to occupy his mind.

He took up sewing. Inspired by the women in the factory and a show he happened to catch on public TV, he found a fabric store on West Broadway, where he bought needles, thread and some material. It took him a week, during which time he ripped out twice as many seams as he sewed, but by the end he had a pair of curtains. He returned to the store for more material and made another set for the other window in his room. To this pair he added backing

to give a better shape to the pleats. He bought a book
on sewing and began to experiment with different
fabrics and stitches. From his frequent visits to the
store he got to know the saleswomen, one of whom,
a career seamstress named Luisa, took a liking to
him. She had sharp eyes, a faint moustache and an
avocation for dolls, for whom she made lavish, designer outfits, classics from Balmain, Balenciaga,
Givenchy. The miniature suits and gowns cost a
fraction of the price of normal-sized clothes, and she
could create whatever she wanted, fashions and
styles that she herself would never dream of wearing. Her enthusiasm rubbed off on Frankie. He
didn't have dolls but he did have the cat, and while
he knew the animal would never permit itself to be
clothed, he started sewing for it anyway. He made a
little coat of satin with tiny buttons and a snap at the
collar. He made velvet pants, booties, a bonnet. The
woman at the store lent him a breathtaking Dior
pattern that took weeks to measure, cut and sew. He
learned beading and appliqué, cutting on the bias
and smocking. He taught himself the rudiments of
embroidery. Every two or three days he brought his
projects to the store for advice and encouragement.
Luisa brought a few of her own, a black velvet
sheath dress with sleeves of sheer crepe, a halter-
neck tunic of forest green silk, a strapless organdy
gown triply flounced and underlined by chartreuse
taffeta. The two of them fell into a fervent, if narrow,
friendship. They had lunch together. Luisa took him
to a doll show in Brooklyn. They talked ruffles, cuffs
and closures. Shirring and the versatility of the
rolled collar. On the train home Luisa asked if

Frankie had ever sewn for men. It wasn't difficult, she said, as long as you kept a firm hand and an even disposition. Good-naturedly, she threatened to introduce him to her son.

At home Frankie put on a different face. He kept the sewing a secret and was careful to hide all evidence of the cat. It was a strain, but he was unwilling to share either of his newfound pleasures. He didn't want to appear soft or vulnerable, fearing that Terry would somehow use it to his advantage. When they were together, his sole objective was to remain in control. Any impulse that threatened that stance had to be kept at bay.

This emotional austerity did not, as a rule, extend beyond Terry. With Edna, Luisa and other more casual acquaintances he was cordial, even openhearted. At times it disturbed him to have such antithetical emotions, and he wished he could feel one way or the other, either vengeful or forgiving, secretive or forthcoming. Living in such contradiction was not only a strain but it seemed artificial, a contrivance of will rather than nature. But then he was an artificial being. Fractured and flawed to begin with. What could he expect?

One afternoon Marcus appeared at the apartment. Frankie had not seen him since returning to the city, and once he got over the shock of a visitor, he eagerly let him in. Marcus was expecting to find Terry, and when he heard Terry was at work, he turned around to leave. Frankie quickly shut the door before he could.

"Won't you stay? Just a few minutes. I haven't talked to anyone for days."

It wasn't Marcus's custom to be alone with someone else's woman, but Frankie was insistent. Reluctantly, he followed her to the kitchen.

"Something hot? Tea? Coffee?"

"A glass of water'll do fine."

"Coke? How about a Coke?"

"Just water. Wet my lips then I'll be moving along."

Frankie got him the water and the two of them sat at the table.

"It's been a long time," said Frankie. "How're you doing? How's your aunt?"

"Haven't heard from Auntie O. She back home with her people. I expect she doing all right."

"You?"

"I got no complaints." He paused, glancing around. "Terry, he didn't leave me nothing?"

"Like what?"

"A little smoke. He said to come on by."

"He didn't say anything to me."

"Course you're right. I should be going."

"Wait." He fumbled for something to to say to keep Marcus from leaving. "How're your guns?"

Marcus looked puzzled.

"Got any new ones?"

"Got my eye on one. A pretty little Smith and Wesson forty-four. I keep telling Terry he ought to get himself a weapon. Learn how to shoot."

"Terry's a pacifist these days."

"Don't matter what you call yourself. You know how to shoot you be whatever you want."

"And what's that?"

"What's what?"

"What you want to be."

He gave her a look. "You foolin' with me? What kind of question is that?"

"Too personal?"

"I got a job, ain't I? I pay the bills. I send a little to the kids. Besides that, I keep to my own business and don't hurt nobody that don't hurt me. A man do all that, I say he's doing all right."

"You're happy then."

He screwed up his face. "Wasn't that me just talking?"

"You make it sound easy."

He stood up. "I best be going."

"Wait." On the spur of the moment Frankie made a decision. "I've got something to show you."

He hurried to his closet, took out his box of creations and brought it to the table. Marcus, whose hands dwarfed the petite costumes, was impressed. He admired the workmanship and attention to detail. He especially liked the diminutive zippers and tiny buttons. They reminded him of the intricate parts of his own toys.

Warmed by his praise, Frankie had an inspiration. He returned to the bedroom for a tape measure, then came back and told Marcus he wanted to sew him a shirt.

Marcus was flattered, but this was moving beyond the realm of propriety. He started down the hall, but Frankie kept at him, blocking his way, insisting. Marcus said something about Terry, and Frankie lied, saying he was already working on a gift for him. He told Marcus a shirt would give him something to do, something to keep him out of trouble. He asked his favorite color.

"Pink," Marcus replied as a joke, seeking to deter her.

"What shade?" asked Frankie. "Salmon, rose, coral, peony . . ."

Marcus shook his head in bewilderment, and Frankie grinned. Undraping the tape from his neck, he took the measurements.

It was harder than he expected, mainly because Marcus wouldn't return for a fitting. Luisa offhandedly suggested her own son as a model, an offer that Frankie politely declined. Taking breaks only when Terry was home, he worked a week straight and ended up with three shirts, one pink, one maroon and one violet. He wrapped them carefully in a box and with a sense of satisfaction and pride brought them to the post office. Once the package was out of his hands, however, his spirits fell. The project had been a respite, but now it was done. His sanity depended on keeping busy. It was a matter of survival.

He wandered home and turned on the TV. It had been a week since he'd watched, and after thirty minutes he became impatient. He went to his room and called the cat, but the cat didn't come. He put out food in the living room and waited on the couch. One of the ribbons he used to tie Terry's hands was lying beside him. It was several inches wide, more a sash than a ribbon, and absently, he started playing with it, tying slip knots and pulling them out, smoothing the wrinkles. He kept glancing at the doorway, expecting to see the cat. An ad came on, and his impatience grew. He thought of Marcus's shirts. He looked at the ribbon. Suddenly, he had an idea.

He took the sash to his room, pulled out needle, thread and some sequins, and sewed a few on. Then he got his embroidery hoop and made a small heart. Liking how it looked, he made another, then popped open the hoop and added more sequins. He draped the sash across the upper frame of his vanity mirror, unfurling it like a banner or strip of holiday bunting. The sequins picked up light from outside. The hearts seemed to be floating in a field of tears.

That night after dinner he brought the sash out. Terry, as had become his custom, was waiting with his hands behind his back. At the sight of the gaily decorated ribbon, his eyes widened.

"You don't like it," said Frankie, deliberately mis-interpreting his reaction.

"I do. It's lovely. I didn't know you sewed."

"When I have time."

"It's for me? You made it for me?"

"Only for you."

Terry liked that. "It's too bad I won't be able to see it. All wrapped up and behind my back."

Frankie paused to give the matter some thought. He too found it unfortunate that his artistry would go unseen. It was something to work on.

The days passed, and he got into his new project in a serious way. To sequins he added paillettes and other spangles, and from simple hearts he moved to flowers and small animals. Inspired by the bras Edna had introduced him to at Bergdorf's, he gave names to the sashes—Intimacy, Rapture, Conquest —monikers he embroidered in a flowing, graceful script. As his designs became more elaborate, Terry became outspoken in his appreciation and praise. His jealousy receded in the face of Frankie's attentiveness, and he took pains to show his gratitude. Frankie fed on this, and his desire to decorate the man grew. He itched to do more than a sash, whose design was quickly hidden once it was tied around Terry's wrists. More than a shirt or pants, which could easily be removed. He had seen insignia on various clothes, alligators, polo men, stitched designer names. He wanted something like that, a badge, a crest, something to remind Terry of his station, to mark him. Something lasting.

One evening he took extra care getting ready before Terry came home. In a magazine he had seen a hairdo that struck a chord, and earlier that day Luisa had taken him to a friend who was a hairdresser. The cut was boyishly short in back and raked up from the jawline on the sides. The hairdresser also did something to take out some of the curl, and then she sprayed it. The faint, cloying scent still hung around his face.

Frankie had read an article on body hair, and for the first time he shaved his legs and armpits. The razor scraped and cut, but he was willing to put up with the discomfort. It was a special occasion, and he chose the skirt and blouse he had worn before. In addition, he put on net stockings and heels with dainty ankle straps. Knowing by now how easy it was to charm and captivate Terry gave him a certain satisfaction, but also it made him sad and a little disappointed. The man was not turning out to be much of an adversary at all. It seemed pointless and unnecessarily cruel to harm him. On the other hand, these games seemed to make him so happy, or what passed for happiness in their strange and twisted affair. In any other setting Frankie might actually have thought the man was thriving.

He was just finishing with his lipstick when the locks turned in the front door. Again he waited until Terry was in the living room to make his entrance. The effect was immediate and predictable. Terry grinned like a kid. The short hair and heels had him nearly creaming on the spot. Without missing a beat, Frankie pulled out a ribbon, a new one he had just that day decorated. It was baby blue, and unlike the others, lacked all form of embellishment, all save a single embroidered word. Bliss. Simple, elegant and impossible to misconstrue. When Terry saw it, his grin got bigger. And bigger still when Frankie told him to take off his shirt.

He obeyed instantly, fantasies of long-denied delights leaping to the forefront of his brain. Greedily, he thrust his hands behind his back.

Frankie found Terry's eagerness pathetic, but it helped set his resolve. He bound Terry's wrists tightly, then went to the bedroom for his sewing kit and a small jewelry box. Inside the box on a square of cotton were the cupid earrings Terry had bought him months before. He held them in his palm.

"Remember these?"

"Do I remember?" said Terry with a smile. "Ask my heart. That's where the little guy got me. Right in the heart."

"I want you to wear one."

"They're for you."

"One for me, one for you."

"I have an earring already."

Frankie lifted one of the cherubs and gently swung it back and forth. "It's shooting arrows. Feel?"

"What kind of guy wears a cupid in his ear?" said Terry. "I'd be embarrassed."

"I wouldn't want that."

"Then we agree."

"Close your eyes."

From the sewing kit Frankie took out a heavy curved needle that was already threaded. Grasping it between thumb and forefinger, he circled the air above Terry's chest.

"Ping, ping," he whispered, drawing the needle closer. "Ping, ping, ping," closer and closer until, ever so lightly, it pricked the skin on Terry's breast.

"The arrow landed." Frankie's voice was innocent, almost tender. "Right where you said. It's your heart, Terry. Your pious, noble, loving heart. Let's put cupid there."

17

In the next weeks Terry's love took wing. By some miracle of patience or understanding, attrition perhaps, or simple fatigue, the barriers between him and Frankie seemed to dissolve. The magnitude of his sin, which had kept him weak and tentative, was overtaken by the power of her forgiveness, and he gave himself fully to her, basking in the glow of her affection. She bought him other earrings, a teardrop, a seashell, a twist, bestowing and attaching them with the same tenderness and care that she had the cupid. These gifts, which at first had seemed so anomalous and ill-conceived, became the symbols to him of Frankie's commitment and devotion. He cherished the cupid's place over his heart, imagined the string of its bow reverberating in his chest and its arrows piercing his heart again and again. The seashell was a sign of the swelling tide of their love; the twist, the entwinedness of their fate. He was more than fortunate to be the recipient of such providence. He felt blessed.

Work became an effort, chiefly because it kept him
from Frankie. Of the two jobs, the hospital, which
required so much more of him, proved paradoxi-
cally to be the less burdensome. The physical toil of
lifting eighty-pound stacks of soiled linen and hoist-
ing waist-high drums of detergent left little energy to
think, and the acrid smell of disinfectant coupled
with the ubiquitous din of the industrial-grade wash-
ers dulled his senses to the point of oblivion. He felt
like a beast whose nature it was to be used, to be
harnessed and ridden. Strangely, he didn't mind,
felt, in fact, that he had finally found a calling. He
welcomed the burden and found himself asking for
more, volunteering for the heaviest loads, the dirti-
est jobs, sheets soaked in blood and excrement, pil-
lows saturated with puke. He was happy, blissfully
so, reveling in the refuse of others, carrying the
weight of Frankie's gifts like a cathedral on his
chest, a sanctified promise, a sumptuous and ongo-
ing meal. His toil signified his passion. He exalted in
love.

At Suter's, where there was little that required or
held his attention fully, it was not so easy. His
thoughts turned on Frankie constantly. He called
her on the phone three and four times a day, drew
pictures of her, scribbled her name on his hand,
wrote poems. Dozens of times a day, hundreds, he
touched his chest, fingering the charms, the bene-
faction of her sustaining hand. The cupid drew him
especially, the plump silver cherub of love that
swayed and beat in time with his heart. He played
with it incessantly and imagined he was playing

with Frankie. He made wishes and vows. He floated on dreams.

It was in just such a state that Brenda found him one day. She coughed to get his attention.

"Join me on break?" she asked. He was too distracted to answer.

"Terry?"

"What?"

"Take a break."

He looked up. "Don't need one."

"C'mon. Everyone needs a break." She reached for his hand, then led him from the counter to the stockroom in back. Once inside, she shut the door.

"Pinkett's been asking after you."

Terry said nothing.

"He wants to know what's going on."

"With what?"

She shrugged, uncomfortable playing the messenger.

"Fuck him," said Terry.

"Right." She lit a cigarette. "I like your cologne."

"He wants something, he can ask me himself."

"He's afraid. Guys intimidate him."

Terry found that laughable. Brenda blew smoke.

"Why do you think he keeps all the women upstairs and all the men down? You, Sal, Benny, Coe. Out of sight, out of mind."

"So? He likes women. Probably the only thing we have in common."

"Cologne," she said. "He drenches himself."

"Frankie likes it," said Terry. "What's Pinkett been asking?"

"He wants to know why you're always late. I told

him to give us a raise, make it worth our while to get here on time. He didn't like that a whole lot."

"I'm working seven days a week. What the fuck does he want?"

"He asked about stocking too. He thinks you're getting behind, says you're forgetting to put in the orders when you should."

"I put in the orders when I feel like it. He wants something different, let him order the books himself."

"You forgot to demagnetize, Terry. Three times this week."

"Big deal."

"It embarrasses people."

He stared into space, disinterested, bored.

"Do I like the man?" asked Brenda. "You know the answer. But he's trying to be nice. He doesn't want to lean on you if you're in trouble, but he has to look out for the store. He asked me to keep an eye on you. Seeing how we're friends."

"Look all you want."

"What's going on, Terry?"

"What's going on?" He gave a brittle laugh. "I'll tell you what's going on. I don't give a shit about this job. Books, Brenda? Words? It's pathetic. These are desperate people we're dealing with here. Fantasy people. They're not real." He grabbed his shirt and with it the charms underneath. "You want something real? This is real. This is life. It's all here, every scribble and word, every book. You want to wallow in something, wallow in this. Wallow in life. You're not willing to do that, you might as well cash it in. It's so obvious. I wish I'd known before."

Brenda stared at him, not knowing what to say. The man was operating on another plane, and for a moment hers seemed flat and gray. She had an urge to defend herself, another to tell him he was full of shit. Alternatively, she thought of finishing her cigarette and walking away.

"Obviously you've got the answers. Tell you what. If Pinkett wants to know something, I'll tell him to talk to you."

"He'd do well to talk to me. There're things he should know. Things I could teach him."

"I'm sure he'd be interested."

"Listen, Brenda. You don't ring up love on the cash register. It's not that kind of thing. When it comes, you ride it. And if you're lucky, it rides you."

"I can quote you on that?"

"You know something? I used to be tired all the time. Working two jobs, busting my ass at home. Now I have more energy than I know what to do with. My mind is always going. I can see what's happening around me, sometimes even before it does. I'm a step ahead. That's the level I'm working at. Blink, and I might be gone. You can see how selling books doesn't exactly get a front-row seat."

"Maybe you need a real break. A week or two. A month."

"What I need is Frankie. I have her, I have everything."

"I hope she can hold up."

"I have to love her enough, that's all. I do that and the sun shines. The moon glows. Day and night."

"Yeah? You might want to check that one out in astronomy."

He shook his head in disappointment. "Obviously you don't understand."

Brenda studied him, trying to decide what to do. At length she stubbed out her cigarette on the floor. "Guess not."

She left but a half minute later returned. Terry hadn't moved, except that now his hand was fiddling under his shirt.

"I like you, Terry. You know I do." She touched his shoulder. "You need help, you let me know."

"I don't."

"Right." She scribbled her phone number on a slip of paper and held it out. When he didn't take it, she stuffed it in his pocket.

"Just in case."

He shrugged.

"I'm your friend," she said. "You keep in touch."

She left, and several minutes passed. Terry had the cupid between his fingers. He didn't need Brenda, and he didn't need help. He already was in touch.

His stomach was growling when he got home, but the sight of Frankie drove food from his mind. He washed and shaved, then took off his shirt and went to the living room to be tied. Frankie used a velvet ribbon he had monogrammed with his own name a few days before. When he was finished with the knot, he had Terry stand back and puff out his chest so he could survey his work.

Since the cupid, he had sewn a half-dozen other earrings on Terry's chest, the last of which, a colored glass dangle, was only a day or two old. The skin where it hung was still red, and when he touched it, Terry winced.

"Sore?"

"A little."

"Do you think it's infected?"

"It's all right."

"Maybe I should stop for a while," Frankie said solicitously.

"No."

"You already have a chestful. The general wants more?"

Terry smiled. This was a game they played.

"Yes. The general deserves full decoration."

"Does he?"

"Yes."

"Does he command it?"

"He commands."

"Is he afraid?"

"Yes."

This stopped Frankie. "The general is afraid?"

"Of losing your love."

"Sit down."

Terry did as he was told, propping his back against a pillow so he was semireclined. A muscle in his jaw began to twitch, and he closed his eyes, trying to calm himself. He heard Frankie remove the ice tray from the freezer and break out a cube of ice. A moment later he felt it on his chest, just above the solar plexus. His face grew hot, and he shivered.

"Your heart is pounding," said Frankie, who was leaning over him. He placed a finger on the point of the pulsation. "Such violence. You are afraid."

Terry shook his head. "No."

"Yes. You're afraid I'll come to my senses and stop this sordid little game. Stop fueling your hate with my own. Stop making it easy for you. You're afraid what you'll do."

"I'm not," said Terry, suddenly worried. He chewed his lip. "I'm not afraid, Frankie. You give me courage. You make me strong."

"I make you weak. You don't want to be strong. You're a violent man. A rapist. Your strength betrays you."

He hung his head.

"Who would dare trust you?"

"No one."

"Say my name."

He did.

"Again."

He said it again.

"Now sit up." Frankie removed the ice and untied Terry's hands. "That's your answer."

"No." He shook his head in distress. "Don't do this."

"Time to grow up, little man. I can't take care of you forever."

"Please. Stop this. Stop toying with me."

Frankie laughed. "You are a toy. Look at you."

He glanced at his chest. "I'll tear them off. I don't want them anymore."

"Don't be childish. You'll hurt yourself."

He grabbed one, but Frankie intervened, prying his hand off. "You're getting too upset. Look, the poor little cupid is trembling." He pushed Terry back against the pillow. "You need to relax."

"Then do what you promised." He reached for the

cube of ice and put it back on his chest. "Don't stop what you started."

Frankie stared at him with a mixture of wonder and disgust. "I want you to remember those words, Terry. When we hit rock bottom, when we're clawing each other's throats, remember what you just said."

"Look," said Terry. "Cupid isn't shaking anymore. He's dancing, like you used to."

"Maybe someday you'll be the one to dance." He tossed the cube away. "No ice tonight. I want you to feel this."

"It'll hurt."

"Isn't that what you want?"

"I want what you want, Frankie."

"No you don't."

"I do."

Frankie felt a stab of conscience, a sickness deep in his heart. He had to turn away.

"Then I pity you."

The actual attachment went quickly, Frankie cleansing the skin with alcohol before pinching it between thumb and finger and lifting it from the chest wall, then inserting the curved needle with a controlled jab to get it beneath the skin. Terry winced but didn't dare cry out. He kept his eyes squeezed tight as Frankie made his passes with the needle. Tonight's trinket was a departure from the others, an Art Nouveau cameo of a horse, nostrils flaring, mane streaming back, eyes ablaze. Frankie had found it in a shop on Church and had been struck at once by the force of the carving. There was

something in the animal's face that was a little insane, that called to mind this project of his, that
begged to be in the center of Terry's chest. It cost
more than he had been planning to pay, but once it
was secure, the thread trimmed, the stitch holes
cauterized with matches, he knew he had chosen
well. He held up a hand mirror for Terry himself to
admire the brooch, had him stand and model it, and
at length said his good nights. Terry, who always
became charged after these sessions, begged him to
stay, but Frankie had had enough of the man for one
night. He retired to his bedroom, where he sat for a
long while before finally undressing. Of late he had
been having trouble getting to sleep and once there,
trouble staying that way. He would wake with a
sense of urgency, convinced there was something he
had to do but not knowing what it was. At times this
disquiet took the form of a recurring dream where
he was being forced into something against his will.
On this particular night he dreamed of being placed
atop a horse, which immediately began to kick and
buck wildly. When he woke in a sweat, covers tangled, pillow pitched to the floor, the source of the
dream for once, at least, seemed clear, and in a re-
versal of logic that seemed logic itself, he returned to
the shop where he had bought the cameo. There
were no others like it, but he did find an alabaster
elephant meant to be worn as a pendant. There was
something about animals that attracted him, some
force or animus he had yet to put a finger on. In the
ensuing days he bought more, enlarging his search,
accumulating creatures at a feverish pace. Some
were stone, some metal, others plastic or clay. By

the end of a week he had a small pantheon of miniatures. To keep up he needed Terry's help, and the
general was at pains to oblige. The decorating became a nightly event, a climax around which the
emotional tenor of each of their days was organized.
Terry longed for the gifts as he longed for Frankie
himself. He could scarcely think of anything else.
Frankie approached their appointments with a similar intensity. The idea of taking this man who by past
conduct had forfeited the right to humanity and systematically dehumanizing him was too intriguing to
resist. The animals represented his descent into savagery. They were his beasts. His stigmata.

It wasn't long before Frankie ran out of room on
the chest and was forced to spread out. Whimsically,
he sewed a row of rivetlike buttons along the lower
margin of Terry's rib cage, so that from a certain
perspective he appeared to be constructed of two
halves, separates that could be detached like skirt
and blouse and used independently. Below the buttons, on the belly wall and around the navel he
sewed animals of the night and the underground,
jaguar, badger, bat. On Terry's arms he attached
reptiles; on his pectorals, animals of the sky, hawk,
toucan, eagle. He had a vague plan in mind, a cosmology of rather routine dimensions. Birds and reptiles above, mammals below, though for the most
part he chose his spots on the spur of the moment.
They had long since dispensed with the ice, Terry
now gritting his teeth against the needle's jab, trans-
muting the pain instantly into evidence of Frankie's
love. So too had they eliminated the ribbons and
sashes, though by habit Terry kept his hands behind

his back. He continued to shave and shower twice a day, and his ablutions now took longer because of the care he had to observe with the ornaments. Frankie was careful to sterilize needle and thread, but some of the sites were always red. Terry used antibiotic ointment, and luckily, none had become infected.

One day in a souvenir shop on Canal Frankie came across a gaudily painted porcelain boar's head brooch. With its hideous snarl, bloodshot eyes and lewd, slavering tongue it was more caricature than animal, the tormented mascot, perhaps, of some sadistic and misguided fraternity. Instantly, he knew it had to be his. The beast seemed somehow at the heart of their drama, its leering, subhuman face emblematic of the man he was trying to tame. He bought it at once, envisioning the obscene head as the crowning point of his zoological garden, the center ring of his fantastical circus. As such, it demanded a unique spot, and on the way home all the obvious choices ran through his mind, each more preposterous than the next. Just thinking of them gave him the shivers. He rubbed the snout and made a wish. He got the giggles. It was going to be one of those nights. One of those rare, uncanny nights. He could barely contain his excitement.

As before, he took pains preparing himself, calling upon all the effects he had learned to use when he was about to push Terry one step further. Nails, hair, perfume: he wondered if every woman's life required such consummate care, such method and attention to detail. He thought of the girl Frankie and what she would have done. Would she have played the game at all, and if so, was this her style, this the makeup she would have used, the hairdo, the clothes? Just where and who was she in relation to him? And what, if any, would have been her particular brand of revenge?

As he did his eyes, he had the boar's head perched on the vanity mirror, a talisman to focus his thinking. He turned his mind to the evening's business. Where should the brooch go? Navel? Forehead? Penis? He felt skittish, as though animals of his own were loose. His hand started to tremble, and for an instant he had second thoughts, doubts about this act, about himself. He forced them out of his mind. Indecision was something he could ill afford. Not now.

He finished dressing and stood at the mirror. Before him he saw a woman in her prime, a woman of unparalleled might and beauty, a woman capable of anything. The sight was breathtaking.

Terry came home slumped and weary, exhausted beyond words, but when he saw Frankie, a light came to his eye. The eagerness to be fixed, to be filled, gave him life, and he hurried through his preparations, then quickly took up his position on the couch.

Frankie did not begin immediately, choosing instead to parade first, flaunting himself, teasing Terry with barely veiled intent. There was an edge to him tonight, a recklessness and power that had Terry wound up like a spring. Terry wondered what Frankie had in store. He felt ready for anything.

Frankie finished his act and told Terry to close his eyes. He brought the head, along with needle, thread and alcohol, to the couch. Terry was semireclined and fully naked, giving Frankie the opportunity to study his work. He had not yet decided where to put the new trinket and tested various sites, holding it an inch or two above the skin while he eyed the lines of motion and energy of his design. The penis had been an early favorite, but on closer examination it seemed too hidden for his taste. The forehead was too conspicuous. On limbs or torso the animal would simply be one of many. He settled at last on the neck, the Adam's apple, gateway of breath and soul. This man, this beast, would carry the head here, so that every time he spoke or laughed, swallowed or cried, people would see and know the emblem of his true voice.

He wiped Terry's neck with alcohol, outlining the brittle cartilage of his voice box, imagining the boar's head in its center. Here was the man's breath, his life, naively vulnerable and exposed. Frankie touched his own neck, marveling at the trust inherent in Terry's gesture, and had a momentary lapse in concentration. He experienced a slight swooning sensation, a wavering of perspective that at first he thought was light-headedness. When the feeling didn't go away, he straightened up and tried to clear his head. He didn't feel dizzy. The room wasn't spinning. Everything, in fact, looked the same, everything, that is, but Terry. And even Terry was the same, prostrate, naked, adorned, except now all the animals, the mammals and birds and reptiles, creatures of swamp, forest and plain, had subtly changed. Frankie's meticulously chosen circus of abuse, his garden of ridicule and debasement, seemed to have transmuted itself. The cobra on Terry's arm no longer looked perfidious but mindful. The elephant not ponderous but majestic. The tiger graceful. The scorpion delicate. One by one the animals shed their previous skins, their bloodthirstiness, savagery and opportunism, and took on other faces, nobler and more virtuous ones, strength, courage, loyalty, endurance, until at last Frankie had no choice but to see. Inadvertently, unconsciously, he had been calling upon Terry's power, his backbone, pinning him with medals to uncover his worth. Contrary to his intent, he had summoned the man's strength, the man inside the man, his hidden prowess.

His eyes strayed to Terry's face. The skin was drawn, the cheeks hollow, giving him a high-boned, almost regal look. His nostrils flared as he waited expectantly; his eyelids trembled like wings. It was a handsome face, or might have been were it not for the air of hunger, of weak-willed and bottomless need. Obsequious was not the word. This was a man who had fawned at the least command, who had surrendered his body to whim, who had begged for his own subjugation. There was no strength here, no courage. On the contrary. This was a man who reeked of weakness and corruption.

Appalled, Frankie took a step back, but he could not distance himself from the next thought. It struck him in the chest like a fist, and when Terry opened his eyes to ask what was wrong, Frankie stumbled backward, too horrified to reply. Terry sat up.

"Frankie?"

It was too much to bear. Frankie forced himself to

move, sliding along the wall of the room until he
reached the doorway. He might have sunk then and
there, quailing before the sordid object of his own
creation, but the man got to his feet. He took a step
forward. Rousing himself, Frankie turned and fled.

Seconds later Terry was at the bedroom door. Had
he done something wrong? Failed to act properly?
Inadvertently offended? He begged Frankie to let
him in.

Frankie told him to go away. He invented a mal-
ady, a headache, which wasn't far from the truth.
He was sick of heart and spirit. He hated himself
and what he had become. Perpetrator, victim, cre-
ator of monsters. This black intent was sucking his
life. It was killing him. He felt frightened, helpless,
out of control. It was the rape all over.

He ransacked the room for a bottle, afraid if he
didn't do something quick, if he stopped for even
half a second to let his recriminations take hold, he
would be overcome with a misery and loathing so
great he would die. He needed help desperately, but
in the whole room there was no liquor. Frantically,
he threw open the bureau drawers, hunting for the
bottle of pills. He found it in a sock and tore off the
cap. There were eight tablets left, four times the dose
he had ever taken before. In a single swift motion he
tossed them down his throat.

18

The phone was ringing. It was ten in the morning, and Frankie was dead to the world. It rang again at eleven and again at twelve. At one-thirty he struggled out of bed, feeling woozy and nauseated. He took a shower, scrubbing his face and body with a washcloth until his skin was sore. He dressed and made himself a cup of coffee. When the phone rang again, he didn't answer. He was too miserable to talk, especially if it was Terry. He watched TV for a while, then went to the bedroom where he tried unsuccessfully going back to sleep. He opened the window and called the cat. He put out food, and ten minutes later the animal came. After it had eaten, the two of them played with the catnip mouse, Frankie grasping its tail while the cat leaped and clawed at the stuffed toy. Afterward, he coaxed the cat into his lap, where the animal, seeming to sense his need, sat for close to an hour before jumping down and trotting away. Frankie got up and wandered aimlessly around the apartment, leafing through books, staring out the window, trying not to sink too low. He didn't trust himself to go outside and felt lost and alone in. He kept returning to the phone, wanting to call someone for help. When it rang again, he jumped, then grabbed frantically for the receiver. At the sound of Terry's voice he hung up, and quickly, before it could ring again, dialed Edna's number.

They met that evening at the apartment. Edna had tried to convince her daughter to come to New Haven, but Frankie was feeling far too volatile to risk a trip of that proportion. Accordingly, Edna had canceled her plans for the evening and taken the train down. She arrived around six, and as she mounted the stairs, she cautioned herself to have patience. Frankie was neither hurt nor ill. This she had learned on the phone.

The door opened, and Edna, fearful of alienating her daughter, stifled an urge to take her in her arms. Instead she clasped her hands at her waist and studied her, searching for signs of neglect. None were obvious, and when Frankie welcomed her with an unexpected embrace, some of the tension went out. Still, she remained vigilant.

They settled in the living room, which, Edna was pleased to note, looked a sight better than it had on her last visit. There were curtains, a new rug, potted plants. No clothes were strewn on the floor, no books or records stacked in haphazard piles. The walls were clean, and there was even a framed print on one. Art to Edna was always a sign of civilization.

Frankie made her a cup of tea and joined her on the couch.

"I put some dinner in. Swanson's. You like chicken?"

"I'm not very hungry. This," she motioned to the tea, "is fine."

"It takes an hour to cook. Maybe later."

"We'll see. The apartment looks nice. You've been busy."

"Have I?" Frankie had trouble recalling just what, if anything, he'd accomplished the last few weeks. "Terry's been doing most of it. Whatever I tell him to. We have an arrangement."

"You're not working, I take it."

"No."

From hints she had gleaned over the past two years, Edna had constructed a distressingly unsavory picture of what her daughter had been doing for money. Because it upset her so, she did her best to ignore it, but now, hearing that the mysterious job was over, she allowed herself a moment of pure anguish before sighing with relief.

"I approve. There's always plenty of time to work later."

"Terry has two jobs now. Three, if you count what happens here."

"Keeping house is always a job. Contrary to popular belief." She looked around. "I like what you've done."

"Have you ever felt like a train?" Frankie asked out of the blue. Edna frowned, then laughed and patted her middle.

"A barge maybe. Never a train."

"I feel like a train without brakes. Like there's some invisible hand pushing me faster and faster."

"I don't know what you mean."

"I'm doing things without thinking. Without even knowing. I can't stop."

"What is it with you, Francesca? There's always trouble, always something. Why?"

"You'd be in trouble too."

"You put yourself in these predicaments, these dramas . . ."

"I didn't ask for this. Believe me."

Edna felt torn between compassion and reproach. She tried not to be too stern. "Sooner or later you have to take responsibility."

"I did," muttered Frankie. "Look where it's gotten me."

"This is life, Frankie. You do your best. You either succeed or you don't."

Frankie gave a coarse laugh. "And what exactly constitutes success here? That's the question, isn't it? What am I going to have to live with?"

"There's nothing wrong with ambition. It gives a person a goal, something precious few of us have. I never did, apart from the family. And family's too unpredictable." She avoided looking at her daughter. "It's not safe to let your life depend on someone else's."

"I had a brush with ambition last night. It was horrifying. I'd rather fail a million times than face it again."

"There you go again. I just don't understand you, Francesca."

"I told you. I'm a train."

Edna shook her head, recalling a time when life had seemed simpler and more rewarding. When she could act without such forethought and be accounted wise merely by virtue of being mother to a child.

"People fail," she said. "It's not the end of the world."

Frankie felt like shouting. "Do you even know what I'm talking about? If I keep going, I'll be worse than him. If I stop, I'll be a victim all over. Either way I'm trapped."

"Victim, victim, victim," snapped Edna. "That's all I hear these days. As though a person didn't have a mind of her own. You do have a mind, Frankie. A good one. You're not a victim unless you choose to be."

"I am," he said helplessly. "Both ways."

"Posh. Have you thought of going back to school? You used to love it so. I've always thought of education as a way of getting on track. Getting oriented. I know you have your own ideas, but it never hurt to learn new ones."

"What are you talking about?"

"You, Frankie. I'm talking about you."

"Somehow I don't think school's the answer."

"What then?" Edna was getting irritated. "You won't come home. You won't try therapy. You won't leave this man. You tell me."

"I don't know."

"Is there something I should be doing? Please, tell me if there is because I don't know anymore. I don't know what to ask, I don't know what to say. You tell me to come down and here I am. Now what? How do we get you out of this one, whatever it is?"

"You're angry. Why are you angry?"

"I'm exasperated. You have all the gifts, Francesca. Youth, beauty, intelligence. What is it you need?"

"Tell me I'm crazy. Look me in the eye and tell me that. Then say this nightmare will be over."

"Oh, Frankie."

"Promise it will."

"You make it so hard."

"You see? You can't. I'm all alone. Crippled, monstrous and alone."

He stopped buying the animals, stopped searching the stores, stopped imagining new ignominies upon which to visit Terry. It left a vacuum in his life, and he got back into sewing for the cat, which rekindled to a modest degree his friendship with Luisa. This helped him through the long days, but nights were difficult. His unilateral retreat from barbarity had not occasioned in him a comparable advance in congeniality. Shame and confusion kept him from making overtures. For the most part all he wanted was to avoid Terry. To Terry this was tantamount to rejection. In response, he wanted Frankie all the more.

Work became an irritant, tolerable only as a place where his preoccupations could run free. He made mistakes and persistently came in late, sometimes half an hour or more. Sal was the principal victim, and one day he took a stand. It was not in his nature to complain, nor to pay that much attention to the world at large, but on this occasion he stopped playing with his gadget of the month long enough to speak his mind. He'd rehearsed the opening line.

"Anything I can do?"

"I already apologized for being late," Terry said.

"I don't mean that. I mean, you know, can I help?"

"Do me a favor and stick to your gadgets."

Sal was tongue-tied. "Look. Even I can see something's wrong."

"Nothing's wrong. Who told you that?"

"I have eyes."

"You want the truth, or you want to stand there mouthing off what someone told you?"

"No one told me anything."

"The truth is I've never been happier. That's what we're talking about, right? Happiness. But scratch that. This isn't happiness. It's beyond happiness. I don't expect you to understand." He was restless and impatient. This was hardly worth the effort. "You think this is me talking, you think this is someone you know, but it's not. I'm not here. I'm beyond this place. Way beyond. It's like comparing fire to rock. Can you do that? You can't. One's alive, the other's dead. I'm burning up. Every day I'm burning more."

Sal was at a loss. He stuttered a reply, offering what help he could. Terry had already lost interest.

"Save your charity for someone who needs it. Now if you'll excuse me, I have to use the phone."

"Don't keep coming in late," said Sal. "I won't keep covering for you."

"You're right." Terry had the phone to his ear. "Time is precious. Moments bleed into hours. The heart suffers that waits. Pick up the phone. Pick it up. Pick . . . it . . . up."

Fundamentals

Lordosis is a U-shaped posture of the spine where the mid-portion of the back is bowed forward while the head and buttock are thrust back. In rats, it is a stereotyped reflex and is accompanied by a slight extension of the hind limbs. In females this posture facilitates penile intromission by male rats.

The behavior is of vital importance to reproduction, and thus plays a central role in the behavioral repertoire of the species. Lordosis occurs at a more or less constant interval following application of appropriate sensory stimuli. The stimuli needed to elicit the reflex are well defined, consisting of pressure on the flanks and genital region. The resultant excitatory impulses travel up the spinal cord to the brain, where they stimulate specific motor centers. Impulses are generated, which, upon transmission down the spinal cord, produce the appropriate motor response.

Lordotic responsiveness in rats is highly sexually dimorphic, that is, there are distinct differences between the sexes. Females are easily stimulated to display maximal lordosis, whereas males are not. The difference has been postulated to lie in the hypothalamus, that area of the brain that regulates such vital functions as growth, appetite, emotion and sexuality. Its anatomy and physiology are strikingly different in females and males. Recently, however, it has been suggested that the observed dimorphic responsiveness, rather than a function of neuroanatomy, is more a result of scientific bias.[14] While true that male rats do not respond to pressure on the flanks or genitals, there is a vast array of other stimuli that has never been tested. It may well be that males do have the capacity for lordotic behavior, that is, when given the appropriate stimulation, they too will thrust out their buttocks and bow in their backs, just as their female counterparts do. Experiments are currently under way.

As the days passed, Terry became a man truly possessed. Finding a way back into Frankie's favor consumed him totally. How he got to work was anybody's guess, because once there he was all but useless. At the hospital he stopped wearing gloves, deeming them unnatural, part of a body not his own. When his supervisor patiently explained the rules of sanitation, not to mention law, Terry replied that cleanliness was a matter of taste. After all, would the man rather fuck with a condom or bare-skinned? An hour didn't go by that he wasn't at the phone calling Frankie, its hollow ringing serving only to egg him on. At Suter's, with the phone right there at the desk, he called every ten minutes. He wrote her name over and over on blank sheets of paper. He scratched it on the back of his hand with a pencil. It had been a week since she had attended to him, seven days without a bauble, without the needle's caress, the reassuring prick of love's devotion. He was getting desperate.

One evening Brenda came down to have a word with him. She hadn't yet decided whether to chew him out or to sympathize, and she stopped for a moment at the foot of the stairs to get a sense of his mood. He was sitting on a stool behind the counter, busy with something in his lap, too preoccupied to notice her. There were other people on the floor, and they, too, were well outside his attention. Brenda reached the counter and waited. Terry didn't look up. She tried to see what he was doing but couldn't. She cleared her throat and when that didn't get his attention, she said his name.

"What?"

"I could've been Pinkett."

"So?"

"Or Elvis risen from the dead."

"What do you want?"

"You need help."

"Go away."

"You look like shit, Terry. And that's being generous. Are you sick? Is it the virus?"

"Leave me alone."

"You using? Tell me you are. Make it easy." She reached over and yanked up the sleeve of his sweatshirt before he could pull away. After a cursory glance she tossed the arm back.

"What gives, Terry?"

"Nothing."

"C'mon, give me some kind of credit. Your eyes are shot to hell, your skin looks like someone's old newspaper, your attitude, shit, your attitude's on another planet. How much weight have you lost? Twenty pounds? Thirty? You look like one of those pictures."

"I'm not hungry."

"Then you better get hungry quick. Before you do yourself some permanent damage."

He didn't answer, returning instead to the task in his lap. Standing on tiptoe, Brenda finally saw what it was. He was digging the tip of a pencil into his palm.

"You'll poison yourself like that."

"You wouldn't understand."

"Try me."

"I'm feeding on love," he muttered.

She rolled her eyes.

"I'm full. You're empty. I'm living in paradise, you're wandering in the desert. Love is the elixir, Brenda. The venom and the cure."

"She better be good," said Brenda. "Real good. She's going to need to be."

The tip finally broke off, causing Terry to wince. Then he looked up. "I pity you. It must be hard staring into the face of what you lack. What you can only dream."

"Someone should do something to your mouth." She was angry and hurt, and grabbed a pencil from the counter. "Here. Why don't you do the other hand?"

Terry watched her storm away, glad to be alone again. He couldn't explain how he felt, the poverty alongside the plenty, the ache at the hollow of desire. His craving had become a thing unto itself, a need demanding constant nourishment, more real at times than its source. He played with the new pencil, feeling on the verge of some climax. He was a man alone, a force beyond reckoning. He dug the tip into his other palm, jamming it down until it broke the skin. This was power. Brenda had handed him the means. Maybe she did understand after all.

The next morning he skipped work and walked to a shop he'd seen advertised in the *Voice*. It was small but clean, and the artist who worked there took him behind a curtain. When he removed his shirt, her eyes got wide. She was always interested in new ideas, and this was one she hadn't seen. Fascinating, she called the job, obviously the work of a fevered spirit. It stimulated her creative juices, and once Terry explained what he wanted, she set to work with a fever of her own.

He came home that afternoon on a wave of euphoria. Love takes two, and somewhere along the way he realized that he'd been holding back. It was amazing how, after taking the last step, making the absolutely final commitment, there was always something more that could be done. A vow, a pledge, a proof. An act of unbridled selflessness. The demonstration of devotion, he discovered, was limited only by his imagination.

Frankie was in the living room watching TV. He was startled to see Terry home so early.

"I skipped work," Terry explained. "I realized I'd been neglecting you."

"You haven't."

"I have. I brought you something to make up for it."

"Please," said Frankie.

"Guess what it is?"

The thought of a gift pained him. It was he, he felt, who needed to make amends, and he tried to put Terry off, motioning toward the TV, where a man was stalking a stage, speaking with great passion and conviction.

"Can it wait? This is almost over."

Terry smiled. The longer the wait, the greater the satisfaction. He settled on the couch. "What's he talking about?"

"Self-confidence. Taking control of your life."

"Does he know the secret?"

"Shh."

"I do. You do too."

Frankie was conscious of Terry's eyes on him, and he slid to the far end of the couch. Terry's unexpected arrival had him off balance, and he tried to focus on the TV, making a wall of his attention. The show ended, and he let the credits run. Terry watched him like a cat.

"You haven't been neglecting me," Frankie said at length. "Maybe the reverse."

"I was angry at first," said Terry, "until I realized, if you'd stopped loving me, there must be a reason. I must not be doing my part. No one loves a selfish man. A man like that doesn't deserve love."

"I don't love you, Terry. I'm still trying not to hate you."

"I understand that. I have to convince you. I have to give you proof." He unzipped his jacket and started unbuttoning his shirt.

"Don't," said Frankie, averting his face. "Please. I've had enough."

"It's right here. Please. Let me show you."

"I'm too ashamed."

"No. There's no place for shame." He slid toward her. "Love is the face of God. What you've done, all this . . ." He lay a hand on his chest. "It's hallowed ground. Touch me, Frankie. Sanctify my flesh. Give me grace."

Frankie wriggled away and retreated across the room. Terry followed her. When she squirmed away from him again, he got angry. He told her to stop moving. He professed his love.

Then the cat came.

It appeared in the doorway and with a plaintive meow trotted to Frankie's side, where it commenced rubbing against a leg. Frankie was relieved beyond words at its arrival. Terry simply stared.

"Where'd that come from?"

"I must have left the window open." Frankie stooped down and picked the cat up.

"I don't like cats," said Terry.

"This one's sweet." Keeping his distance, he cradled the animal in one arm and with the other rubbed behind its ear. "We're friends."

"It shouldn't be here."

"She's probably hungry. Why don't you pour her a saucer of milk?"

"I was talking to you, Frankie. I don't like to be interrupted."

"Listen to her purr. She loves being rubbed right here."

"I said I don't like pets."

"C'mon." He motioned Terry over. "She won't bite."

Terry came, but instead of a gentle touch he snatched the cat away and tossed it to the floor. Frankie was too startled to intervene, and by the time he tried, the cat had already bolted. He chased it to the bedroom window, then watched helplessly as it scampered down the fire escape. He returned to the living room in a cold fury.

"What is the matter with you?"

"Animals don't belong here."

"No? Then maybe you should take a hike."

He looked away from her. "I don't like sharing your attention."

"It's a cat, for godsakes."

"Can I show you what I got? What I did today?"

"She better be back."

"It's for you, Frankie."

Frankie glowered. "Do I have a choice?"

"You'll like it. I know you will." Eagerly, he unfastened the rest of his shirt buttons. "Close your eyes. Count to ten."

"You're so excited. You count."

He did, and when he reached ten, Frankie opened his eyes. Facing him was Terry's back, muscled from the laundry work, broad and sinewy, especially across the top. Tattooed on one shoulder blade was a boar's head, a copy of the charm Frankie himself had bought. Its eyes and tongue were red as flame, its lips a lurid blue. Intertwined in the stream of its saliva Frankie's name was written in a flowery pink cursive.

Frankie was stunned. He had never seen anything so hideous, so grotesque, so horrifyingly misjudged. His skin crawled. A wave of nausea rose in his throat.

"What's wrong?" asked Terry, who had turned. His face, at first so bright and eager at the thought of regaining Frankie's affections, now recoiled in panic.

"I can't look at you."

"It's for you. I did it for you."

"Don't say that."

"Look." He twisted the shoulder and proudly pointed at Frankie's name with a finger. "You're a part of me. Permanently."

"I have to leave. I can't stand this."

He took a beleaguered step, and then, as though breaking free of chains, rushed from the room. Terry followed close on his heels, and when Frankie tried to shut himself in the bedroom, Terry stuck a foot against the door and forced his way in.

"What's the matter? What did I do?"

"This is sick," said Frankie. "You're sick. I'm sick. This whole thing."

"Here." Terry pulled the boar's head from his pocket. "I found it between the cushions. It's yours."

"It's not. I don't want it."

"Sew it on. Please."

"You're insane."

"I beg you."

"I won't."

"Please, Frankie. Like old times. Keep the fire burning."

"You disgust me."

"No. Don't say that."

"Look at you. Listen. It turns my stomach to be in the same room with you. The same building. The same planet."

"I'm driving you away, aren't I? My love, it's too strong."

"Your love is pathetic. What man would do what you've done? Snivel like you. Grovel."

"What would you know of men? The love that's in

our hearts. The need.'' He was shouting now. ''The pain.''

''You forget who I am.''

''Sew it on, Frankie.'' He shoved the charm in her face. ''Finish what you started.''

Frankie raised his hand and slapped the charm away. It sailed through the air and struck a wall. Terry watched where it landed. Then he turned back to her.

''I am a man,'' he said.

''Go away.''

''You should give me what I want.''

He pulled her roughly forward and kissed her on the mouth. She twisted away, but he put a hand behind her head and forced her back. He pressed his lips hard against her own, flattening them and prying them open. He drove his tongue into her mouth.

Frankie finally got him off by yanking on one of the animals. Terry gave a yelp and backed away. His eyes were glazed. There was spittle on his chin. Frankie grabbed the shears as a weapon, holding them point out and waist-high. They faced each other for what seemed like hours.

At length Terry got a grip on himself. He frowned as if at some unpleasant thought, and an instant later the life drained from his face as he became aware of what he had done. He stood in quivering silence, lacking the strength and self-respect for even the lamest of apologies. When Frankie ordered him from the room, he obeyed without a whimper.

In the living room he sank abjectly to the floor, certain beyond doubt, beyond prayer, that he had finally driven her off. Had he the will he would have wept, and a minute later, or an hour, when Frankie appeared in the doorway dressed as before, no suitcase in hand, no coat for the night air, no shoes, it still did not occur to him to hope. As a matter of grim formality he muttered the question, the statement to which he already knew the answer. And when, brandishing a look of surprise, of mild alarm as if at some trivial misunderstanding, Frankie said no, she had no intention of leaving, far from it, she could see how what he said was true, how they had to finish what they started, Terry's heart leaped. The gloom lifted, and all at once he located the strength, the will that was in fact hers, and borrowing it once again, taking it for his own, he wept.

19

Frankie sewed his lips shut with size A silk thread, careful to keep the line straight and the needle steady. He used an overhand stitch and allowed a quarter inch of play so that Terry could speak. He fastened each end with a small knot and snipped the excess thread with his embroidery scissors. He blotted the droplets of blood with a handkerchief.

Terry's wrists were bound but not tightly. He was face-up on the couch with a towel underneath his head. When the job was done, Frankie undid the sash and gave him the handkerchief to hold. Then he went to the bathroom for a washcloth to wipe the few drops of blood that had dribbled down his chin. By the time he had Terry cleaned, the puncture wounds had stopped bleeding. The tiny dots of coagulated blood ran like code across upper and lower lip. Between them coursed the narrow zipper of black thread.

Terry tentatively touched his lips. They felt puffy,

though in truth, Frankie had exercised such care that there was little swelling. He pushed his tongue against the thread, making little ridges of its soft flesh.

"You could have washed my mouth with soap," he mumbled.

"Soap?"

"It's a joke."

Frankie eyed him solemnly. "Why do I get the feeling I'm playing into your hands?"

"Mine?" He tried to laugh, but the sutures wouldn't allow it. "Believe me. You're doing the right thing."

"You're so eager."

"I need help, Frankie. I'm not in control."

"I wonder."

"I can't be trusted."

"I need to trust you. Now more than ever."

"You can't."

"People learn. I did. You can too."

"If you say."

Frankie sighed. Standing before Terry, he ran a hand down his body, outlining his breasts, his waist, the curve of his hips.

"Tell me what I am, Terry."

He looked at her hungrily but was afraid to reply.

"Use your eyes. You know. You know because you see, because I'm here, because I tell you. Do you understand? This is what I am. This, and nothing else. If I can learn, you can too."

The next morning Terry called in sick to both jobs. His speech was remarkably clear, save for certain

consonants, principally b and p, which lacked
strength. Other than a little residual soreness he felt
well. Frankie made a sumptuous breakfast, eggs,
toast, fresh fruit, none of which he could get into his
mouth. They didn't have a blender, but later Frankie
went out and bought a package of straws and a bottle of juice. They spent the day at home, mostly
watching television. Frankie cleaned Terry's lips
with alcohol-soaked Q-tips and did a little house-
work, refusing to let Terry help. He served the juice
and, with Terry's hands tied, held the glass while he
sipped through a straw. Later, he gave Terry a
sponge bath and shampoo, after which he put him to
bed.

Terry called in sick again the next day. He had
slept well and apart from hunger pangs felt uncommonly refreshed. His lips were practically healed,
which he attributed to Frankie's skill and solicitude.
He was looking forward to another day at home.

Frankie, however, was not quite so upbeat.

"Bad night?" asked Terry.

"My nights are my own business."

"I slept like a baby."

"Is it too much to ask to have coffee ready when I
get up?"

"No problem." He went to the kitchen. "You want
some breakfast too?"

"I make my own."

"I dreamed of food. Big plates of it." He paused,
remembering. "You were in the dream too."

"On second thought why not? You know how to
fry an egg?"

Terry grinned. "With my hands tied."

"You think this is funny. I'm glad. I want two. Bacon, toast and coffee. You like jelly?"

"Sure."

"Put some on the toast. Bring it to my room when it's ready. Knock first."

He left, and ten minutes later Terry knocked at the bedroom door. Frankie had him wait before letting him in. He motioned to his vanity.

"Put it there."

"Can I stay?"

"It's rude to watch someone eat."

"I'll have juice."

After a moment's thought Frankie shrugged and told him to do what he liked. He settled down to eat, and Terry brought back a half-filled glass of orange juice.

"We're running out."

"So go get more."

Terry lowered his eyes. Frankie chewed his food, allowing the silence to grow.

"I'd be embarrassed."

"That's a tough situation."

"Will you go? Please."

"I have plans."

Terry couldn't contain himself. "What's wrong today?"

Frankie considered what to say. He had woken that morning with the tail end of a dream, a vision remarkable in its clarity. In it he was no longer a victim, his epicene birth no longer a source of torment and affliction. On the contrary, it was as if something immanent had fallen into place, a restitution of sorts, a blessing. In the dream his transformed self was far fuller than either he or the girl had been before, and this filled him with such a sense of wonder and well-being that it made a mockery of his vengeance. He was a better man than that. A better woman.

Sadly, though, the vision had been fleeting, or perhaps it was simply too late in coming. Too late to mock himself, too late to turn back from vengeance. It had been a fine moment, an inspiration, but now it was gone. Its loss was bitter, and bitterness is what laced his reply.

"I don't know what you mean," he told Terry.

"Did I do something? The coffee? Is that it?"

"The coffee is fine."

"What then?"

"You think about it."

"I don't know. You're not used to having me home? Is that the problem?"

Frankie wiped his lips with a napkin and regarded him coldly. "Habits are habits, Terry. Facts are facts. No one gets used to a toothache."

Frankie spent the day out of the apartment, not returning until nightfall. He was empty-handed, and Terry made due that night with water. The next day he again called in sick. When both supervisors asked how long he'd be out, he told them indefinitely.

Frankie was in a better mood that morning and made a point of going out first thing to get some juice for Terry to drink. He even poured and served it as he had done before. Unfortunately, the straws had mysteriously vanished, and Terry had to drink from the glass itself, whose rim didn't quite reach far enough past his lips. As a result, much of the liquid spilled. Still, it was better than nothing.

The sutures were now virtually healed, the sleek black threads almost as much a part of his body as the charms on his torso, his gnawing hunger and inverted pride. They tended to pull when he yawned, and he could neither laugh nor smile, but this was of no great consequence. He was moving beyond those simple emotions, and as the days passed without food, his transcendence grew. The more he was denied, the more he eclipsed himself. His heart begged to be stripped bare.

Several days later the cat returned. Terry was as decent as a minister. He watched without complaint as Frankie fawned over the animal and cradled it in her arms. At her command he poured it a saucer of milk and stood by attentively as it lapped it up. The next day he did the same, and Frankie, as if struck suddenly by the answer to a terribly difficult riddle, let out a sound.

"This is terrible. It just occurred to me, you must be starving."

Terry shrugged.

"No," said Frankie. "Don't pretend." He coaxed the saucer from the cat. "I insist. Please. Have what's left."

After that, Frankie made sure that Terry got his share, unless the cat was particularly hungry. Drinking from the saucer was even harder than the glass, but often the cat, who had taken an interest in this curiously bejeweled human, would lap his skin wherever the milk had spilled. Terry liked the feel of its rough tongue, but it was no substitute for

Frankie's own touch. This she bestowed capriciously, without discernible rhyme or reason. Some days she doted on him as a child would a doll. Others, she was as distant as the moon. He never knew what to expect and as a consequence was always on edge. That was the thrill.

Frankie sometimes read to him, often from one of the surgical texts. He would curl up alone or with the cat and make his way through a page or two, savoring the precise and unembellished descriptions as one might a poem. Other times he read Terry articles he had culled from women's magazines about beauty, devotion and grace. The messages were anything but abstruse, and there was plenty of fodder for thought.

One day he came home with a bag of magazines and a full-length mirror that he propped against the living room wall opposite the couch where Terry slept. All but two of the magazines had to do with bodybuilders and athletes, and after leafing meticulously through the pages, Frankie cut out photographs of the best male specimens. These he taped around the mirror's wooden frame, leaving an open space at the very top and bottom. The last two magazines were girlie sheets, and he carefully clipped out the naked female centerfolds and taped them in the remaining spaces. Stepping back, he regarded his creation. It was an altogether new pantheon and had taken a full morning to assemble, but it was well worth the effort. In the ensuing week he had Terry model before the mirror, matching poses to the ones in the photographs, creating his own, exhibiting his wares. Sometimes he'd be bare-chested, sometimes in briefs, sometimes naked to the bone. The tattoo had ceased to bother Frankie. While he continued to find it limitlessly grotesque, it no longer held any special power. It was on Terry's skin, not his own. Terry, not he, was the victim.

Frankie was a hard taskmaster, but there were times when he retreated to his bedroom or left the apartment completely. These were difficult hours for Terry. He didn't like being alone, both because he didn't know what to do with himself, and because he had to deal with the mirror. At first he'd been shocked by the reflection, the haggard, gaunt face, the starved eyes. It seemed more specter than man, a skeleton, skin draped over bone. At one point he covered the mirror with a sheet, but Frankie tore it off and told him never to do it again. The fact was there was no escape, and with time he found a way to handle the tormented figure that shared his room. He did what he had done with the charms and the sewing. He transmuted pain into pleasure. Pious men throughout history had starved themselves in the name of love and devotion. He was no different. His was a holy mission, his wretched body a saintly vessel. Thus it was he experienced moments of exhiliration, fleeting epiphanies of understanding and acquittal. Briefly, his emptiness would be filled, his hunger placated. But it took an effort, and as the days bore on and his weakness grew, the deceit was difficult to sustain. More and more he saw himself for what he was, cowering, contemptible, self-devouring. He was losing substance by the hour. One day he would wake up and be gone.

The following week Frankie had an idea. He fiddled with the radio until he found a station with a good beat, then had Terry strip to his briefs. He turned up the sound and settled comfortably on the couch, where the cat joined him. Placidly stroking her fur, he told Terry to dance.

Terry did his best to comply. He hopped on one leg, but his weakness made him stumble, then fall. Picking himself up, he tried the other, the baubles bouncing and jangling in mock time with his jig. Frankie ordered him to face the mirror, better to see the man he had become. Terry obeyed, but soon he was out of breath. Panting, he asked if he could stop.

"I'm proud of you," said Frankie. "Not many men would do what you have."

Bent over his knees and trembling, Terry barely registered the mockery.

"Would you like me to dance?" asked Frankie. It was a brash impulse, a heedlessness that was testimony to the essential ludicrous impenetrability of the situation. "For old times?"

"You?"

"I'll have to tie you up. You understand. For safety's sake."

He cinched a sash around Terry's wrists, then stood up and stretched. He had on tight jeans and a clingy sweater, each of which he took care to smoothe and contour. Feeling bold and inspired, he began swaying with the beat, rolling his head and shoulders. He moved a leg, and some of the memory came back. He rocked his pelvis. Framing him in the mirror were the sundry hulks of the world, the stallions and studs, the swaggering gods of muscle and splendor. Highlighting them were the two goddesses, sanitized, hairless and naked, one in diaphanous veil, the other in torn panties and blouse, both smiling as if sharing a joke. He rolled his hips and shook his breasts, and all at once the moves flooded back. Closing his eyes, he danced for real, wildly and with abandon. He could feel the power. It came from inside and reverberated through the room.

The Body of the Beloved Becomes
A Geography of Personal Meaning

Lesch-Nyhan syndrome is a sex-linked recessive genetic disorder characterized by mental retardation, motor abnormalities and aggressive self-mutilating behavior. Its symptoms usually become apparent by the second year of life, and being recessive, it affects only males. The mental retardation is moderate to severe and the motor abnormalities both spastic and choreoathetotic. The self-mutilation involves the fingers and mouth. If unchecked, a patient will typically chew off his lips, parts of his cheeks and the terminal digits of all his fingers. These compulsive and uncontrollable acts are invariably accompanied by great pain, so much so that the sufferer routinely cries out for help and restraint.

By contrast is the self-mutilatory behavior of borderline or psychotic patients. Their acts tend to be sporadic and their self-inflicted wounds far-ranging, varying from cigarette burns, skin carving and head banging to acid-dripping, face-sandpapering and breaking of the bones with a hammer. Feelings of pain in at least half of these cases are either diminished or fully absent, and it has been postulated that the neuro-endorphin system of such individuals is altered so that the release of endogenous opiates that normally occurs with painful stimuli is greatly increased.[15]

In Lesch-Nyhan patients, the abnormal behavior has been traced to a genetic abnormality on the long arm of the X chromosome, which results in the defective activity of a single enzyme. How it is that such a narrow chemical event can have such far-reaching and devastating effects is the source of active investigation.

Genetic studies are also being carried out in the non-Lesch-Nyhan cohort of self-mutilating patients, but as yet no consistent abnormalities have been identified. Etiological explanations have taken a more psychological orientation, and accordingly, some investigators have theorized that these patients may suffer the obverse of what Kernberg calls the primitive condensation of love and hatred that allows aggression to be neutralized by incorporating it into the fabric of sexuality.[16] *In Kernberg's view, sadism, masochism, hatred and love are normal developmental experiences in the life of the infant. To be willing to suffer for the sake of the loved one and to demand that the loved one suffer in return is an expression of trust and commitment. This holds for adults no less than children. Healthy erotic behavior depends on a person's ability to successfully handle—and fuse—these basic contradictory emotions. For those who cannot accomplish this task, love and hatred may remain forever split, making ambivalence intolerable and aggression, which in a healthy person sublimates into erotic desire and mature sexual love, a source of dysphoria, perversity and malignant self-abuse.*

One night, growing bored with their normal fare, Frankie brought out his costumes. It was the first Terry had seen of the diminutive creations, and though he had grown weak to the point of listlessness, he managed to revive enough to show interest. He complimented Frankie on the care and affection she had obviously shown: being also a product of her hand, he felt a certain kinship with the miniatures. When, however, he discovered that much of what she had sewn was inspired by the cat, he became jealous and demanded an outfit of his own. Frankie gave the idea some thought.

"Four legs," he said at length. "That's who I'm sewing for these days."

"I have four." Terry showed her. "Two arms, two legs."

"You don't understand."

"No. I do." He kneeled on the floor and leaned over, planting his palms and locking his elbows. He offered her a ride.

Frankie swung contemptuously onto his back, and Terry started to crawl. After two steps he collapsed.

"I'm too weak."

"Weak in body, weak in spirit," observed Frankie. "Obviously we have to beef you up. I can't have you fading on me. Not now."

For the next few days he fed Terry protein drinks, chalky and horrible-tasting affairs that settled heavy in his shrunken stomach and were sticky when spilled. The cat would have nothing to do with them, and often they stayed on Terry for hours, spotting his clothes or drying and caking his skin. What entered his system wasn't enough to build his mass, but it did give him more energy. By the end of the week Frankie had him up and bathing himself, shaving and doing his toilet. Once, briefly, he even got Terry to dance again.

Satisfied that he could, when necessary, rejuvenate his charge, Frankie decided it was time for a visitor. There had been calls, from Brenda, Sal, Marcus, but Terry had refused to speak to anyone. Frankie had not pushed the point, content to have his own time with the man, but now the situation had ripened. With a deaf ear to Terry's pleas, to his whimpering self-pity and shame, he dialed Marcus's number.

They set a date a week away, a period of time that Frankie deemed sufficient. He stopped feeding Terry the protein drink, resuming his diet of water. All trace of fat had long since vanished from his body, and what little muscle was left seemed to melt away. He was bone now, skin, bone and failed will. His face looked truly skeletal, his limbs like matchsticks. Too weak and broken to pose a threat, he no longer had to be tied. When Frankie ordered him about, he obeyed without hesitation. When she told him to sit, he sat; to get out of her sight, he huddled in a corner and tried to disappear. When she was gone, he gazed at himself in the mirror, incapable of recapturing hope, much less love, dully wondering what life had become.

Frankie knew what was happening. He could see the walls of Terry's prison growing, thickening, becoming more and more impervious to escape. He could feel the suffocation. He knew what it was to suffer, to be trapped and violated. He knew helplessness. It pained him, but pain, it seemed, was the coin of this world, the price of release. He had tried hope and he had tried kindness. There seemed only one recourse left.

Two days before Marcus was scheduled to visit, Frankie removed the sutures. He clipped them with the embroidery scissors and tugged them gently out with a tweezers. There was a minimal amount of bleeding, which stopped within minutes of direct pressure with a tissue. The jaw was too stiff to open more than an inch, but the lips seemed fine. Maybe not as robust as before, but then nothing about Terry was.

That night Edna called to chat. She asked how things were going, especially wanting to know if Frankie had made any progress solving her problems.

"Great progress," said Frankie. He cocked his head. "Wouldn't you say, Terry?"

At his insistence Terry was in the process of polishing his charms. He stopped immediately when Frankie spoke and looked up.

"He's become very, what? Docile? Even-tempered? Certainly more willing to do his part. It's a big improvement. You should see."

Edna expressed her happiness and suggested a visit sometime soon. Or dinner, maybe all three of them.

"What a nice idea," answered Frankie. "We love visitors."

They chatted awhile longer before hanging up. Frankie turned to Terry.

"You're in demand. I don't think you appreciate it."

He shrank from the threat.

"Your friends care about you. Even Edna. They call and want to know how you are. They miss your smiling face. Your charm. Your cheery presence."

"I'm not fit to be seen."

"Don't start with that. Look in the mirror. What you see is a testament to what you are. You yourself said. How can anyone be ashamed of love?"

"I'm wretched."

"You're not. You're heroic." He came to Terry's side and took his head softly against his breast. "My general. My sad, beautiful general."

On the day of Marcus's visit Terry became so agitated that Frankie lied, saying he'd called Marcus back and canceled the plan. Which was no reason, he explained, that Terry shouldn't look nice. So saying, he drew a bath and helped him into the tub. The charms on looser threads floated to the water's surface, bobbing about like miniature bath toys. Frankie soaped his man down, careful not to disturb them. He gave him a shampoo and a shave, and when he was done with the face, he took the razor to Terry's chest and armpits, explaining that it was easier to control the odor that way. Afterward, he got him out and dried and onto the couch, then went to his own room to get ready.

About an hour later the buzzer rang. Frankie went to the door and peered through the peephole.

"It's Marcus," he said over his shoulder. Terry,

who was following him at a shuffle, was panic-
stricken.

"Don't let him in."

Frankie undid the first bolt. "We must have gotten
our signals crossed."

Terry reached out and covered his hand. "Don't, I
said."

"We can't just tell him to go away." He shook
Terry's hand free as if it were a leaf. "He's your
friend. We should be gracious."

"No. Tell him to come back. Tell him I'm sick."

"Don't you think you're overreacting just a tiny
bit?"

"Please, Frankie. Don't." He was naked and
shivering. There was terror in his voice.

"All right," said Frankie, touched by Terry's fear.
He resolved to be merciful and get rid of Marcus.
"Go in my room. Shut the door. I'll get rid of him as
fast as I can."

Terry disappeared from the hall, and Frankie
flipped back the last bolt. Marcus greeted him with a
smile and a hug, then ducked through the doorway.
Frankie led him to the living room, where Marcus
looked around.

"Where's my man?" he asked.

"Terry's resting."

"He didn't know I was coming?"

"He thought maybe you'd forgotten."

Marcus frowned but let it pass. He gave Frankie
the once-over. "You lookin' good."

It was an understatement. Frankie was wearing
the sleeveless dress Edna had bought him, the deli-
cately draped white one that had seemed so femi-

nine at the time. With his pale complexion and the white silk ribbon he had tied in his hair, he looked to Marcus like some kind of angel.

"Drive the men crazy lookin' like that."

Frankie smiled. "Terry likes it when I dress up. I do it for him."

Marcus glanced around. "Place looks good too. You been workin'."

"Some. Mostly Terry. The man's a miracle."

"Bonified. I hear he's been bustin'."

Frankie wasn't sure what he meant. "Hey," he asked, "you get my shirts?"

"Shirts?"

"I mailed you three."

"Sure you're right. Three button-downs. Tell me something. Where'd you get those colors?"

"You didn't like them?"

"Who said that? They's wild, that's all. Gets me all kinds of attention. 'Specially from the ladies."

"You and Charles."

It took him a moment to register the compliment. Then he grinned. "That's right. Me and my man Charles."

A minute or two passed. Frankie asked Marcus about work.

"I got my eye on something new. Something technical. No more mopping and slopping, rubbing and scrubbing. Let someone else do the cleaning." He hesitated, working up to something. "Some of the fellas in the laundry, they be talking. Say how Terry be pushing it awful hard. Too hard, making other folks look bad. He ever say anything like that?"

Frankie shook his head. "Never did."

"He been off work awhile now. He sick or what?"

"He's in the bedroom."

Marcus glanced down the hall. "Tell you what. How 'bout you go in and tell him Marcus be here. Tell him I come all the way down to see his ugly face. That oughta get him up."

Frankie wavered. He had resolved to be merciful, and yet real mercy, it seemed, lay in finishing things off as quickly as possible. With that in mind he took Marcus's hand. "How about you come with me?"

Marcus thought it over. "I could do that too."

They went down the hall, Frankie knocking once on the door before throwing it open. Terry was in bed, and at the sound of their approach, he had pulled the blanket up over his head.

"Wake up," called Frankie. "Someone to see you."

Terry cowered and clutched the covers tight.

"Now now," said Frankie. "Don't be shy. It's your friend Marcus."

Leaning over, he yanked the blanket off the bed. Terry uttered a cry and curled into a ball. But not so fast that Marcus didn't see.

"Sweet Jesus."

"I should have said something," remarked Frankie.

"Who is that?"

"It's Terry. I'm sorry. You shouldn't have to see."

"That's not Terry. No no." Marcus, who prided himself on his unflappability, could not conceal his horror. "What is it? What's he got?"

Terry grabbed for the blanket, but Frankie pulled it away.

"Answer the man."

"I seen sickness like this on TV. People starving. Guys with AIDS. He got AIDS?"

Frankie crouched at his side. "You sick, babe? Tell Marcus."

Feebly, Terry shook his head.

"You're a big boy. Use your words."

His reply was barely audible.

"What's them things hanging off his skin?"

"What are they, Terry?"

He shrank away.

"He needs a doctor."

"No," Terry managed to say. "No doctor."

"Terry is a doctor," said Frankie. "Did you know that? Three quarters of one anyway. He went to medical school. I bet he was first in his class. That's something to be proud of. Medical school. A fine profession like that."

"Something nasty going down here," muttered Marcus. "Some bad ju-ju."

"It's sad, isn't it? Poor baby." Frankie pulled the blanket back over Terry, patted him on the head, then straightened up. "Rough day for the man of the house. Maybe we should leave. Let him get some rest."

"He needs help."

"I've been trying, Marcus. What can I say? A man gets help who helps himself. You told me that."

Marcus felt stuck. His allegiance was with Terry, but life had taught him to trust the women in matters of health and home. He let Frankie lead him out.

"I be calling you," he told Terry at the door.

"Don't think I won't. You start doing like the lady says. Get some meat on them bones."

Frankie ushered him out of the apartment. "Thanks for coming by. It means a lot to him. To both of us. I know it'll help."

"You call me," said Marcus. "You let me know."

Frankie gave his assurance, then shut the door and went to the kitchen. The largest knife they owned measured eight inches from tip to heel. It was made of tempered steel with a polished wooden handle. Frankie took it and returned to the bedroom. Terry was huddled under the blanket.

"One humiliation after another," said Frankie. "Doesn't it get old? Don't you get tired?"

Terry hugged his knees to his chest.

"I'm your nightmare, Terry. The evil in your dreams a thousand times magnified. The wickedness of your sick and twisted mind. As long as I live, you're a dog. You're a pushole. A piece of shit. You're fucked, Terry. Fucked to the wall."

Frankie sat on the bed, forcing himself through this last impersonation, this final emptying of his spirit. His manner softened, as he folded back the blanket and made Terry sit up.

"Hate and more hate. Insult upon insult. Embarrassment. Humiliation." He placed the knife on the sheet between them. "How far do I have to go?"

Terry stared dully at the weapon, and when he looked up, Frankie had pulled down the bodice of his gown. His breasts were pink and bare. The tip of his heart beat silently against his ribs. He slid the knife handle into Terry's hand, undid the white ribbon from his hair, then put his hands behind his back and loosely wrapped them.

"Now we finish what we started. Just like you said." He closed his eyes and thrust out his chest. His body was trembling, but his voice was firm. "I don't think I need beg."

Terry stared at her and then the knife. Was this the love he had craved, the holy passion? If so, why did he feel so hollow and raw? So degraded. Something was wrong. He hadn't planned it like this. Love was supposed to work miracles.

It came to him then, the will that had been so long absent. On a wing, a prayer, it woke like a flame. Frankie was right. There would be no more begging. In this, too, she was his guiding light. He raised the knife and held it aloft. Summoning the last of his failing strength, he plunged the blade down.

20

Late at night the girl is sitting. She is in a cushioned, metal-backed chair in a small, dim room. A machine nearby periodically clicks on and off, and the faint hiss of oxygen issues from a nozzle in the wall. She shifts position, draws her legs under her, pulls the blanket tighter about her shoulders. She is tired but cannot sleep. Recent events have altered what for a time seemed so clear.

A bed takes up most of the room. In it is a man whose eyes are closed. Tubes extend like jointless limbs beyond the sheets. Through them flow pale pink, yellow and clear liquids. The man has a three-day growth of beard. Except to breathe, he does not stir.

A young woman wearing white enters the room. Dark-haired and self-possessed, she resembles the woman in the chair. She checks the man in bed, takes his pulse, makes notes on a clipboard. She adjusts one of the machines and asks the visitor if she'd like a pillow. The woman shakes her head.

Why sleep? she thinks to herself. What dream could possibly rival this?

She is wearing jeans and high-tops. A cowl-neck sweater, no makeup. She has arrived in this room by a circuitous route. She has been here before but the place, it seems, was somewhere else. Circumstances are hard to pin down. Lately, she just hasn't been herself.

There is a small window in the corner of the room where time is measured by light. As the red in the sky turns violet, the woman in white returns with a syringe that she injects into one of the man's bags. The girl in the chair watches, trying to make sense of the roller coaster that has marked her days. Is there no middle ground? she wonders. Something less frantic, less grievous and deranged. Doesn't my coming here, sitting patiently, waiting, count for anything?

The call was made, she knows that, because people came and took the bloody man to the hospital. Others came later, asking questions, giving commands, taking the knife. She stayed behind, feeling hopelessly depleted, anesthetized, forgetful. Had she fed the cat? Was the stove on? Hadn't she made plans to meet someone for lunch? She took a shower and went to the bedroom, which smelled of metal. She opened a window for air and stripped the bed, mopping the floor with the part of the sheet that wasn't wet with blood, then tossing it in a corner with the gown. After that she went to the kitchen and took out the other large knife and tried to kill herself. She poked the tip against her belly, her rib cage; she teased the edge along her wrist. Romeo,

Romeo, she could not do the deed. Angry with herself and furious with the man for his betrayal, she tossed the knife away and locked herself in the apartment, vowing never to leave. She would starve herself, tie a sash around her neck and hang from the ceiling, drown herself in the tub. That was her vow and her promise. Somehow she would find a way to die.

But her fury could not sustain itself, and as it bled away, as the storm diminished, so too did the urge for self-destruction. She wondered how she had come to so misjudge the man. His last-minute defiance, as much as it had enraged her, showed character. It showed courage, a measure, even, of self-respect. She was curious.

She left the apartment and went to the hospital. It was the third day since the stabbing, and the man remained in the ICU for another week. After that he was transferred to the floor, where his condition steadily improved. The kidneys kicked back in, the deep layers of his belly wound closed, his weight increased. It was a rosy picture to hear the doctors talk. Another patient salvaged to walk the good earth. All that remained, they said, the last little piece of the puzzle, was for the man's consciousness to return.

The girl shifts in her chair. Nine nights, the woman said, nine and then freedom. She has been here three weeks, marking time, sitting vigil. By whose measure, she wonders, is it nine? By what calendar? Whose hourglass drops the sand by which to count the days to recover one's nature?

She could leave. She could always leave. But she

stays. Day upon day she returns and waits. Is that what the woman meant? Is staying freedom?

For all these weeks the man has been cared for by others, bathed, fed, sustained. The orderlies change him, the doctors prescribe, the nurses minister. All do their part while the visiting woman waits. There has been endless opportunity to help, to reach out, but she has done nothing, nothing save come and sit. The man's blood is on her hands, hers on his. Blood brothers. Sisters. If she knew a lullaby, maybe she could sing.

The light in the window turns orange, and she rises from the chair. It is daybreak, another night gone. Desire gnaws at her heart as she steps to the bed. There is something she must do, something to break the stalemate. The man revealed his strength. He tried to redeem himself. She must do the same.

He is childlike in the depth of his slumber, his face still, his lips slightly parted. She tries to imagine what he is thinking, if anything. Are there dreams? Nightmares? Is he embattled? At peace? She brushes back a strand of hair that has fallen across his forehead. The skin underneath is beaded with sweat. Fever? she wonders. Is he suffering?

She finds a cloth and dips it in a pitcher of cool water. She wrings it out and fluffs it in her palm. Leaning over, careful not to disturb any of the life-giving tubes, she wipes the man's brow.

Notes

1. Koskinen, H. "Kokeiden äänifrekvenssien vaikutus keskushermostoon," Suomalainen lääketieteen aikakauslehti 43 (1989): 17–29.

2. National Center for the Study of Disease. "Collaborative Study of the Neural Effects of High-pitched, Alternating-frequency Sound," *Journal of Neuro-medical Mechanics* 71 (1987):132–39.

3. Ibid.

4. Sacks, O. W. *The Man Who Mistook His Wife For a Hat* (New York: Summit Books, 1985), p. 39.

5. Luria, A. R. *The Man with a Shattered World, The History Of a Brain Wound* (New York: Basic Books, 1972), pp. 98–100.

6. Adapted from Bizjak, T. "Bringing Up Beauty." In the *San Francisco Chronicle*, October 1, 1987.

7. Baudelaire, C. *Intimate Journals*. Paris, 1857 (translated from the French).

8. Cunningham, M. "Measuring the Physical in Physical Attractiveness: Quasi-Experiments on the Sociobiology of Female Facial Beauty," *Journal of Personality and Social Psychology* 50 (1986): 925–35.

9. Ibid.

10. Al'Nembuli-Lehim, C. "The Future in the Past: Evidence of Labile Bipolar Reproductive Behavior," *Perspectives in Archeology* 7 (1991):432–51.

11. Ibid.

12. Adapted from *Cosmopolitan*, November 1986.

13. Kisch, E. H., M.D., *The Sexual Life of Woman* (New York: Rebman Company, 1910).

14. Flower, M. L. "Structure Collides with Function: The Folly of Fixed Dimorphism," *Archives of Neuro-ontogeny* 16 (1990): 123–27.

15. Winchel, R., and Stanley, M. "Self-Injurious Behavior: A Review of the Behavior and Biology of Self Mutilation," *American Journal of Psychiatry* 148, 3 (1991):306–16.

16. Kernberg, O. "Sadomasochism, Sexual Excitement and Perversion," *Journal of the American Psychoanalytic Association* 39, 2 (1991):333–62.